A SUMMER McCLOUD PARANORMAL MYSTERY

THE CASE OF
MISSING BOOKS

book 6

NIKKI BROADWELL

AIRMID PUBLISHING
TUCSON, ARIZONA

The Case of Missing Books

Formatting by Polgarus Studio

CHARACTERS

Ames: a sleepy Connecticut town where strange things happen.

The Victorian: a turn-of-the-century large house owned and recently renovated by Agnes and where most of the ghosts live.

Summer McCloud: amateur sleuth and now a PI—owner of Tarot and Tea, an occult shop specializing in Tarot cards, essential oils, figurines and books on mythology. Can see and talk to ghosts.

Cutty: Summer's terrier mix.

Mischief: Summer's black cat.

Tabby: Summer's shop cat that now lives at the cottage.

Jerry Brady: a former detective on Ames police force and newly married to Summer.

Agnes Weatherby: now Agnes Anderson, Summer's best friend.

Sam Anderson: Jerry's best friend and former colleague, and Agnes's husband.

Sammie: Agnes and Sam's eighteen-month-old baby son.

Lucia Brady: Jerry's mother.

Douglas Weatherby: Agnes's father and also a ghost—currently involved with Lucia.

Emilia Browning: a ghost who frequents Tarot and Tea, and resides in the Victorian.

Becky Henderson: Valerie's daughter who owns the bakery down the street from Tarot and Tea.

Valerie Henderson: a psychic and Tarot card reader, former friend of Summer's dead mother, Lila.

Daniel Booker: owner of Booker's Bookstore next door to Tarot and Tea.

Philippa Booker: Daniel Booker's missing wife, presumed dead.

Isabel and Henry: old friends of Lucia's.

Marguerite Powers: high priestess of the local coven.

Byron Forsyth: high priest of coven and Marguerite's significant other.

Corinne Samuels: Therapist who Summer has seen in the past.

PROLOGUE

"Am I a witch, Mama? The kids at school say I am."

Lila turned to her nine-year-old daughter. "Why do you think they say that?"

"Because I can see things they can't? And also I knew Susie was going to fall before she got on the slide."

That's not magic, Summer, it's a premonition. Being a witch requires magic that comes directly through you." She placed a comforting hand on her daughter's head.

"I don't want to be a witch."

Lila smiled down at her. "Why is that? I'm a witch and your grandmother was a witch, as well as her mother before her. It runs in the family."

"Because no one likes it," Summer whined, looking up.

"There are those who don't understand it. They find it scary, like the dark night when the moon is absent."

"When I worry about monsters?"

"That's right. Once you grow up you'll find out how much freedom it gives you—how much help you can be to others."

Summer frowned, her lips moving into a pout. "I don't want to ever be a witch."

1

Lila laughed, a tinkling sound that reminded Summer of the wind chimes hanging on the tree behind the house. "You'll see it all in a different light once you grow up and I'm gone."

"Where are you going?" Summer asked in alarm.

"Where everyone goes sooner or later. Don't worry— I'll always be there for you." She leaned down, her green eyes meeting her daughter's hazel ones. "And you'll have a book to help you understand your gifts." She pointed to the shelf of books on magic against the wall behind them.

"Which one, Mama?" Summer asked, moving to examine them.

Lila smiled a secret smile. "It will come to you when the time is right."

~And it's strange, so strange…
You got to pick up every stitch…
Must be the season of the witch~
~Donovan

1

Sunlight wafted through the distorted antique glass window to the right of the front door, pooling on the new wood flooring. My store had been set ablaze over a year ago and I'd had to do a lot of internal repairs, including the new pine flooring. But updates had been long overdue and in a way the entire fiasco had been a blessing in disguise.

It was August, a time when the lingering summer sunshine kept people wearing flip flops and shorts, and yet a cold wind had come up this past week, sending leaves whirling. Flowers had been ripped from their stems, both rhododendrons and roses looking stripped. I hated to think what fall and winter might be like. Many of my customers had already fled for warmer climes or were buying their essential oils, specialty teas, crystals and sage bundles on the Internet where they could probably get them cheaper. Tarot and Tea was still afloat, but for how long could I compete with cheaper prices?

I pulled my gaze back to Valerie who had just recounted a hard to believe story about the store to the right of mine, owned by Daniel Booker. Valerie was my friend Becky's mom, and also the one client I could count on. "But why would someone steal a bunch of musty old books?" I asked, responding to what she'd just said.

Valerie turned toward the door just as Daniel Booker entered, her gaze returning to me. "See, Summer? I told you he was on his way over to talk to you."

Was everyone in this town psychic? I let out a sigh and smiled at the owner of Bookers.

"I heard you have a new line of work," the slightly stooped gray haired man said, suspicious eyes darting around the store.

"Hi, Mr. Booker," I said, trying to get him to focus on me. It did no good as his nervous gaze roamed the room as though scanning for ghosts. I glanced around, noticing Mrs. Browning and Douglas in the stacks looking at goddess books. They qualified, but I doubted the staid and conservative Daniel Booker, who rarely left his store or apartment above it, would have recognized them for what they were. "Valerie says you have a small problem you wanted to talk with me about?"

His gaze finally settled on me. "You're a private investigator?" he whispered.

After Jerry's resignation from the police force he and I had gone into the PI business, bringing a long-standing dream of mine into reality. So far we'd had very little interest in our new venture, but then again, Ames was a small town. Business would pick up—eventually. "Yes." I pulled one of our cards out of my pocket and handed it over:

Jaguar Enterprises
Brady and Brady Investigators.

Jerry had chosen the name after our last case in which a spirit jaguar had saved my life and the lives of several other desperate women. It had happened on our honeymoon and I'd nearly died in the process—but no point in going down that particular road again.

I brought my attention back to the present and the bloodshot and worried eyes of Daniel Booker. "What do you need to investigate?" I asked, glancing at Valerie who had just told me the entire story.

Daniel gave her a sharp look and then turned back to me. "Can we speak privately?"

"Can you watch the store for a few minutes?" I asked Valerie.

She nodded, her conspiratorial wink escaping Daniel who was now facing the shelves. "Take all the time you need."

I led the way into the back and through the door into what had once been the kitchen of this house—my dead mother's house, to be exact. I gestured to the kitchen table and chairs. He sat and I sat facing him, waiting for him to begin.

He let out a long sigh, running his fingers through his thinning hair, his gaze going to the tabletop. "About a month ago a theft occurred in my store. I told the police but...well...you know how they are."

"I do know since I'm married to one—or at least he used to be one...he..."

He glanced up, a frown deepening the lines in his

forehead. "I know all about Jerry Brady and his new profession," he said, cutting me off.

"We're partners," I said defensively. "It isn't just *his* new profession. Please go on."

He chose not to look at me, his gaze going everywhere in the small cluttered room.

Instead of hauling extra merchandise upstairs I had gotten into the habit of depositing the boxes in here, telling myself I'd organize them soon. But so far the stacks were getting higher, teetering precariously.

"This theft couldn't have happened and yet it did," he continued. "The store was locked from the inside with no sign of a break-in and I was upstairs at the time."

"And what was taken?" I asked, knowing full well what had been taken. Better let him tell it.

His eyes finally met mine, an uncertain expression in them. "All the books on magic. Every one of them is gone."

"Do you have any idea who would do this, or why?"

He shook his head, his thin lips pressing together. "It doesn't make any sense to me. They weren't worth anything, and they..."

"Were they old? Maybe they had some esoteric value, or..."

"Some were very old. Some were first editions. But selling them wouldn't be worth the trouble."

"Maybe the thief knows something you don't. Any titles you can remember?"

"*Witches and Warlocks, Black Magic and the Occult...*" he waved his hands in the air, his eyes narrowing. "I've been in the book business for forty years and I know which ones are worth money. And if that was the motive why take the used paperbacks?" He shook his head. "Makes no sense."

"If they aren't worth anything then why do you care?"

He glared at me. "Someone managed to get into my store, cart off two shelves of books without making a peep, and I'm supposed to ignore it?"

"Do you know exactly what day it happened?"

"Yes. It was midsummer, the longest day of the year."

"The summer solstice."

"Yes, I suppose, if you're into that sort of nonsense."

"Well, it seems that your thief might have been into that sort of nonsense, as you describe it. Don't downplay the old ways, Mr. Booker."

"The old ways? This is the twenty-first century. No one believes in those rituals anymore."

"And yet people walk around talking about an old man in the sky who will grant them what they want if they only go to church and get down on their knees and pray to him?"

Daniel scoffed. "I suppose you're right. Superstitions abound, don't they? I guess it doesn't matter how far we've come."

"In my opinion we haven't come very far," I muttered.

"What was that?"

"Never mind. Who has a key to your store?"

He shook his head. "My wife did, but she's long gone."

"Gone as in dead, or moved away?"

"Come to think of it, Philippa was into the occult," he continued, as though I hadn't spoken.

"So not dead…could she have done this?"

He looked up from where he was staring at his hands.

"Philippa died seven years ago."

I let out a huff of frustration. "Mr. Booker, can you concentrate, please? "I'm trying to determine if there is a spare key floating about that you may have forgotten. Did you keep one under a planter, or…"

"No!" he said emphatically. "No one unlocked that door and walked in and took those books. The door was bolted from the inside. Deadbolts."

"Okay. Did you actually see the shelves of books that night? Could they have been taken earlier? Maybe one of your clients came in during the day and…"

No!" he yelled. "I'm telling you exactly what happened. I check the store every night before I head upstairs to my apartment. The books were all in place at nine p.m., and gone when I came down the next morning at seven. I noticed their absence immediately."

I pulled out a notebook and wrote down what he'd told me already. "And it was only the books on magic that were missing?"

"Yes! Why do I have to keep repeating myself?"

"I just want to make sure I'm not missing an important piece of information."

"Like my dead wife?" He stood up abruptly, knocking over his chair. "Maybe I should consult a real firm instead of talking with a woman who seems immersed in the occult, and believes she can talk to ghosts."

"Mr. Booker," I began, rising from my chair. "Any private investigator will need to question you to get all the facts straight…and…"

But he had already exited the room and was striding across the store. By the time I reached my desk he was out the door, the slam rattling the antique glass panes.

"I take it that went well?" Valerie asked innocently.

I shook my head and watched Daniel Booker's stooped form hurrying across the grass toward the bookstore. "He thinks I'm untrustworthy because I can talk to ghosts."

Valerie smiled. "Perhaps that gift of yours will solve the enigma of the missing books."

I swiveled toward her. "Did you see that in a vision, or are you just speculating?"

She shrugged. "What's the difference? He'll be back, Summer. No cheapskate like him wants to pay the big bucks to hire some hotshot firm, nor will he want to admit to normal investigators how much this means to him."

"Losing those books means a lot to him?"

Valerie's savvy gaze met mine. "Of course. Why else would he have ventured out of his safety zone to talk with you about it? He's a complete recluse."

"He seemed so down on anything pagan or out of the ordinary."

"His wife was very involved with the occult. She was a member of the coven."

"Really?"

"And me thinks the man protests too much," Valerie continued, sotto voice. "There is something about those books he isn't saying."

At home later that evening I described the meeting to Jerry, trying to get him interested. This was our first case and I, for one, wanted to dig in and solve it. Jerry needed something to occupy his mind and I needed to stop worrying about Tarot and Tea and why I had so few customers.

But instead of being intrigued he said, "Just let it go. The guy's a curmudgeon who will drive us both crazy if we take him on."

Jerry and I were in our first year of marriage and still getting used to the constant togetherness, especially since he'd quit his job on the force. He was here when I got up in the morning and here when I got back, his obvious restlessness coming out in little ways that I found increasingly frustrating. He left clothes lying around on furniture, wet towels on the floor in the bathroom, and dirty dishes in the sink. And he never thought to take Cutty, our terrier mix, out for a walk, or do anything useful around the house. I was still the one who did all the shopping, the laundry and the cleaning.

"But the missing books on magic—don't you find that at all interesting?" I asked, picking a shirt off the couch and carrying it to our stacking washer and dryer.

"Not as much as you do, but I have to admit that getting in through a bolted door piques my curiosity."

I laughed, coming back to sit next to him on the couch. But when I leaned in to nuzzle his neck, he moved away and stood up. "Need a beer," he said, glancing back at me with a wary look.

I stared after him, surprised. Jerry never turned down my advances—normally by now he would have dragged me into the bedroom. "What's going on, Jer?"

"What do you mean?" he called, opening the fridge.

"You just snubbed me."

"Snubbed?" He laughed. "Just not in the mood right now." He came back to the living room, but instead of sitting next to me, he chose the chair.

"What have you been doing all day?"

"Drumming up business—there's this guy at the station who Sam told me about, who…"

"Sam's pimping for you now, is he? I thought he was doing police work."

Jerry took a long swig of beer before saying, "He's thinking of bringing me in as an independent contractor on some of the more confusing cases."

I let out a snort. "Some of the more confusing cases in Ames? Give me a break! Hardly anything happens here. And besides that, what about me? Are you planning to go solo?"

"We've had our share of stuff, Summer. Don't forget the school shooting."

Yes, Ames had had a very puzzling school shooting a couple of years back, but that had been an anomaly.

"And don't forget your brother, the serial killer."

I felt the blood drain from my face, changing the subject as quickly as I could. "But those things are a rarity," I muttered. "I don't know what you were thinking when you decided to quit the force. Boredom is going to drive you up the wall."

Jerry stared into space, his gaze opaque as he downed the rest of his beer. "Maybe I shouldn't dismiss the Booker case so easily—talking it over with a man might help."

"A man? Oh brother." I shook my head. "I'm sure you're right—misogyny is alive and well in Ames."

"Don't be like that. We're a team."

I ignored him as I went into the kitchen and pulled leftovers out of the fridge. Jerry was bored. And Jerry bored was not a good thing. I hated to think what would happen if we didn't take on Daniel Booker's case. This PI venture was new territory, and I doubted Jerry hanging around the precinct would help.

While I was heating up the food Jerry came in for his third beer, his eyebrows pulled together in a frown. "What is going on with you?" I asked him, feeling a prickle of apprehension.

"Quit asking me that!" he yelled, stomping into the living room again.

Judging from Jerry's anger and the wary look in his eyes, something was definitely on his mind, but if he wasn't willing to talk about it there was no point in pestering him. I turned back to the stove, trying to keep my attention on not burning the food instead of worrying about why my husband was drinking too much and not interested in sex.

2

When I woke in the morning Jerry was already gone, his pride and joy Indian motorcycle missing from the side yard where he always parked it. He'd paced for hours the night before and then watched shows on his I-phone instead of coming to bed. Recently he'd begged me to get a TV, but so far I'd held out. But with Jerry out of sorts my resolve was beginning to slip. His recent change of careers was taking its toll, not only on him, but on our intimacy as well. My passionate Irish Italian lover had turned into a brooding, grumpy beer drinker who rarely seemed interested in ravishing me.

I sighed and rolled out of bed, my gaze going to Cutty, who sat on the floor staring at me with a woeful expression, one ear up and one down. "What's wrong, little guy?" When I checked his doggy door I discovered that Jerry had left the lawnmower parked against it on the outside, blocking Cutty from his route into the yard. And the lawn had not been mowed, the grass a foot high. Another sign that my husband was preoccupied. I let Cutty out the back door and walked over to move the mower to the shed where it belonged before heading back inside to make coffee.

In our newlywed days and before, Jerry had brought me cappuccinos in bed that he made with his costly and elaborate espresso machine. Now he left without drinking coffee, heading to the local coffee shop to meet Sam, or to the precinct to hang around and find out what was going on. Although no longer working there, his interest in police business was always front and center.

When my cell phone rang I hurried to the counter where I'd left it, hoping it was Jerry.

"Summer?"

"Hi Agnes. What's up?"

"I hate it when people say that," she grumped.

"It's just a figure of speech instead of saying, *what do you want.*"

"Well, that's just rude," she said.

"I know. That's why I chose, *what's up*. Why did you call?"

There was a sigh and I heard her baby wail before she said, "Jerry's at it again."

"What does that mean?" I asked, placing the phone on speaker on the counter as I poured ground coffee into the filter cup. I tamped it down and attached it carefully and pressed the on button.

"It means he's disrupting my marriage."

"He mentioned that Sam was helping him with a consulting job. Is that what you're talking about?"

"No. Jerry and my husband are hanging out in my living room early in the morning, and sometimes again in the afternoon. What's going on with you two?"

"I bet baby Sam likes him," I muttered, attempting to keep my espresso cup from overflowing.

"Yes, of course Sammie likes him. What's that got to do with anything?"

"I don't know—just stream of consciousness."

"And speaking of that, why aren't you pregnant yet?"

I burned my fingers and let out a yelp before I moved back to where I'd left the phone. "We have a business together, Agnes. I don't want to get pregnant right now."

"Jerry wants a baby."

"He told you that?"

"Not in so many words, but I can see it in his eyes when he plays with Sammie."

"If he wants a baby he's certainly not attempting to make one."

There was a long pause before Agnes said, "Sorry about that—you two have always been...."

"I know what we've been, but we aren't now," I muttered, adding cream to my overflowing cup. It dribbled over the sides and dripped onto the floor. "Crap!"

"What are you doing?"

"Attempting to make coffee. Jerry usually does it."

"Please talk to him, Summer. Sam's susceptible right now and Jerry's a bad influence."

"We have a case. Maybe that's where he went this morning."

"I just told you he was here this morning."

"You did? I didn't get that part."

"He was here when I got up and here when Sam left for work. He would have hung with me except I told him I had chores to do."

"What the hell?"

"That's what I'm saying. Please do something or I'll

have to turn into the rude bitch that lurks beneath the surface."

I laughed and hung up, sipping my distinctly mediocre coffee as my mind went to Jerry's odd behavior. He'd dated Agnes once, but that was ages ago. A twinge of jealousy knifed through me. He preferred hanging out with Agnes to rolling over in bed and taking me on the wild ride I'd come to expect? What in hell was going on?

⤫∞⤸

The sky was clear, the aroma of dried leaves and wood smoke making it seem more like late September than August on the drive to Tarot and Tea. I wanted to listen to the radio but I'd left my car unlocked a week or so ago and someone had ripped it out. It was an antiquated model, not much good for anything, but whoever had stolen it must have hoped to make a few bucks. Anyone that desperate was welcome to have it.

Today would be busy for me since I'd received a shipment of essential oils and I had to categorize them, price them and place them on the special shelf with the others. I parked in my usual spot in front of the store and hurried to unlock the door, hoping to make some headway before customers arrived. Inside I shoved my CD of Back concertos into the player, turning up the volume before I got to work. The first one was his concerto in D minor, the piano work astounding.

I was humming along with the music, bent over the box of oils when the chain of Tibetan bells on my front door signaled my first customer. I glanced up as Valerie waltzed inside, her gray streaked hair windblown and her cheeks pink. Instead of saying hello she hurried by toward the shelf where I'd placed the books on goddesses and magic.

It was sometime later that she arrived at my desk holding a small figure of Freya, the Norse goddess of magic, love and divination. She placed it down and reached into the heavy bag slung across her shoulder. "Freya is my new best friend," she whispered.

"Why are you whispering? It's only the two of us."

Valerie glanced around, her gaze finally settling on the statue. "Freya's been visiting my dreams of late. I have an idea why, but I'm waiting to see if things pan out."

"Pan out? What are you talking about?"

Valerie smiled. "I hesitate to say until I know more."

"Becky?" I asked, knowing that her daughter's love life was always on Valerie's mind. Becky had nearly died from one horrible relationship and since then she'd been single, spending all her time at the bakery she owned and ran.

Valerie lifted her brows and changed the subject. "Will you meet with Mr. Booker today?" she asked, putting her credit car in the small machine on my desk.

I rang up the sale and wrapped her figurine in turquoise tissue paper. "I'm not sure he wants my help. And Jerry took off this morning before I got up. I'd hoped he'd help me with this one."

Valerie's eyes narrowed as she cocked her head to one side like an inquisitive bird. "I thought you two had a business together."

"So did I, but he's been..." At that moment the door opened and Daniel Booker walked in, his brooding gaze going to me.

"Good morning," I said pleasantly, trying not to be

disturbed by the pinch of his eyebrows. I rose to turn the volume down on the music.

"It may be for you, but it isn't for me. Your husband promised to meet with me this morning and so far he hasn't shown up."

"Really? He never mentioned it to me. He left early and I haven't seen him since."

Daniel Booker made a huffing sound, his thin lips pressing together. He glanced away, his hands turning into fists at his sides. "I need to get to the bottom of this. Have you come up with anything?"

"I thought you didn't want me on the case."

He let out a sigh. "I don't have much choice now, do I? Your husband isn't reliable at all—at least I know where to find you."

"Have you looked into other PI firms?"

"In Ames? Are you kidding? I did contact the police again, but they have no interest in pursuing it."

"I'd like to see the scene of the crime," I said, glancing at Valerie with my eyebrows raised in question.

"Yes, dear. I can watch the store."

"Thanks, Valerie. I shouldn't be long." I gave her a grateful look before I followed Daniel Booker out the front door.

Daniel Booker strode purposely toward the turn of the century building that housed his bookstore and the second story apartment where he lived. Tarot and Tea was in a nearly identical building, both of them constructed around the same time. But he'd let his go, paint peeling and several roof tiles missing, as well as windows that needed re-puttying. Weeds had grown up along the front walls, giving a seedy feeling to the entire place. Both houses were on the historic registry, but mine had been repainted, the single pane windows replaced with double panes. I glanced back at Tarot and Tea's recent paint job, the cream wood accented by deep green trim. His was yellow with brown trim, colors that had gone out of style years ago.

When I caught up to him Daniel was unlocking the front door, swinging it back to reveal the dark interior. The front window hadn't been washed for quite some time, and the books displayed there were covered in dust. I almost said something but stopped myself—it wasn't my place to comment. Bookers was an institution in Ames, and Daniel was now on his own, with no help aside from the occasional young person during the holidays. I suddenly felt sorry for him as I noticed the bald spot on the back of his head, the threadbare jacket he wore.

He disappeared down the hall between his messy and overflowing bookshelves, coming to a stop at the very the back of the store. He pointed. "This is where they were."

The shadows seemed to deepen, sliding from darkened corners to fill in the area where we stood. "Can you turn on a light?" I asked, squinting.

When he flicked a switch I heard a hum and then a pop as one of the bulbs in the ceiling blew out. "Damn these light bulbs," he muttered. "Cost a fortune and don't last."

"You should try LED's," I said, glancing upward. "They last a a lot longer and they don't use as much electricity." My neck prickled for a second, indicating that there was something supernatural at play. "Did your wife have much to do with the store?"

He let out a heavy sigh and ran a hand across his unshaven

face. "Of course she did. We worked the bookstore together."

"I heard she was part of the coven."

His eyes widened in anger. "What in god's name does that have to with anything?"

"All your books on magic are gone, Mr. Booker. Was it your wife who collected them for the store? From what you've told me it doesn't seem like you would have wanted them, or even cared once they were missing."

"Philippa bought all of them. Despite my warnings she was very into magic."

"Your warnings? About what, exactly?"

"Is this really relevant?"

I glanced at the dust-covered bookshelf, the darkened corner where the books had lived. They'd been placed in the most obscure part of the store where no one would find them unless they knew where to look. "Yes, I think it is."

He shook his head and stared at the floor. "A few of her coven friends met here once a month. They practiced spells. I wasn't in favor of this and warned her what could happen if they dabbled in the devil's work."

"Most witches don't believe in the devil, Mr. Booker. Were you afraid of repercussions?"

His dark gaze met mine. "I'm a god-fearing man who warned my wife not to continue her unnatural pursuits. Yes, I was afraid of repercussions."

"How did your wife die?"

His mouth tightened. "She...she just disappeared one night."

Something indistinct and wispy caught my attention but when I turned to look it was gone. "So you don't know for sure she's dead?"

Anger narrowed his eyes. "She wouldn't have left me alone here. We...we..."

"Okay, "I said, jotting down what he'd told me. "If we assume she's dead—were the books always in this part of the store?"

"I moved them after her death."

I noted his use of *her death*, as though her disappearance was the same thing. "I think I have enough information for right now," I mumbled, the sudden need to be out of his store coming over me. I pocketed my notebook and hurried toward the front door where a single beam of sunlight beckoned.

My hand was on the handle when he said, "Please figure this out. I'm losing business."

I turned. "Losing business—why?"

"Because I've closed up shop, that's why," he barked impatiently.

"Because of a theft? Are most of your customers interested in magic?"

He shook his head, rubbing his face again, his eyes going to the ground. "You don't understand," he muttered.

"Perhaps I don't, but if you want me to solve this you have to tell me everything, Mr. Booker."

"I've told you as much as I'm going to," he growled.

"Fine, then. I'll do what I can with the information you gave me." I opened the door and hurried into the light, releasing my held breath. But as soon as the door closed behind me the sun was obscured by dark clouds, a rumble of thunder sounding in the distance.

When I entered Tarot and Tea Valerie rose from behind the counter, moving to give me room. I waved her back. "I need a cup of tea. Do you want one?" She nodded, the look in her eyes questioning. "Tell you in a minute," I said, hurrying into the back.

I made tea from the small container of powdered chai, my thoughts on Booker and the missing books. I wondered if the ghost of his wife was wafting about, trying to get his attention, but whatever I'd seen didn't jive with that theory. And Mr. Booker didn't believe in all of that anyway. She could appear right in front of him and he'd probably chalk it up to a seizure or something.

I carried the mugs up to the desk and handed one to Valerie. "I thought it was odd how he kept referring to his wife's death—as far as I know her body's never been found," I said before taking a sip of the hot aromatic liquid.

"I remember Philippa's vanishing act," Valerie said, her gaze on her mug. "She was very unhappy. Daniel had forbidden her to go to the coven meetings."

"Did my mother know her?"

Valerie looked surprised. "Of course, dear. Lila and Philippa were around the same age and both into the occult. They were close friends."

"What do you think happened to her?"

Valerie stared into the distance, a faraway look in her eyes. "At the time I was afraid she'd committed suicide. Now I'm not so sure."

"What do you mean?"

Valerie's pellucid gaze met mine. "She either left him or he killed her."

"I got the feeling he loved her."

One shoulder lifted. "It could have been accidental."

I let out a sigh. "This case is more complicated than I thought."

Valerie nodded. "You might be investigating a murder as well as a theft."

"Should I contact the police?"

"Aren't you married to a former detective?"

My mind went to my absentee husband. "If this turns into murder Jerry will definitely want to be involved."

Valerie laughed. "The bright side," she said, putting down her empty mug and heading toward the front door. "Thanks for the tea."

Several customers were in the store, including Mrs. Browning, who I hadn't spoken with since the surprise party at the Victorian Jerry had arranged to announce his resignation from the police force. That night he'd also declared his commitment to our PI business, even coming up with a name for it. But that was almost two months ago now and nothing had been said about it since. I sighed, thinking about the lack of cases and Jerry's subsequent restlessness.

I looked up as Mrs. Browning approached my desk carrying a small Ganesha.

"So nice to see you, dear," she said, placing the elephant god on the desk in order to retrieve her money. "How are you faring with Daniel Booker? His wife was a saint to put up with him."

I didn't bother to ask how she knew about the case—she was a ghost and ghosts knew things before they happened. "His wife is the one who interests me. She was the one who purchased those missing books on magic."

"Yes, yes she did. She was quite a beauty. I always wondered what she saw in him."

"Why didn't I know her? I never saw her at the coven meetings."

"It was before your time, dear. Lila knew her quite

well—especially with these two buildings being so close together." Her dark eyes sparkled for a moment. "These houses were built before prohibition."

I wondered what prohibition had to do with anything, but I didn't ask. "What do you think happened to her?"

Mrs. Browning's eyes glazed over, a furtive look coming onto her face. "I'm sure I don't know."

That signaled that she knew exactly what had happened, but I knew better than to question her. Ghosts were notorious about keeping details to themselves. "Valerie thinks Daniel might have killed her."

Mrs. Browning's eyes widened, her hand going to her mouth. "What a terrible thought!" She placed the money for the statue on the counter, and before I could question her further she was exiting the store.

When the other customers trooped out behind her without buying anything, my heart sank. The bill for my essential oils stared up at me, reminding me of how little money I was making these days. Luckily Jerry was filthy rich now, after inheriting a chunk of change from his mother's sale of the family home. But some stubborn streak in me refused his help. When my cell rang I answered it quickly, happy to see Jerry's name on the screen.

"Finally," I said. "Where have you been?"

"I spoke with Daniel Booker this morning. Where have *you* been?"

"You did? He told me you missed your appointment."

"I missed making it to his store, but I spoke to him a few minutes ago."

"And what have you been doing since you left the house at the crack of dawn?"

There was a long silence in which I could hear him breathing. "I saw Sam…and…"

"Yes, I'm well aware of that. Agnes told me. What else?"

"I've been doing some thinking. We'd best talk about this later after you've calmed down."

"Calmed down? I'm only asking where you've been—how hard a question is that?"

When the call suddenly ended I figured the question was harder than I thought. I stared around the deserted store before I punched in his number.

"What?"

"What do you mean, *what?* You just hung up on me. Where are you?"

"I'm at the precinct."

"I should have guessed," I muttered. "When will you be home?"

"Not sure. I need a few days to myself."

My mouth opened and I shut it, unable to utter a sound. When I finally was able to speak my voice came out in a whisper. "A few days…to yourself…why?"

"Because I do. Listen, Summer, I have to go now. I'll see you after the weekend."

Before he hung up I heard Cutty bark. He'd lied—he was at the house. Anger rose up, worry and confusion adding to the rage. Since there were no customers in the store I locked up and hurried to my car, speeding toward home to catch him before he took off. *After the weekend?* He'd never mentioned one word about needing time to himself. My mind raced, my stomach churning as my foot pressed down on the gas pedal. I barely noticed the swiftly forming storm clouds hanging low over the town of Ames.

3

Jerry's motorcycle was gone by the time I reached the cottage, and his backpack was missing from the shelf in the closet. I stared around the bedroom, surprised by how empty it felt. Despite the recent lack of intimacy, we did share a bed and eat dinner together, talking over our day. I tried to remember any possible clues to explain his sudden need to get away, but nothing came to mind aside from his obvious restlessness. I sat on the bed, my mood darkening further as I attempted to untangle the past few weeks. Had I said something or done something to drive him away?

Cutty's whine brought me out of my funk, his whiskered face peering at me from the bedroom doorway. When I glanced at him he trotted off, looking over his shoulder to see if I was following. In the kitchen the two cats were curled up on top of the cupboard together, their faces obscured. Mischief, a black female who'd been living wild, had arrived at my front door one day and decided that being fed regularly and having a warm place to sleep was better than her former life. Tabby had been my shop cat, but now there was no way of separating him from Mischief; after a bumpy start, the two of them had become fast friends.

"What is it?" I asked Cutty, scanning the kitchen. He wagged his stub of a tail, his nose pointing toward the kitchen table and the square of paper that lay there. I picked it up.

Dear Summer,
   I know I've been a pain lately. Some things are going on in my life and I need to be alone to sort them out. Don't worry about me. I'll be back before you know it.
   Love,
   Jerry

What? What things? *A pain* hardly covered it. I reached in my pocket for my phone and called him. But when he didn't answer I hung up and called Agnes.

"He didn't say where he was going?" Agnes asked after I spewed out what was happening.

"No. What has he said to you?"

There was a slight hesitation before she said, "Nothing much, other than complaining about his mother's behavior."

"His mother...she's still living at the Victorian, right? Isn't she with Douglas, your dad?"

"Lucia's involved in the coven now."

"Are you kidding? Wow. I never would have expected that."

"Neither did Jerry, apparently."

"But why didn't he tell me?"

"Because he knows how you feel about witches and magic and all that?"

"I thought he accepted my involvement in the coven and the ghost thing. This man is a constant surprise."

Agnes let out a scoff. "He acts like he accepts things, maybe even thinks he does, until…"

"Until he suddenly realizes he doesn't. Yeah, I do know that about him. But we're married now. If he can't share his life then maybe we shouldn't be together."

Agnes was silent for so long I thought the call had been disconnected. "Are you still there?"

"I think you'd better speak to Sam," she finally said. "He knows what's going on a lot better than I do."

When we hung up a minute later I had the distinct impression that Jerry had divulged things that she didn't want to tell me. I was suddenly cold all over. When my phone rang a minute later I grabbed it and answered, hoping it was Jerry.

"Miss McCloud?"

"Yes. Who is this?"

"This is Mr. Booker's lawyer, Wendy Werner. He asked me to call regarding your inquiry into the theft at his store."

"Yes, what is it?"

"He asked me to tell you that he's solved the case. Your services are no longer needed."

"My services…okay. Why didn't he call me directly?"

"He said that you can be very persistent, and he didn't have the wherewithal to argue."

"Thank you, I guess."

"You are very welcome. Have a nice day."

I placed my phone on the counter. Two disturbing calls in fifteen minutes. Were my stars out of alignment? And how on earth had he solved the case?

Leaves swirled across the road as I drove back to Tarot and Tea, my shoulders tensing as I continued to mull over my husband's odd behavior. When a black cat came out of nowhere and ran in front of me I swerved to miss it. It looked like Mischief—but then again black cats were a dime a dozen and most were shorthairs like her. I shrugged and continued on, ignoring the little prickles moving up my arms.

When I reached the store there were several irate customers waiting for me. I was late.

"It's too cold to be standing out here," Valerie hissed.

"I'm sorry," I said, inserting the key into the lock. "It was an emergency."

A man and woman I'd never seen before headed by me to peruse the shelves while Valerie followed me to the counter. "I sense a distinct shift in your energy, Summer."

I gazed at her as I turned up the heat. The store was freezing. "Jerry's mother has joined the coven, and apparently it upset Jerry so much that he had to spend some time alone. And Daniel Booker had his lawyer call me to basically fire me from the case."

Valerie frowned. "Jerry didn't tell you he was leaving?"

"Not until right before he left. Agnes was the one who told me about his mother."

Valerie glanced at the couple in the back of the store. "Who are those two? I've never seen them before."

"Me neither. Maybe they're visiting."

Her gray-green eyes met mine. "Something's afoot—I can feel it. What will you do about Daniel?"

"If you can stay here for a few minutes I'll go next door and find out what's going on."

She placed her hand on my arm. "Try not to read too much into Jerry's behavior. It could be his stars." A frown puckered her forehead. She sniffed the air. "I'm picking up a distinct aroma of sulfur."

"Like the devil?"

"No, not like the devil. Someone just lit a match. You don't allow smoking, do you?"

"No." I glanced into the back of the store where a tendril of gray smoke wafted upward, but I didn't have the energy to confront the person who had lit up. "Jerry lied to me too, told me he was at the precinct when in reality he was at home getting ready to leave."

She gave me a little shove. "Go talk to Daniel. It will take your mind off it."

I nodded gratefully and hurried outside, my gaze going to a sky that had turned darker than the far reaches of hell. A storm was definitely on the way. Bookers was closed up tight, a closed sign on the door. I knocked, expecting no answer, surprised when the door flew open to reveal his haggard face.

"What do *you* want?"

"I got a call from Wendy telling me the case had been solved. How'd you figure it out?"

"I no longer need your services," he mumbled, trying to close the door.

"But who did it?" I asked, moving my foot between the door and the jam.

"No one. I misplaced them."

"Mr. Booker, I know that isn't true."

"Just leave me in peace, would you?" He kicked my foot out of the way and slammed the door.

The rain began as I was on my way across the grass toward Tarot and Tea. I put my head down and began to run, nearly colliding with Douglas and Lucia on their way inside. "Good to see you both," I murmured, waiting for them to go ahead of me up the steps. Once we were inside I closed the door, turning to them. "What a change in the weather!" I smiled, trying to appear my normal cheery self.

Jerry's mother gazed around the store, her gloved hand tucked into Douglas's elbow. "Has Jerry spoken to you about me?" she whispered.

"No, he hasn't, but I heard a rumor."

Lucia frowned, her gaze on Douglas. "Your daughter has broken my confidence."

"I'm sorry, my dear," Douglas said, patting her arm.

"She only told me because Jerry took off yesterday."

Lucia's eyes went wide. "Took off? Do you mean he's abandoned you?"

I smiled. "I hope not. He said he needed a few days."

"Why is he so impetuous?" she asked, looking up at Douglas again.

"He's passionate like his mother," Douglas replied. He glanced at me and winked.

"See you later," Valerie said, coming toward the three of us standing by the door. She gave me a sharp look before she exited the shop and closed the door, hurrying toward her car on the other side of the street. I watched her hair lift in the wind, her dark skirt billowing as she tugged her car door open.

I turned to Lucia. "Why would this revelation hit him so hard? He knows about my involvement in the coven—he knows you're a ghost," I added, glancing at Douglas.

Lucia shook her head. "Oh no, Summer. Douglas is certainly not a ghost." She giggled girlishly, her dark lashes fluttering.

When I glanced at Douglas he shook his head ever so slightly. "Lucia's involvement in the coven is merely a way to accommodate my needs. She wants to participate in my life as much as she can."

"Yes, that's right. I am not normally a person who embraces the occult."

"And you've been to a meeting?" I asked her.

"Well, yes. One or two."

At that point the smoking couple I didn't know emerged from the back with several books in their hands. They glanced furtively in our direction before the woman whispered something to the man.

"Isabel, is that you?" Lucia called out.

The older woman with dyed red hair stopped in her tracks, her cheeks going pink. "Lucia, what a surprise. I'm sorry, but we really don't have time to chat right now. Henry and I are late for an appointment." She held out two books. "Can you hold these for us?" she asked me.

"Of course." I took the books and moved to place them under the counter. A moment later she and the gray-haired man with her rushed through the front door and hurried off.

Lucia adjusted the mink-lined collar of her coat, her surprised gaze on the door before she walked up to the counter. "How odd. I haven't seen Isabel and Henry in years, and they can't even stop to say hello?"

The man and woman were getting into a dark car on the other side of the street. "Who are they?"

"Friends from when I was married to Jerry's father. I'm surprised they were here in your store. As I remember they're staunch Catholics, just as I am…or rather, was." she added, looking up at Douglas.

Jerry's father, who had been chief of police, had committed suicide a few years back after being caught on fraud charges. Lucia had been a different person back then, a woman who couldn't abide my involvement with her son. I understood later that the death of her husband had taken a huge toll on her. Jerry was her favorite, the youngest, and out of her five children, the easiest one to manipulate. At least now we'd grown past all that, and although not close, she accepted me.

I pulled the books out, checking out the titles: *Spells and Potions* and *The Power of Black Magic*.

Lucia gasped when she saw them. "Why on earth?" She stared at me wide-eyed, as though I could explain their choices.

"Maybe they're gifts?"

But Lucia was not convinced. Douglas and Lucia left a few minutes later, leaving me by myself. The store felt cold, as though ghosts were wafting about. I thought of recent events, from Jerry's sudden need to be alone, to Daniel Booker and his dead wife and the missing books, to this odd couple in my store and their choice of books—not to mention Lucia's sudden interest in the occult. Experience had taught me that when there was a cluster of unusual happenings it could indicate an incongruity in the fabric of reality. Something was seriously off.

Those two had left a lingering energy that I didn't like, and it wasn't just the cigarette smoke. After thoroughly smudging the store I sat on the stool behind the counter and tried to think. Daniel Booker had not solved the case—that was one thing I was sure of. And my intuition told me that these two former friends of Lucia's were somehow involved. I should have asked her if they knew Mr. Booker.

My gaze wandered Tarot and Tea, a wispy shape in the shadows catching my eye before it evaporated. There was definitely a ghost present. "Who are you?" I whispered. There was no answer aside from a breath of cold wind that touched my cheek.

When I left the shop around five a black cat was sitting on my stoop. But when I called out it took off, disappearing around the corner of the building. Probably just trying to keep dry. I stood there under the porch roof watching the rain pour down and wondering why I felt like my world was falling apart.

⁘

A storm blew in the next morning like a beast waiting for the opportunity to tear all memory of summer from our hearts. The temperature plummeted, the first frost casting a white glaze across the lawn. The kitchen window was fogged over, my fingers making a squeaking sound as I rubbed them across the glass, attempting to see outside. Pale icing covered the patch of lawn in the front, bushes that had been happy just yesterday now withered and dead looking.

I paced, trying to make sense of everything that seemed off kilter, my mind grappling with my husband's sudden need to be alone. We'd been married less than a year and already he was so tired of me he needed weekends to himself? It wouldn't have been so bad if he hadn't lied, saying he was at the precinct when in reality he was at home packing his bag.

Anger rose up, the sudden need to throw something making my fingers itch. But when my gaze lit on the vases, figurines, and decorative bowls that presented themselves to be hurled into bits, I realized they were all antiques I'd inherited from my mother. I sat on the couch, trying to turn the swirling energy into something more productive. It was time to go to work and I still had several chores to do.

My black cat appeared in front of me, her green eyes staring into mine. Her food dish was full and I'd even given both cats canned food this morning. Something about the way she was looking at me made me feel kind of prickly all over. "What do you know?" I whispered. Mischief probably knew a lot more than I did about most everything, but I couldn't decipher her message. By the way she stalked off I figured my uncomprehending gaze had annoyed her. "Sorry, kitty," I called, watching her jump on the counter and then up onto the top of the cabinet. "I'm just dense."

I made it to work with just moments to spare, barely getting the door unlocked before a couple breezed in searching for Tarot cards. I showed them the many decks I had, explaining their origins and what each one had to offer. After a few minutes they chose a traditional Rider-Waite deck, paid me in cash and left.

After that the store was oddly empty. Even Valerie was absent for the first time in weeks. I figured she was at home meditating on Freya and trying to influence her daughter's future in a good way. I put in a CD of Donovan, a favorite of my mothers, and now a favorite of mine. *Season of the Witch* seemed apropos, I thought as my gaze went to the front window, watching leaves twist by in the wind. The sky was filled with fast moving clouds, their color somewhere between the ocean during a storm and dirty dishwater. I used the quiet time to straighten shelves and dust, hoping that more customers would show up later on. The prickly feeling came again, my heart racing when I noticed a pale shape wafting in the shadows behind the shelves. Ghosts had never made me nervous—why was I feeling this way? When I went to investigate there was nothing there but dust motes and the lingering aroma of burning sage.

4

On Saturday I decided to do inventory, putting the shut sign up on the door so that I could count out my merchandise and see exactly what I had and what I needed. But really I was taking a mental health day in order to process my life. The weather was even worse, if that were possible, wind whistling and dark clouds scudding. I wondered if the early winter had to do with global climate change—I'd never experienced an August this cold or this stormy.

The night before I'd transferred my summer clothes into the cedar chest and pulled out my sweaters, wool skirts and tights. I'd even made a fire in the fireplace, although having a hot toddy and staring into the flames was not the same without the man I loved. I sighed and put in an Enya CD, turning it up to drown out my thoughts and letting the calm of her music settle into me as I sorted through the shelves and made lists.

Jerry had been gone since Thursday and hadn't called. Agnes had been no help, and I had yet to catch up with Sam. As for Daniel Booker, I was still wondering what to do. Was it my place to keep digging into a theft he didn't care about? Yes, if it involved others and could possibly solve his wife's death. I was a sleuth, after all, and I couldn't just walk away from this mystery. And besides that, there was a ghost involved. Who this ghost was and how to communicate with him or her, was another matter. Most times they entered my dreams, asking for my help, but so far I hadn't had any visitations. The reluctant ghost, I thought, giggling to myself.

I was on my knees in front of a cabinet filled with surplus statuary when I heard a rap on the door. "Summer? Are you in there?"

I rose and crossed to the door, opening it to see my friend Becky standing there, a warm coat over her butter and flour stained apron. Her bright red hair wasn't braided today, wisps of it in her face, which was flushed and wet from running through the rain. "Did you hear?" she asked breathlessly.

I ushered her inside and closed and locked the door before turning the music down. "Did I hear what?"

"There was a murder last night."

"Who?"

"Not so much who, as where. It happened at the coven meeting—and by the way, why weren't you there?"

"I…"

"Does Jerry disapprove or something?"

"No, I just…Jerry isn't even here right now. I forgot the date. I'm surprised you had it in this weather."

She raised her eyebrows and smiled conspiratorially. "The weather cleared for the hours we were there. Write it on your calendar, Summer—it happens every full moon.

40

Anyway, this woman I've never seen before was there. Lucia knows her, or knew her, I should say."

"Don't tell me, her name is Isabel."

"That's right—how did you know?"

"She and her husband were in my store yesterday. Who killed her?"

"That's the thing. No one knows. She was standing next to her husband while we were chanting, and then she collapsed."

"Did the police come?"

"Yes. Sam was the officer in charge. All he could find was a bruise on the back of her neck, which hardly explains why she died."

"And what about her husband?"

"He says it wasn't him. There was no murder weapon on him or anywhere around."

"Motive?"

Becky shrugged. "I found out she was good friends with Daniel Booker's wife, the one who disappeared a few years back?"

"Did you hear about his books on magic being stolen? He called me in to help, but then he told me he'd solved the case."

"I heard about it last night from Isabel's husband, Henry."

"Was that before or after his wife was murdered?"

"Before."

I thought about what Lucia had said about Isabel and her husband being staunch Catholics. "Why were they there last night? Lucia said they didn't believe in Wicca or pagan stuff."

"I got the feeling Lucia invited them. But from what I observed they seemed pretty into it."

"Daniel wasn't there, was he?"

"As a matter of fact, he was."

"But he...he told me he's god-fearing—those were his exact words. He was totally against his wife's involvement in the coven."

"I know that—Mom told me. Do you think...?"

"I don't know, but the coincidences are piling up." Becky and I often had the same thoughts, our communications punctuated by unfinished sentences.

Becky stared at me. "Philippa's body was never found."

"I know, and I also know that Daniel keeps referring to 'her death', as though he knows something. Otherwise wouldn't he be inclined to think she might still be alive?"

"I would, if it were me. And what's with the missing books? That's just plain weird."

"Here's what we've go so far," I said, ticking things off:

"1. Missing books on magic at the store of a man who hated magic—missing wife of same man.

2. Isabel murdered at the coven meeting.

3. Isabel and her husband Henry, who according to Lucia were not into the occult, asking me to hold books on spells and black magic."

"Really?"

I nodded. "I doubt Henry will be back to get them now."

"Henry is being held on suspicion of murder."

"He is? I thought he said he didn't do it."

Becky laughed. "He was standing right next to her. He's the most likely candidate."

I scoffed. "Jerry will kick himself for missing this one," I muttered.

"Where is he?"

"How do I know? He just decided he needed to think."

"What about? Don't you two have a business now?"

"He's bored, Becky. And according to Lucia he's upset that she joined the coven."

"That doesn't sound plausible—why would he care?"

"He hasn't confided in me about any of it."

Becky frowned. "He can really go off the deep end, can't he? I wonder what goes on in that head of his."

"His head was formally occupied with police work—now he has too much time on his hands."

Her gaze met mine. "Maybe this Jaguar Enterprises wasn't such a good idea after all."

"That's what I've been thinking. But I don't know if he can be reinstated at the precinct."

Becky chuckled. "Maybe he'll have to give out parking tickets."

I shuddered. "Over his dead body."

"I've got to get back to the bakery. Let me know if you find out anything."

"Same goes for you," I said, walking her to the door. "I might have to talk to Sam about Henry. This case seems like it might overlap with the missing books."

"Books on magic are the common denominator, right?"

I opened the door. "And death."

"Talk soon?" she said, pausing on the stoop.

I nodded and locked up, watching her run down the street toward the bakery. When I went back to the shelf where I'd been working I was sure I saw a shadow in the corner. But when I went to investigate there was nothing there.

I finished up the section where I was working and decided to continue in the morning. Becky's visit had put a damper on my concentration.

Before I left the store I used the landline to call Jerry's cell, sure that he would want to know about the murder. When he didn't answer I tried to leave a message, but his mailbox was full. How could his mailbox be full—where was he? I suddenly had a vision of him with his arms around a statuesque red-haired beauty. They were laughing—about to kiss. My stomach twisted as I registered the possibility that he was having an affair.

In my car fifteen minutes later I called Sam's cell, glad when he finally answered. The vision of Jerry wouldn't leave me alone—I had to get my mind off it. "I heard about the murder, Sam. Do you think Henry did it?"

There was a pause before Sam said, "You know I can't discuss the case with you, Summer."

"Can you at least tell me if there are any other suspects?"

"No, I can't."

"Do you know where Jerry went?" I blurted.

Sam let out a heavy sigh. "Maybe you should come by tonight for dinner."

"You know something."

"Come over around five, okay?"

"I'll be there." He was having an affair and Sam knew about it. I let out a little cry, my eyes welling.

At home I hurriedly fed Cutty and the cats, surprised when Mischief sidled up to me purring, her glassy green eyes staring into mine as though she had a message for me. "Again? I'm sorry, but I don't understand cat," I told her, rushing off to change my clothes.

⌘

Agnes opened the door, her tight sleeveless black velvet shirt showing off the colorful tattoos on her arms. She'd lost the baby weight and looked thin and gorgeous.

"You look tired," she said immediately, her kohl-rimmed eyes meeting mine.

"A lot going on," I muttered, pulling off my raincoat and hanging it on the coat rack.

I heard a squeal of baby laughter as Agnes led the way to the living room, Sammie's laughing face coming into view as Sam swung him up into the air.

"Hey, Summer, good to see you," Sam said, placing the eighteen-month-old on the floor. He came toward me and kissed my cheek, a look of worry appearing on his face.

Agnes appeared from the other room with two glasses of white wine, placing one on the table in front of me. "How's the store?"

I raised my eyes to hers. "I'm doing inventory."

Agnes chuckled. "Glad it isn't me. I guess you heard about the latest excitement in sleepy Ames."

"I did." I glanced at Sam. "But when I asked, Sam wouldn't divulge anything about it."

Sam made a face. "You know I'm not allowed to, Summer."

"That didn't stop you when Jerry was on the force."

He shrugged and took a swig from his bottle of beer.

"Did Henry do it?"

Sam laughed. "You don't give up, do you?"

But underneath his laugh I saw the worry in his eyes. I felt the tension build. I couldn't smile, my nerves as taut as piano strings. These friends of mine were about to tell me something that I didn't want to hear. The redhead appeared in my mind again, a scornful smile curling up her beautiful mouth as she stared at me. Jerry stood behind her, his eyes dark with desire, his hand reaching for the strap of her dress. I let out a moan and pulled my arms around my body, trying not to cry. I turned to Agnes who was watching me as she placed her glass on the coffee table.

"More importantly," she said, her eyes on mine, "we have some news regarding Jerry."

Here it was, the news I didn't want to hear. "I figured that's why you invited me. If he's having an affair I don't want to know."

Agnes and Sam exchanged a look, some signal passing between them. "He's not having an affair, Summer," Agnes said softly, her hand gently touching mine before moving to her lap.

"He's at Boston General for some tests," Sam continued.

I let out my held breath. "He's at the hospital? What kind of tests?"

Agnes leaned forward, her hands twisting nervously. "He asked us not to tell you. He didn't want you to worry."

"What kind of tests?" I repeated, my pulse speeding up.

"Cancer screening," Sam supplied, looking down at the coffee table.

I went cold all over. "Cancer…what kind of cancer?"

"Prostate."

I placed my glass carefully down, shock making my hands shake. "Why didn't he say?"

"He…"

"Yeah, I get it. He didn't want me to worry. But we're married. If I wasn't so worried I'd be furious with him right now. I can't believe he'd share this with you and leave me in the dark."

"Have you heard from him?" Sam asked.

"No. Have you?"

"He called when he reached the hospital, but I haven't heard anything since."

He called when he reached the hospital. I thought of the calls I'd made, the ones he hadn't answered, and the full mailbox. I stared at the baby playing with blocks in the corner, listening to his coos of contentment. Tears threatened. I glanced at Sam. "I'm so angry right now I don't even know what to say."

A look of surprise crossed his features. "You're angry?"

"Yes. And I'm also completely freaked out. I always thought we were best friends. I feel betrayed."

"Summer," Agnes began, rising from her chair.

But I was already standing and half way to the door. I grabbed my coat and flung the door open and slammed it behind me, running for my car as the tears I'd been holding back slid down my cheeks.

I drove like a maniac, unable to see the road through my tears. Jerry wasn't having an affair, he was seeing a doctor because he might have cancer. I let out a howl of pain, slamming my hand into the steering wheel. Why hadn't he told me?

5

After calling and calling Jerry's number and being frustrated by not being able to leave a message, I cried myself to sleep. I was hurt, terrified, and furious, all at the same time. When I finally fell into a crying-induced stupor, my dreams took me to hospitals with white clad doctors tiptoeing down deserted white corridors. When I entered a room Jerry was in bed, his face as white as the sheets. He held up the covers to show me the blood soaked bandages between his legs. I let out a scream, waking myself up, my entire body filled with adrenaline.

In the morning I was worn down to a nubbin, my eyes red and swollen. Thank goodness I was still doing inventory and wouldn't have to face customers.

The animals crowded around in the kitchen as though sensing my mood and wanting to comfort me. I fed them and grabbed my coat and bag and hurried out the door.

When Agnes called the store phone later I almost let it ring, but then I thought better of it—she might have heard from Jerry.

"Just wanted to check on you," Agnes said when I answered.

"I called Jerry a zillion times last night and he never answered."

"He's probably in a place with no cell reception."

"Don't make excuses for him. I'm…I don't what I am. I can't think. Have you heard from him?"

"Since last night? No. But he said he'd be back on Monday, which is tomorrow."

"His note said after the weekend."

"I can understand how you feel. If Sam did this I'd be beside myself. But Jerry's proud and probably feeling very vulnerable."

I hated her telling me this, hated that he'd shared the most intimate details of his life with her and left me out. "Why did he think something was wrong?"

"He told us he's been getting up to pee in the night and it burns when he goes."

"That could be due to other things."

"I know it could, and I told him that. Did you know his dad had prostate cancer?"

"No, I didn't." Another secret shared with Agnes and Sam and kept from his wife. "No wonder he's worried," I muttered.

"One more thing, and *please* don't tell him I told you— Sam doesn't even know about this."

Oh god, what now?

"He said he's been having difficulty with erections."

A shock wave passed through me. "He told you *that?*"

"Yes. And it's a symptom."

Anger boiled to the surface of my mind—how dare he share this with Agnes? "That can also be caused by stress," I heard myself say, trying not to yell at her. Jerry's behavior wasn't her fault.

"Did he mention this problem…or…"

"Our sex life is a wasteland," I interrupted. "When I tried to snuggle with him the other night he got up and went to the kitchen. And he's drinking too much. And he basically didn't come to bed that night."

"That was the night before he went to Boston?"

"Yup. If he slept at all it was in the guest bedroom." I sniffled, trying not to cry again. "Now I'm terrified."

"He's young and strong and there's lots of treatments for it. Try not to worry."

"I can't believe he talked this over with you and never mentioned a word to me. If I didn't love him, and want to be there for him, I think I'd divorce him."

"Remember who he is—a proud passionate man who has never had anything go wrong with his health."

"You're right about that. But…if we're going to have a good marriage he has to be able to talk to me. Without that I'd rather be single."

When we hung up I tried to quell my worry, turning back to the elephant gods in plastic bags and drawing one out to stare at it. "Please help Jerry," I said, holding it close to my heart. "You're the remover of obstacles," I whispered. "Please remove this one."

Later on that afternoon I called and ordered a TV for our house. I didn't want it, the thought of the noise and the flickering lights making me feel slightly ill, but I did it anyway, knowing it would make Jerry happy. It was due to be delivered Monday morning. To keep the living room free of electronics I planned to have it installed in the spare bedroom. That way he could watch his sports and news while I stayed in the living room and read.

I cried myself to sleep for a second night in a row, feeling like my heart had been cleaved in half. I woke an hour later struggling between anger and misery until I noticed Ganesha sitting on my bedside table. "Please help him," I whispered. "And please help me forgive him." After that I fell into a restless sleep, dreaming I was tumbling down cliffs and running into walls in my car when the brakes refused to work. Jerry came to me, his eyes sunken, his face ravaged. The pain in his eyes woke me, a scream on my lips as I registered the reality of what was going on. He could die.

"Where you want it, lady?" the uniformed man asked, holding the dolly with the giant cardboard container. I held the door wide and pointed the way to the spare room.

I made coffee, listening to him banging around in the room. Having this monstrosity would probably insure that once dinner was over I'd never see Jerry again until we went to bed. But then I remembered what was happening, the precariousness of the future, my eyes filling with tears. Damn him!

Once the TV was installed and the directions for how to use it on the kitchen table, I fed Cutty and the cats and left for Tarot and Tea. The day seemed to be holding its breath, the rain gone for the moment and not a hint of wind. But in the distance I saw a bank of charcoal colored clouds, occasional jagged lightning within them. The Ganesha was in my purse, my fingers reaching for him every time my mind turned to what might happen. I flipped the heat on high as my teeth began to chatter. *Soon,* I told myself. *He'll be home tonight and you'll know.* But that thought did little to help.

Once I'd opened and turned on the heat I slid my CD of Tangerine Dream into the CD player, needing something ethereal to take my mind off reality. Valerie was my first customer, her breezy attitude allowing me to let go of the tangled knot in my stomach.

"Are you investigating the murder?" she asked me right off.

"Sam won't tell me a thing about Henry. Were you there that night?"

"I was. And I was standing directly across from Isabel and Henry."

"Do you think he did it?"

She gazed into the distance. "I haven't had any premonitions about this one. Perhaps I should consult the cards."

"But why would Henry kill his wife?"

She shrugged. "I have no idea—and I don't know them. Lucia might be a better person to ask."

"True. Maybe I'll go over to the Victorian later. I have some other things I need to speak with her about."

Valerie eyed me. "You're worried about something. Is it the murder or something else?"

I shook my head and turned away as my eyes filled. "I can't talk about it."

Valerie frowned and gazed at me for a moment before she asked, "What about the missing books? Any progress on that front?"

"Not yet. Still digging."

"Good girl. Now…where is Emilia?" she asked, turning toward the door. "She was supposed to meet me here."

The door opened a second later and Mrs. Browning appeared, a purple beret covering her steel gray hair. "The world has gone topsy-turvy," she said, glancing at me. "We've never had a murder during the coven meetings. I'm afraid of what this might mean."

"What could it mean, other than someone wanted Isabel dead?"

"Oh, my dear, this is so much more than that," she answered. "Wouldn't you agree, Valerie?"

Valerie nodded. "I'm afraid it could be a sign."

"A sign of what?" I asked, but both women had retreated into the stacks, their heads together, whispering.

I spent the rest of the day trying not to think about Jerry as I took money from customers and attempted to appear normal. When Becky arrived just before closing time I couldn't hold it together anymore.

"What is it?" she asked when she noticed my welling eyes.

"Jerry may have prostate cancer," I blurted, letting the tears come.

Becky didn't say anything for a moment, her eyes narrowing in thought. "Has he tried any natural herbal remedies? I know a few I could recommend."

"He hasn't even told me about it, Becky. I only found out from Sam and Agnes."

Becky moved forward to hug me. "That's not right," she whispered. "You're his wife, the first person he should turn to."

"That's what I think too, but he didn't tell me he was worried, or that he was going to Boston for tests. What do I say when he comes home tonight?"

"You listen and then tell him exactly how you feel about being left out."

"Even if he's seriously sick?"

Becky's gaze went into the distance for a moment before her clear eyes met mine. "My intuition says he's fine."

I stared at her. Becky took after her mom and her intuition was usually spot on. "Really?"

"Yes, really. Now stop worrying and get to work on the missing books and the rest of it."

I let out a long sigh. "Thanks, Becks. You always make me feel better."

◦◦◦

It was close to six before I heard Jerry's motorcycle pulling into his parking spot. My stomach twisted with nerves as I tried to think what to say. I sat very still on the couch, determined not to behave like an idiot. But as soon as the door opened I was there, flinging my arms around him before he could get inside.

"Hey? What's all this?"

"I missed you," I muttered. "And I had no idea why you left. I thought...I thought you..."

He caught my arms. "Thought I what?"

"Didn't love me, or..." The tears I'd been holding back slid down my face.

"Summer—what's going on?"

"I know, Jerry. Agnes and Sam told me."

Jerry's eyes went dark, his brows pulling together. "I told them…"

"You told them not to tell your wife you were going for tests? How could you do that to me?"

Jerry shook his head and pulled off his leather jacket, hanging it on the iron coatrack. "Can't trust anyone," he muttered.

"What did you find out?"

His eyes met mine and slid away. "I don't have it."

"Thank the goddess!"

"But the tests showed I have a low sperm count."

"So what? That isn't a fatal disease."

"It is if you want a baby."

I just stared at him, unable to speak. "I thought we…"

"Summer, you're in your thirties. If we're going to do this we should do it soon."

"I'm barely thirty—hardly 'in my thirties', but…what did they say about the erection problems? Is that part of the low sperm count thing?"

"God dammit!" Jerry exploded. "That was in confidence!"

"So you tell my best friend you're having a problem getting an erection, but you don't even mention it to the woman you love? Do you want a divorce?"

Jerry stared at me. "I…"

"There's no excuse for this, Jerry. I don't even know what to say." I stomped away, my eyes filling again as I hurried into our bedroom and slammed the door.

I was face down on the bed when he came in a while later and sat next to me. "You bought me a TV?"

I turned, wiping my eyes. "I knew you wanted one."

Jerry's dark eyes went soft, his fingers pushing the hair off my wet face. "I'm sorry about all this. I couldn't tell you—I was too ashamed."

"About the prostate or the erections?"

"Both. The doctors couldn't explain it, but they did suggest some drugs."

I sat up. "So your mother joining the coven had nothing to do with this?"

"My mother…what in hell are you talking about?"

"Agnes said you were upset because Lucia is now going to the coven meetings with Douglas."

Jerry frowned, his lips pressing together. "Why would I be upset about that? She can do what she wants."

"I thought that sounded off. I guess she was trying to explain your bad mood without telling me the truth. As far as drugs, there's nothing wrong with you aside from stress."

"Stress—from what? I'm doing nothing."

"That's why. We need to talk."

"Isn't that what we're doing?"

"You haven't been happy since you quit the force. This PI thing isn't working for you."

"Summer, I…"

"You know it's true. And another thing—if you ever, and I mean ever, tell Sam and Agnes something this personal again before you tell me—you're out of here. I really mean it. I can't believe you kept this from me. I'm your wife. I thought you trusted me—I thought we were best friends."

"I…I felt…I was scared. I want to be a husband to you, not unable to perform and need you to take care of me."

"All this time you've been avoiding sex I thought it was because you weren't attracted to me anymore."

His eyes welled. "Of course it wasn't."

"How was I supposed to know that if you kept it from me? And why didn't you ever mention that your dad had prostate cancer?"

"I never really thought about it until my symptoms started."

I stared at him. "Did you never think I might have been able to help?"

He made a grimace. "I've never needed help before."

"When you join the force again I bet this so-called problem will disappear."

He stretched out on the bed and leaned back against the pillows. "I can't rejoin the force now."

I moved beside him. "Why not?"

"Because they've moved on. Sam's next in line for head detective."

"Maybe there's another position open. You mentioned a consultant job a few days ago. From all the time you've been spending there I figured you might have something worked out."

His gaze went into the distance. "Yeah, there is that, but not sure if…" His expression changed, a thoughtful look appearing.

"What?"

"Let me check it out first. I don't want to jinx it."

"Guess I should go make us some dinner," I said, pushing myself off the
bed.

He leaned forward and grabbed my arm. "If you were

serious about helping me with my problem, now might be a good time."

I let him pull me back onto the bed. "Are you sure you're up to it after your stressful weekend?"

He grinned. "That's where you come in."

As it happened it took one minute of me 'helping' before Jerry's supposed problem disappeared.

6

When I woke in the morning Jerry was on the way into the bedroom carrying two cappuccinos. He placed one on the table next to me and headed around to his side. "Feel like a new man," he murmured, gazing at me.

I pulled myself up to sitting, glancing at his naked body. "More like the old Jerry, "I said, chuckling. "I think the suggestion of getting back on the force released your stress."

He slid into bed beside me. "Released—good word."

"This sperm count thing—does it fluctuate like cholesterol?"

"I don't know. I've been smoking a lot of dope. Could that affect it?"

"You idiot—of course that's what's doing it!"

"Really?"

"Yes, Jerry—don't you know anything?"

After coffee Jerry told me he needed my help again, a grin lifting the
corners of his sensuous mouth. "Likely story," I said, glancing down.

"How'd that happen?" he asked with a puzzled frown.

I laughed, relief and love flooding through me as I pulled him close.

I was putting on my coat, ready to leave for work, when Jerry finally asked about the case.

"Daniel told me he solved it, but he didn't tell me how or who did it. Did you hear about the murder at the coven meeting?"

Jerry shook his head, his eyes widening. "Who was murdered?"

I told him what I knew, finally adding, "Glad it was me and not Sam who filled you in."

But Jerry was already lost in thought, his detective skills in high gear. "Hmm?" he said a few minutes later, looking up after I asked a question.

"Do you think Henry killed her?" I repeated.

"I'm still back on Daniel Booker's wife. I remember that case. We never found a body."

I glanced at the clock in the kitchen. I didn't have the time to discuss it. "What do you have planned for today?"

"I'm heading to the precinct."

"Good. See you later."

I was nearly out the door when he grabbed me and spun me around. "I love you, Mrs. Brady. I hope you forgive me."

"Didn't last night and this morning give you a clue?"

He scoffed and then he pulled me close and kissed me.

༄

The worsening weather couldn't bring down my mood as I drove around flying trash and detritus on the road, turning on my wipers to sweep away the ice filled raindrops on my windshield. Jerry and I were solid again and he wasn't sick. I let out a whoop of happiness, swerving a second later to avoid a trashcan rolling across the street.

I had barely walked through the door into Tarot and Tea when my cell rang. "You already miss me?" I chirped.

There was a pregnant pause. "This is Daniel Booker."

"Oh, I'm sorry. I thought…how are you?

"Not very good, thanks to you."

"What are you talking about?"

"Apparently I'm a suspect in this latest murder. An officer came by this morning to question me."

"Why do they think you had something to do with it?"

He sighed. "They found an ice pick and traced it to me."

"How can you trace an ice pick?"

"It was a birthday gift and it has my initials on it. Not sure how it came to be there."

"Did it have the victim's blood on it?"

"I don't think so."

"And they didn't arrest you."

"Not yet, but I have a feeling they will. I told them I hadn't seen that ice pick since the night my wife disappeared. We had drinks together in the early afternoon and I had to use it to break apart the ice cubes."

"Have you called your lawyer?"

"Yes, but if you're willing, I'd like to enlist your help as well."

"Shall I come by?"

"I know you're busy—I'll come there."

Daniel Booker arrived at an opportune moment when they were no customers in the store. He'd changed his tune completely from the last time I'd seen him, all smiles and politeness.

"I need you to solve my wife's murder."

"How can I solve it when there's no body?"

"There is a body," he whispered.

My mouth dropped open. "You know where it is?"

He nodded. "Come by when you close up and I'll show you."

As the hours went by I grew more and more nervous. Did I trust him? What if he murdered his wife and was planning to murder me too? But why would he want me dead? Would I have to drive with him to some remote area where he could dispose of my body once the deed was done?

The questions rolled around inside my head until I thought I might scream. I considered calling Jerry but didn't want to get him involved, especially at this juncture. If there was indeed a body, he could come examine it and get in touch with the ME. But then I remembered that Jerry wasn't on the force—he had no access to the medical examiner—and yet...as I remembered they were good friends. Perhaps he could ask the guy for a favor?

By the time I closed and locked the shop I was still undecided about what to do. But when I found myself hurrying across the rain soaked grass to Bookers, I figured I'd made up my mind.

The door opened before I knocked, Daniel Booker standing there wearing his frayed jacket and a button down blue oxford shirt underneath. His pants were well-worn corduroys, hanging loosely around his thin legs.

"Come in," he said, holding the door wide.

"Is she here?"

"In a manner of speaking."

He led the way into the back of the store and I followed, already regretting my decision. The shadows coalesced the further back we went, the hair on the back of my neck registering the uncanny. When he kicked a throw rug aside and pulled up a trap door, I let out a little gasp.

He glanced up at me. "Don't worry. I'm not planning to kill you." A ladder led downward into darkness and he moved onto it.

"What about a flashlight?"

"There's a light switch down here. I'll turn it on as soon as I get to the bottom."

I waited until he flicked it on before I turned backward and followed him down. It smelled of damp and mildew and dirt, cobwebs hanging from the low ceiling. "Where are we?"

"These tunnels were built during prohibition. One of them leads directly to Lila's house."

"You mean my store, Tarot and Tea?"

"Yes, that's what I meant," he said, heading off.

I followed at a distance, not happy when the lights flickered and then died. I pulled my cell phone out and turned on the flashlight feature.

"That's clever," Daniel said, turning. "Do all phones have that now?"

"I think so." What in hell was I doing following this man into tunnels that no one knew about? If he locked me down here...*don't go there*, a voice warned.

"Here's where I found her," he said suddenly, stopping abruptly in front of me. I nearly ran into him, putting on the brakes just in time. I peered into the shadows, shining my light where he pointed. I let out a little shriek that echoed.

"I didn't move her or disturb her," he said, kneeling reverently next to the skeleton.

The pale bones still had bits of fabric stuck here and there from what she'd been wearing the day she died. A scarf covered in cobwebs and dust lay a few feet away. "What happened? How did you find her?"

"I killed her, Summer. It was an accident."

"You…but you just said…"

"I know what I said!" he shouted.

"Please, Mr. Booker—I didn't mean anything. Just tell me the details."

"I pushed her and she tripped in the dark and hit her head."

"Why were you down here?"

"I was showing her…never mind that. When I checked she wasn't breathing."

"Why didn't you go to the police?"

"Because they would have accused me of murder."

"But you reported her missing, why are you telling me now?"

"Because I think you can help me. I can take a polygraph, or…"

"They could have determined how she died seven years ago. Not sure they can now, unless she has a crack in her skull. Why did you push her?"

"Because she said something…something that made me very angry."

His answers sounded rehearsed, spoken quickly and without emotion.

When a woman's voice called out, Daniel froze, his eyes

widening. "Wait here," he said, staring at me as several emotions played across his features.

Before I could react he was running toward the ladder. I ran after him, but in my haste I dropped my phone. In the meantime I heard the slam of the trap door and the sound of something heavy being pulled across. A moment later there was a surprised shout from Mr. Booker and then the murmur of a woman's voice. I stood at the base of the ladder and strained to hear the voices that were now moving away. My pulse raced. When I climbed the ladder I couldn't budge the trapdoor. "Mr. Booker!" I screamed until I was hoarse. I was trapped down here in the dark while he consulted with his lawyer—who else could it be? Maybe he'd come back in a while.

I crawled in the dirt, searching for my phone, and then I shouted again, finally giving up to crumple into a ball on the damp ground. Why did he ask me to solve his wife's murder when he was the one who did it? He might get off with manslaughter, but even so, he would surely go to jail. That is if I didn't die down here too. My tears came then, hot against my cold cheeks.

A couple of hours must have gone by before I decided to look for my cell phone again. I didn't find it. I sat down with my back to the tunnel wall and tried to think. Daniel said these tunnels connected to Tarot and Tea. But how could I ever find the right one in the dark? I was still sitting there when a wispy indistinct shape wafted toward me. A woman's pale and barely perceptible face peered at me, a finger pointing. "Are you Philippa?"

She didn't answer, her translucent glow leading me down the tunnel. I rose and followed.

The heavy wooden square at the top of the ladder was stuck. Straining to keep my balance, I pushed up on it as hard as I could, glad when it finally gave a rasp of complaint and opened. I pushed it back and climbed into the kitchen of Tarot and Tea and collapsed, my muscles trembling from the effort. When I turned to say thank you to the ghost, she was already gone.

After I switched on the lights in the other room I called Jerry, shaking so much I was afraid I'd punched in the wrong numbers.

The phone had barely rung when he answered, his voice cracking with emotion. "Where are you? I've been calling your cell for over two hours!"

"I'm at Tarot and Tea. Can you come get me?"

"Don't you have your car? What's happened? You sound like…"

"Like I'm about to have a nervous breakdown? Just come, please. You can leave your motorcycle here and drive my car home."

"Summer…"

"Please hurry."

I was waiting by the door when he arrived, only unlocking it after he climbed the steps. He took one look at me and pulled me into his arms. "What the hell is going on?"

After clinging to him in silence for a minute I pulled away, locking the door behind us. "There's a dead body in the tunnels between Tarot and Tea and Bookers, and I think Daniel Booker just tried to kill me."

Jerry's thick brows drew together in confusion. "Tunnels? What tunnels?"

"I guess they were built and used during prohibition—but that's not important. Daniel's wife is down there."

Jerry waited, his gaze on mine.

"He told me he accidentally killed her. I told him I'd help him with the police, and then he locked me down there. I lost my cell phone, and..."

"Jesus, Summer! I should call Sam."

"Yes, you'd better. Are you on the force yet?"

Jerry took his jacket off and put it around my shoulders. "You're shaking like a leaf. And no, I'm not on the force, but there's a good chance I'll have some sort of position soon." He reached into the pocket of the leather motorcycle jacket he'd placed around me and pulled out his cell, punching in numbers as he walked away. I heard him talking but I didn't register the words, my mind going in circles.

He ended the call, his measured steps bringing him back to where I sat on the stool behind the counter. "Sam's on his way. Where's the body?"

"It's actually a skeleton. Do you think this is all connected—I mean Philippa, and then Isabel's murder and the missing books?"

Jerry grinned. "Your teeth are chattering but you're still sleuthing—that's my girl."

"I forgot to tell you the most important part. Philippa's ghost showed me the way out." When I led the way to the open trapdoor and started down the ladder, he grabbed my arm.

"Let's wait for Sam. We need to do this properly." He glanced around the kitchen. "How about I fix you a cup of tea."

I pulled myself out of the opening and collapsed in a chair. "That would be heavenly."

I was feeling decidedly better by the time Sam arrived. Jerry let him in, the two of them whispering together before they arrived in the kitchen. "You up to showing us where she is?" Jerry asked, gazing at me worriedly.

"I can try, but what about Daniel Booker—he…"

"Sam brought back-up, Summer. They're already knocking on his door."

I felt a wave of relief as I climbed down the ladder, the beam of Sam's flashlight comforting where it bounced off the stones and dirt as he walked beside me. When we came to a turning I had him point the light at the ground, searching for my footprints. "This way," I said, heading to the left.

When we reached Philippa's skeleton I stopped to listen, able to hear the rumble of furniture being moved and the sound of male voices.

"Over here!" Sam shouted.

Jerry was already kneeling beside her, the small light from his cell phone tracking across the curves of her pale bones as he examined her. "There's a fracture here," he told Sam, both of them shining their lights on the back of her skull. "And one here," Sam said, examining one of her legs.

"He told me he pushed her and she tripped and hit her head."

Jerry's face looked eerie in the light shining under his chin. "Looks like more than that," he intoned.

A second later two men in uniform joined us. "There's no one in the house," one of them told Sam.

"Not even in the apartment upstairs?" I asked.

He glanced at me and shook his head.

"So he really planned to leave me down here," I muttered, half to myself.

"Looks that way," Sam said. "Can you fill me in?"

I explained the woman's arrival, and how Daniel hurried off and told me to wait. "And then I heard him move a piece of furniture. When I tried to push the trapdoor up it wouldn't budge."

"It had a bookcase over it," one of the men said. "We wouldn't have noticed except the rug was bunched and there were scratch marks on the floor."

"Thank goodness for the ghost," I murmured.

"Ghost?" the same man asked.

"Summer's just being dramatic," Sam assured him, glaring at me.

I let out a huff of annoyance before I grabbed Jerry's sleeve. "Can we go now?"

He put his arm around me. "How about we take a look for your phone first?"

We found it a few minutes later, close to one side of the tunnel leading toward Bookers. By that time Sam and the other two men were headed toward the open trapdoor.

"What now?" I asked Sam.

"We get the ME down here and take a more thorough look. The man is already a suspect in Isabel Franklin's murder."

"You should also take a good hard look at the apartment," I whispered, glancing at the other two cops who'd gone ahead.

"Yes, that too," Sam agreed, glancing at Jerry. "Have you made up your mind?"

Jerry turned from where he was helping me up the ladder into Bookers. "Need to talk it over with Summer first."

"I could use you right about now," Sam muttered, closing the trapdoor behind the three of us.

We were in the car on the way home, when Jerry chuckled, glancing at me. "That ghost remark was pretty funny, Summer."

"I thought the entire police department knew about me by now."

"The old contingent may know, but these guys are new. You should have seen the look on his face."

I giggled. "I wasn't thinking clearly at the time."

"Yeah. I need to get you home and into a hot bath. I'll make us some toddies."

The thought of being cozy in my house with Jerry had me sighing with contentment. "What is it you need to make up your mind about?"

"We can talk about that tomorrow. You need a night to recover."

I glanced over at him, wondering if he had any tricks up his sleeve to help me 'recover', but his expression was impassive as he concentrated on the road.

At home Jerry fixed me a hot toddy with lemon, whiskey and honey, and forced me to eat some crackers and cheese. An hour later I was in the bath, letting the hot water work its magic. After I soaked for a while Jerry joined me in the tub, his fingers working shampoo through my hair. Once he rinsed the shampoo out I leaned back against him, letting out a sigh of pleasure. "So glad we're getting along again."

"Me too," he whispered in my ear, his hands wandering.

He had a plan after all.

7

The next morning over coffee I questioned Jerry about his possible 'new' position. "So not as a detective, but some sort of special consultant? How does that work?"

"I'd be on the payroll but not involved in the day-to-day running of things at the station. And it would give me time for our cases."

I lifted my eyebrows. "Sounds about perfect, Jer. It will keep you from going crazy in between our cases."

He smiled. "That's what I thought too. And right now Sam needs help with this mess."

"Any news?"

"Haven't spoken with anyone this morning. I'll call and let you know once I'm sworn in."

"Sworn in? That sounds kind of official."

"It won't be much—I'll sign some papers."

"Who's chief now?"

"Carrie Lancaster. She's a battle-ax—tough lady."

"Because she isn't a beauty?" I said indignantly.

Jerry smirked. "She's no beauty, but I didn't mean it like that. She's gray-haired and keeps the guys in line—there's no messing around with her."

"What would be the equivalent term for a man, Jerry?"

"You and your feminist crap. Give it a rest, would you?"

I turned away and finished my coffee. "If you want to pick up your bike you'd better come with me," I said, putting on my coat. I glanced outside at the trees that had lost nearly all their leaves in the last few days of wind. At least today the sky was a pale blue and the sun was peeking out behind a thin layer of cloud. But when I opened the door I let out a shriek. "It's freezing!"

Jerry chuckled behind me. "Want me to warm up your car for you, milady?"

"Would you?"

He grabbed the keys and set off, turning to smirk at me before he opened the car door.

❧

I was at my desk in Tarot and Tea when I got a call from Sam.

"We found something interesting in the apartment," he said after greeting me. "There was correspondence between Daniel Booker and Henry and Isabel Franklin. They were working together against the coven in what you might term a counter cult devoted to getting rid of all things pagan."

"Were there details?"

"A few. It looks like Daniel Booker and the group were planning a book burning, but the books were stolen before they had a chance."

"And now Daniel's disappeared. Did he kill Isabel?"

"I don't think either one of them killed Isabel. They were all on the same team. There's someone else involved in this."

"Did you talk to Jerry?"

"Just spoke to him. He asked me to fill you in."

"What now?"

"We keep digging. Please be careful, Summer, and don't do anything without Jerry."

"What about Philippa? Did the ME examine her?"

"Yes. Her skull was fractured and her leg was broken in two places."

"But how did she die?"

"Could have been the head injury—looks like she was bludgeoned to death. She's still doing tests."

I looked up when Mrs. Browning walked in. "Got to go, Sam." I ended the call and stuck my phone away, still reeling from the vision.

"I heard you found a body," Mrs. Browning whispered, coming close to my desk.

I gazed at the older woman, noticing the canny look in her pale eyes. "Yes. There was a skeleton down in the prohibition tunnels. You knew, didn't you?"

She didn't answer, her lips pulling together. "Philippa was a friend of mine. At the time her disappearance was disturbing to all of us involved in the coven. Witches worry when one of their own is taken."

"Taken? Why would you call it that?"

"Taken is only a term to describe what we feared had happened to her. There are those in this town who don't approve of us."

That was a major understatement. "Do you know who they are?"

"Of course, dear. Daniel Booker and his friend, Henry, were at the top of the list at the time. I always wondered about Philippa—has the person been identified?"

Something about the way she asked the question led me to believe that things were not what they seemed. "He led me to her, but then he locked me down there."

She scoffed. "Those tunnels are like a labyrinth, but there are many ways out."

"Not just between Bookers and Tarot and Tea?"

"The bootlegging circulated between many places."

Before I could ask her more, she'd moved off, her expression closed. If what she said was true, then maybe he hadn't intended to kill me after all. And now that I thought about it, I'd assumed it was Wendy, his lawyer, who called out to him—what if it was someone else? It was definitely a woman's voice I heard.

Jerry called me while I was having a quick cup of tea.

"Are you all right?"

"Yes. Why wouldn't I be?"

"Well…you slept like the dead last night."

"And whose fault was that?"

Jerry laughed. "Guess you had too much toddy."

"Is that what you're calling what you did to my poor unsuspecting body?"

He chuckled. "Had to take your mind off the tunnels, didn't I? Did Sam call and give you the news?"

"He told me about the correspondence. Sounds like there's more to the case than a couple of murders."

"That woman in the tunnels Daniel Booker claimed was his wife? She isn't."

"The skeleton isn't…?"

"That's correct. Anita's doing DNA tests to try and identify her."

"Wow. This just keeps getting…"

"More and more interesting?"

"I was going to say complicated. He must have known it wasn't her—why would he say it was?"

"For some reason he wanted you to think it was. Maybe if and when she's identified, it will shed some light on what's going on."

"But he implicated himself in her death. Mrs. Browning keeps mentioning the illegal bootlegging going through those tunnels, but that was nearly one hundred years ago. And what about this counter cult Sam mentioned? Did Henry confess his part?"

"Henry is cooperating fully with the police, but I'm not privy to what he's said."

"And Jerry, the woman I heard calling to Daniel Booker—maybe it wasn't his lawyer. Has anyone reached out to Wendy Werner?"

"Not sure, but I'll check on her."

"And I think Sam should get a search team down in those tunnels. Whenever Mrs. Browning mentions something more than once I figure she's trying to steer me in the right direction."

Jerry chuckled. "I'll talk to Sam."

It was near closing time when Valerie burst through the door, wet leaves blowing inside with her. "Have you heard the latest?"

"No—what?"

"Daniel Booker was murdered—his body was out by the river."

"Who would want Daniel dead? He was just a tired

middle-aged man trying to locate a few missing books."

"And yet you thought he tried to kill you."

"True, but I've changed my mind now. Jerry said the skeleton down there wasn't his wife after all."

"Maybe Philippa's alive after all. Do they know who the skeleton belongs to?"

"Not yet. So if there's a connection between these deaths, maybe Philippa killed him—maybe she killed Isabel too."

Valerie shook her head. "Philippa was not the type of person to hurt anyone. Whoever killed Daniel wanted him out of the picture for some reason."

"If he didn't kill his wife why would he tell me he did?"

Valerie shook her head. "He must have known who that skeleton belonged to."

"Maybe the person responsible killed him to keep him from talking. When that woman called to him from the bookstore he got the strangest look on his face. And then he pulled a bookcase over the trapdoor. Why would he do that?"

"You don't think it was his lawyer?"

"I don't know—Jerry's checking into Wendy Werner. My head feels like it's about to explode."

She patted me on the arm. "I'll consult the cards tonight."

I turned to my CD player and replaced the lively Irish music with a disc of Indian chants, hoping to calm my frazzled nerves. When I turned back to speak with Valerie she was gone.

8

The rain had stopped by the time I drove home, patchy clouds blowing across the deepening night sky. When I reached the house Jerry was already there, the door opening while I was walking toward it.

"Jesus, Summer. Where have you been?"

"Is it late?" I asked, moving past him into the kitchen.

He padded after me, his expression concerned. "It's after six. Daniel Booker is dead and I was worried about you."

"I know. Valerie told me," I said, pulling out the wine bottle and pouring a glass.

"When did she hear about it?"

"I don't know—earlier today?"

Jerry frowned, watching me. "There is no way Valerie could know this. The police found Daniel's body two hours ago."

By his tone and expression I could tell he found this significant. "You aren't thinking Valerie had something to do with it?"

"How else could she know?"

I shrugged and carried my glass into the living room,

slumping onto the couch. "I can't think anymore, Jer."

"You aren't concerned?"

"About Valerie? No. She could have seen his body earlier, or…"

He leaned over me, his eyes dark. "And she told *you* before notifying the police?"

"Valerie is not a murderer." I took a gulp of wine and placed my glass down. "Has Henry revealed anything else? Seems like he's the best lead at this point."

"Henry was released."

I sat up. "Since when?"

"Since early this morning. They couldn't hold him any longer without evidence."

"So he could have killed Daniel."

"Possibly. They need to do a post mortem to find out when he died and if it looks like murder."

"Valerie thinks it was murder. And what about Wendy Werner? Did you speak with her?"

"I couldn't get hold of her. Did Valerie tell you that Booker was murdered?"

"Yes. She said he was murdered and his body was out by the river." I picked up my glass and leaned back. "I'm beginning to hate this case," I muttered.

"I find it puzzling that Valerie would assume his death was murder. When the police found him he was lying in the mud and there was no sign of a struggle."

"How did he die?"

"Now that's the odd part. There were several places on his body that were blue, like the skin was bruised. But the area around the bruises had deflated and turned gray."

"So no clue as to what caused his death?"

"The ME is stumped and doing blood tests to see if it was some kind of poison."

"I'm going to bed," I announced, rubbing my eyes.

"You're not hungry?"

I shook my head, got off the couch and staggered into the bedroom. I was barely able to get my clothes off before I fell asleep.

I watched a stocky dark-skinned man climb down the ladder and reach up to grab the box of bottles from the man above. When he placed it in the cart another man dragged the cart away into the dark, the sound of the wheels echoing as they bumped over the uneven ground. I ran after the cart, trying to discover where they were taking it. The tunnels were lit with strings of lights, the sound of men's voices growing louder as we reached the end of the first tunnel.

"You do the honors, Ike," the one pulling the cart said in a heavy Irish brogue. When he turned my way I sucked in my breath. But instead of looking at me, his gaze went right through me toward another cart about to arrive. He was wearing a vest over a heavy wool shirt and baggy pants, a cap over his thick hair, and his resemblance to Jerry was uncanny.

"Where's the rest of my rum?" a deep voice called out from above.

"Sorry, sir. It's coming. We had some trouble this time. Some ladies from the temperance league were hanging around and we didn't want to appear suspicious."

"Fine, Brady. But get the rest of it up here tonight. I have customers to serve."

Brady? I glanced up at the light coming from the trapdoor that in my time led into Tarot and Tea. In whatever time this was, my store was a speakeasy. A woman popped her head into the opening. "You have my beer?" she called out.

"Yes, Mrs. Franklin. It's on its way."

"And tell that no good husband of mine to get his be-hind up these steps. I need help in here."

"Where's Booker? He said he'd be here by now. You don't think the coppers got him, do ye?" a bright-haired young man wearing a cap asked.

Jerry's look-alike turned from where he was unloading another case of bottles. "Booker's meeting the boat."

I heard running feet, turning to see a black man approaching from another tunnel. "You gots to stop now!" he called out. "They's caught up with Mr. Booker. If they don't kill him first they'll haul him off to jail!"

"Close it up!" someone yelled. A second later the tunnels went dark.

I woke with a gasp and turned on my light. Jerry lay sleeping beside me, his thick hair mussed. His doppelganger in the past was just as good-looking, maybe even more appealing because of the Irish brogue. But what did bootlegging have to do with today's case? Was this just an elaborate dream or did I really just witness the past?

In the morning Jerry was up before me, humming as he made espresso. I was about to share my dream when he got a call, his eyes on his phone as he headed away to talk. When he came back he seemed distracted, barely registering my presence.

"What is it?"

He turned. "There's been a development."

"What kind of development?"

"Someone in town reported seeing Daniel with a dark-haired woman the day before we found his body."

"Philippa had dark hair, didn't she?"

Jerry nodded, running a hand across his unshaven chin.

"Valerie said Philippa would never kill anyone."

"Maybe it was Valerie and she was wearing a wig," Jerry muttered, turning away.

"She didn't do it!" I yelled. Jerry ignored me and went to grab his coat. A moment later he was out the door and I heard his motorcycle start up. I didn't get a chance to tell him about my dream.

⤳∞⤲

"And the bootleggers were unloading into Tarot and Tea?" Valerie asked.

I nodded. "And there was a woman with the last name of Franklin, a man named Booker, plus the Jerry look-alike, whose last name was Brady."

Valerie laughed. "Sounds like Alice in Wonderland."

"But that was a dream where she put in faces of people she knew—this was real, Valerie. At least I think it was. I hope it happens again so I can determine why I was there. There's obviously something I'm supposed to see or learn from this."

"Knowing you, you're probably right. But what could rum running have to do with now?"

"The only thing I can come up with is the tunnels. They have to be the key."

"When I tried to do a reading last night the cards refused to cooperate. I don't remember the last time that happened."

"Why do you think that is?"

"If the secret to solving this case is in the past, perhaps

the cards were unable to go there—they normally forecast the future."

"I want to explore the tunnels."

"I can see that, but I would wait until Jerry's with you."

"Don't worry—I won't go alone."

It was early afternoon when I called Jerry, sweet-talking him into re-visiting the tunnels. "Who knows?" I said. "Maybe there are other bodies down there."

Jerry let out a snort. "I've never known a woman so obsessed with death," he muttered.

"It's not about death, it's about solving a case," I said, indignant.

"Okay, okay. "I'll meet you there when you close up shop for the night."

Jerry arrived at Tarot and Tea at five o'clock with two large flashlights and a skeptical expression on his face. "Not sure what you expect to find down there, but I'm willing to take a look if it gets you off my back." He led the way down the ladder, pointing the flashlight upward so I could see when I followed him.

Once we were in the tunnels I explained my dream, pointing out what I'd seen. "This is where they were storing bottles," I told him, shining the light on an indented section of wall. I felt along the wall to see if there was a secret doorway, but there was nothing there.

"This is getting a bit too woo woo for me," Jerry muttered, watching me.

"I saw the entire thing."

"In your dream."

"It wasn't a dream, Jerry. I was really there."

"With some guy named Brady who looked like me? I don't think my family lived in Ames back then—what year did you say it was?"

"I don't know what year it was—it was sometime during prohibition."

"That covers quite a few years, Summer."

"Whatever. It doesn't really matter in terms of my dream." I led the way forward, rounding a bend and heading down a tunnel we hadn't explored. When we came to the end I pointed my flashlight toward the ceiling, spying another trapdoor.

"Whose house is this?" Jerry whispered.

"How should I know? Should we knock on the trapdoor?"

"No. What exactly are we looking for?"

"I wish I knew."

And that's the moment when I was plunged backward in time, the tunnels changing before my eyes.

"Hey, lady—whatcha doin' here?" a man asked, peering at me.

"I…I work at…Mrs. Franklin's establishment," I stuttered.

"You'd best get back now. This is no place for a lady."

"I got lost—where is it?"

When he got closer his eyes went wide. "Aren't you that McCloud woman—the one who does the spells?"

"Spells?" I racked my brain for my roaring twenties relatives, trying to come up with first names.

"You know, the magic spells."

"Oh—yes, yes. I do them."

He relaxed. "Douglas told me about you—said I should get my cards read." He let out a guffaw. "Nonsense, I told him."

"It isn't nonsense, Mr..."

"Mr. Pederson—Carl Pederson. The place up this end is mine."

"Another speak-easy?"

"Mine's a bit different—got me a Negro jazz band."

"What's the name of it?"

He laughed. "Pederson's Place. In the day it's a normal café, but at night..."

"Aren't you afraid of being caught?"

He shook his head. "We got a few coppers on our side. Truth be told I'm not much lookin' forward to when all this ends—I'm making money hand over fist."

"When prohibition ends, you mean? How long will it be?"

He shrugged. "That's the way there," he said, pointing down another tunnel. "Pretty gal like you shouldn't be down here alone."

I was about to say thanks when I was plunged into the present. I heard my name being called and felt a painful slap on my cheek.

"Ow! What are you doing?"

"You've been lying there in a trance for twenty minutes!"

I sat up. "I was there again, except this time I was really there. Apparently there was a McCloud back then who worked magic spells."

Jerry frowned, grabbing my hand to haul me to my feet. "You were doing spells?"

"No, but the man who showed me the way out asked if I was the spell woman. I told him yes."

Jerry scoffed. "Of course you did."

"And Jerry—there may be a new player. The last name is Pederson."

"Pederson. Wasn't he written up in the news recently for opening an occult bookstore?"

"I...didn't hear anything about that."

"That's because you never read the paper. The house was left derelict for years until this dude shows up and says he owns it. Turns out he's related to the former owner—his great grandson or something." Jerry fiddled on his phone for a minute, a scowl on his face as he concentrated. A minute later his eyes met mine. "We're right under his store—I checked on Google earth."

I glanced up at the trapdoor. "What a coincidence."

"Yeah, right."

I grinned, glancing at Jerry. "Are you saying it isn't a coinkidink, Mr. nothing woo woo?"

"Let's get out of here," he hissed, grabbing me none too gently to haul me back the way we'd come.

⤖

We were in the car on the way home when I finally voiced my suspicions. "If a relative of Carl Pederson lives here now he could be the killer."

"Or the person who stole the books."

"Or both." I stared out at the blowing leaves that appeared in the circle of the headlights. "He mentioned Douglas. I wonder if it was our Douglas."

"Guess you'll have to ask him."

I nodded, thinking. "Mrs. Browning knows something—I'm sure of it. Maybe Douglas does too."

"But will they tell you?" Jerry asked, slanting a glance my way.

I shrugged. "And what motive would this Pederson guy have?"

"That's for us to find out."

Was Jerry actually taking me seriously? It was hard to know.

At home Jerry went to take a shower while I connected my Bluetooth speaker with my phone to play some Indonesian Gamelan music. The dissonant sounds of the instruments seemed to activate my third eye, and right now the intuitive part of me definitely needed to be stimulated. I turned it up and settled on the couch.

I was enjoying the strange sensations in the middle of my forehead when I heard a shout from Jerry. "Shut that crap off!"

I turned to see him standing in the doorway of the bedroom wearing a towel. I clicked the music off. "What's wrong?"

"That music makes my head feel funny."

I laughed. "That's why I put it on—it activates the third eye."

Jerry frowned, staring at me darkly. "I can't think when that shit's playing, Summer."

"That's the whole point."

He shook his head, turning toward the bedroom. "I need to think," he muttered. "This case is getting the best of me."

9

On Sunday I put the shut sign up so I could visit the Victorian and talk to Douglas and Mrs. Browning about prohibition times. Jerry had headed off to the library early, planning to look for records about prohibition days and find out who lived in the houses connected by the tunnels. We'd only found three, but I was sure there were more.

The Victorian's wide French doors were open, several people sitting on the patio in the rare sunshine drinking coffee. Douglas and Jerry's mother were two of them. Douglas stood when he saw me, gesturing me over to their wrought iron table.

"How have you been?" he asked, pulling out a chair for me—such a gentleman.

"Fine, thanks—well…that isn't entirely true. I'm still trying to solve Daniel Booker's missing books, and…"

"But Daniel Booker's dead!" Lucia interrupted.

I turned to her, noticing how her skin glowed and the brightness in her brown eyes. Living with Douglas was doing wonders for her. "The books are still missing and I think there might be a connection to that and his death."

"Jerry mentioned that yesterday," she said, turning to

glance at Douglas. "He seems to think it was murder."

"Were you around here during prohibition?" I asked Douglas.

Douglas glanced at Lucia before turning back to me. He shook his head, a frown appearing. "How could I? That was a hundred years ago."

I laughed uneasily. Lucia was still clinging to the falsehood that Douglas was a living breathing person. "There was a man who lived here then—Carl Pederson. Have you heard of him?"

Douglas put one hand up to his chin, staring into the middle distance. "Pederson. Sounds familiar—isn't he the one who just opened a bookstore?"

When Lucia wasn't looking I made a face at him. "Yes, but apparently Pedersons have owned that property for some time."

Douglas shrugged. "Can't help you, my dear."

Irritated, I stood up, scanning for Mrs. Browning.

"If you're looking for Emilia, she isn't here today."

"Where is she?"

Douglas chuckled. "I think she's with that Pederson character you just mentioned."

I frowned at him and left, heading to my car to go check out the new bookstore. Maybe that store was why my sales had dropped off.

Pederson's Books was newly painted and refurbished inside and out. The aroma of new paint and wood finish filled the air where new bookcases had been set up and stained dark. There were shelves and shelves of books on magic, many of which I was sure I'd seen at Bookers years ago. Since there was no one around I wandered about until Mrs. Browning appeared from the back looking disheveled and distracted. She adjusted her hat and straightened her long jacket, her face turning pink when she saw me. A minute later an older gray-haired man wearing a wool vest came into view, his brow furrowing when he noticed me.

"Summer—what are you doing here?" Mrs. B hissed.

"Came to see what all the fuss is about," I said, watching the man approach.

When he reached us Mrs. Browning smiled up at him and introduced me.

"Ah, my competition!" he chuckled. "Wondered when we'd meet."

"Nice to meet you, Mr. Pederson."

"Please call me Carl," he said, giving my hand a brief shake.

I smiled, scanning for the trap door I knew was here somewhere. "This building has been in your family for a long time, correct?"

He frowned and looked wary for a second before he responded. "Yup. It was built in 1910, around the same time as the others in this area, including yours. My family has owned it ever since."

"There are tunnels under my store and Bookers, and they lead here too, I believe. Do they connect to any other buildings?"

Carl glanced at Mrs. Browning. "Did you mention this?" he asked her.

"I did mention prohibition, but I wasn't aware that your building was on the rum runners route."

I could tell she was lying by how she fiddled with her hair, adjusting her hat. "It was you who mentioned the tunnels, Mrs. Browning. I only discovered that they led here the other night when Jerry and I..."

"You were down there?" Carl asked, his eyes narrowing.

"Jerry and I were trying to determine the extent of the tunnels, but we didn't get very far. I think we were at the bottom of the trapdoor leading up here."

Carl seemed to pale, his hand rubbing nervously across his closely shaved chin. "I must nail that thing shut," he muttered.

"Were you aware that books were stolen from Bookers?" I asked brazenly, glancing around.

"Books? No, I was not. I did hear about his wife's skeleton, though."

"Actually, the bones we found don't belong to his wife."

"Is that so? Well, then, who is it?"

"Yet to be determined." I turned to examine the closest shelf. "These books are used, aren't they?" I asked, running my fingers across the spines.

"I have both used and new books for sale," he answered, moving to block me from going any further.

A moment later Mrs. Browning took hold of my arm, steering me toward a shelf filled with small figures. "You simply must see Carl's collection of statuary, Summer."

I let her lead me, knowing that I was making both of them very uncomfortable. I examined his collection of Greek goddesses and figures of Mary and Jesus. "Very nice," I murmured. When the front door opened I looked up to see Marguerite Powers, her gaze scanning until she noticed Carl walking toward her. "Just the man I want to see," I heard her say, as she waltzed up to him. She seemed to be in a flirtatious mood, the tight fitting jacket she was wearing showing off her full bosomed figure.

Mrs. Browning gave me a quick glance, her eyes darting to where Marguerite stood talking with Carl. "Don't say anything more," she whispered.

"Do you promise to fill me in?"

She nodded before she picked up a small statue and carried it to the front of the store. When Marguerite smiled, bending her head to Carl's, Mrs. Browning's shoulders tensed. By the look of it she was jealous. But before she reached the two of them Carl opened his mouth to reveal fake vampire teeth and bent to Marguerite's neck. Mrs. B stopped in her tracks, her rheumy eyes widening.

"Stop that!" Marguerite laughed, pushing Carl away. He laughed and pressed his mouth against her neck before pulling back to gaze at Mrs. Browning.

"Emilia," he said in a fake accent. "Your friend does not wish me to drink her blood."

Emilia and Marguerite exchanged glances before Emilia drew close and put her arm through Carl's. "You can drink mine," she said, laughing up at him girlishly.

In the meantime I quickly examined two shelves of books, my attention drawn to the leather bound copy of *Black Magic and the Occult*. I'd never heard of this book until Daniel mentioned it. I pulled it out, noticing the handmade look of it, the leather worn from use. When I opened it I felt an electric shock go through my hands and up my arms. The copyright was 1890.

I was trying to study it further when I noticed Carl behind me, a frown on his face. Before I could turn the page the book snapped closed on its own, and when I tried to open it again it was like it was glued shut. I slipped it back and hurried by Carl, hoping to speak with either Marguerite or Mrs. Browning, but by the time I got to the front they'd both left the shop.

"Are you through snooping around?" Carl asked nastily, arriving next to me.

"I was checking your supplies, hoping our inventory didn't overlap too much."

"A likely story," he muttered. "I have the sense that a lot of your clients are shifting their allegiance."

"Yes, you do have more books, but I have Tarot decks, essential oils and incense and more of the pantheon of gods and goddesses. I wish you well," I said, turning toward the door.

"I suggest you keep whatever false ideas you've come up with to yourself," he said. "I wouldn't want anything untoward to happen to you."

My neck prickled and I didn't look back, closing the door solidly behind me.

⌘

"He threatened you?" Jerry's expression was one of disbelief, brows lowered in anger.

I fell onto the couch, the aftereffects of my visit finally getting the best of me. "Sounded like it to me."

"I don't like this, Summer. And I can't keep you safe."

"He won't do anything unless I do. He's just warning me off."

Jerry shook his head, his mouth tightening. "Couldn't find out much about the tunnels—looks like they may have been kept secret—until now, that is. During prohibition Ames was a big rum running town, boats with shipments of booze coming up river in the dead of night. I have the sense that half the police force was in on it."

"Interesting."

Jerry sat next to me. "I don't want you involved anymore. From what you just told me Carl stole those books and he knows you're on to him."

"From what I observed he and Mrs. Browning are close. He may be a ghost."

"Ghost or not, he can hurt you."

"I want to revisit the tunnels and see if I have any more visions. There's a piece missing."

"There are a lot of pieces missing—like who that skeleton belongs to."

"I think she has something to do with Carl. Have they done a DNA test yet?"

"They're working on it, but without anyone to match it to, it's like finding a needle in a haystack."

"Maybe I'll have a vision."

"Summer, I mean it—I don't want you messing around. It's too dangerous."

"If you go with me?"

"You are the most persistent and stubborn woman I've ever known."

I shrugged and raised my eyebrows. "Isn't that why you love me?"

10

We dressed in black and drove toward my store, parking the bike a couple of blocks away before skirting around trees like thieves in the night. Luckily there was a cloud cover, any moonlight or stars absent as night deepened. Jerry had the key and opened up, shoving me inside before closing the door and locking it behind us.

"How'd you get the key?" I whispered.

He scoffed. "Took it out of Sam's desk."

I chuckled and went ahead of him toward the open trapdoor. "They took the bones, right?"

Jerry nodded. "I'm wondering about other tunnels. I bet we haven't seen half of them."

I turned on my flashlight and led the way down the ladder. "I think you're right. I just hope there aren't other bodies down here."

"Daniel Booker's wife, maybe?"

"Yup. Or is she still alive?"

Jerry shook his head and hurried by me, disappearing into the darkness. I ran to catch up, glad when my flashlight joined his, illuminating the dust and cobwebs and the uneven ground in front of us. The damp made me sneeze, the sound reverberating off the stone.

We were walking down a new tunnel when I was suddenly catapulted into the past, the tunnel lit with strings of bulbs hung on iron hooks along the walls. *Someone ran by me carrying a case of bottles, another man running by in the other direction as they hurried to get their work done. "We need to wrap this up!" a voice shouted from down the tunnel. "The coppers are coming."*

And that's when I saw Carl Pederson, anger emblazoned across his features as he stared at me.

"What the fuck are you doing here?" he hissed, his face close to mine.

"I…"

He shoved me against the tunnel wall. "You need to stay out of my business."

"Hey, Pederson—who are you talking to?"

He turned. "No one. Where's Louise?"

"She's upstairs waiting for the latest load. Why?"

"I thought I saw her down here. Wouldn't want anything to happen to her."

"It won't, boss. Unless you want it to."

Carl blanched, glancing at me before he hurried off.

"Summer?" I felt Jerry's hand on my arm, the sudden darkness like a blanket pulled over my eyes.

"I'm okay."

"You threw yourself against the wall—I thought you knocked yourself out."

"Carl threw me against the wall—he could see me but the others couldn't. And Jer, I think that skeleton is Louise, Carl's wife."

Jerry hauled me to my feet. "You're trembling again."

"He didn't mean to tell me—the guy with him made a comment that if he wanted her out of the way, they'd do it for him," I elaborated, my arms hugged around my body.

Jerry hugged me close, keeping an arm around my shoulders as he led me toward Bookers. "I'll contact the ME tomorrow and also check out the newspaper archives at the library. Maybe we'll get lucky."

At home another hot bath was in order, my nerves slowly coming back to normal as I basked in the warmth.

"Do you delight in scaring the shit out of me?" Jerry asked, coming into the bathroom.

I turned to look at him. "Seeing Carl in the past leads me to believe that he's involved in all of it—he's not a normal human being."

"Maybe he's like you."

"Like me? No, Jerry, he lived back then and he's alive now."

"What is he then?"

"I don't know, but he has to be either a ghost or some other supernatural creature."

Jerry grabbed my hand and hauled me out of the tub, wrapping a towel around my body before rubbing me dry. "I'll handle things from now on," he muttered.

"But Jerry, I'm the one who can…"

"No buts, Summer. If something happened to you I'd never forgive myself."

I let the towel drop and reached for my pajamas. "I'm a big girl. I'm not your responsibility."

He grimaced and left me to it, the tension in his shoulders saying it all as he exited the bathroom.

I was at Tarot and Tea the next morning when Jerry called. "We discovered her identity. Louise wasn't married to Carl, she was his manager who he suspected of conspiring with the police."

"How'd you find that out?"

"Newspaper clippings."

"They said she conspired?"

"The article said she disappeared under suspicious circumstances. Carl was jailed after that due to his part in the rum running business. And apparently he ratted everyone out to save his own hide."

"So, they did know about the tunnels. But if so, why didn't they find her body down here?"

"Assuming that skeleton is Louise," Jerry said. "Or he could have dumped her body after they let him go."

"Can they determine her identity?"

"I think so, since there are hospital records. She had a stillborn baby in 1919."

"That's lucky."

"Not for her at the time."

I looked up as Douglas came into the store, his face seeming more worn than usual. "Got to go, Jerry." I ended the call as his Douglas approached, his eyes dull with either anger or exhaustion or possibly both.

"Summer, I must speak with you," he said, leaning his forearms on the counter. "I thought I made it clear that Lucia is unaware of what I am. I'd like to keep it that way."

"But I thought you explained the ghost thing months ago."

"She refused to believe it and I didn't push it further. She knows, but she doesn't want to acknowledge it."

"I'm sorry if I caused a problem. Did you know that we have another ghost in residence?"

"And who might that be?"

"Carl Pederson. I've seen him here and in the past. He's not a nice man."

"Oh dear."

"Mrs. Browning knows him and I think they may be entangled in some way."

Douglas ran a hand over his face. "She told me all about it the other day."

"Was she around in 1920?"

He nodded.

"And you were here too."

"Yes, I was here, but I wasn't involved in the rum running. Emilia's in love with Carl, has been since she met him in 1918."

"So she knew him back then? I think he killed his manager, Louise."

"Emilia and Carl were hot and heavy during the rum running years. She wasn't personally involved in the business, but I have the sense that she did her part whenever he asked. She thinks very highly of him. What leads you to believe he killed Louise?"

"The tunnels sent me back in time and one of his men made a comment about Louise. I doubt he did it himself, but I think Carl was responsible for her death."

"I do remember the scandal about the bootlegging. A lot of people went missing during those years. Carl was let off, as I recall."

"He told on everyone involved in it."

Douglas looked down. "I'm not sure Emilia knows this—if she did I think her feelings for him would have dimmed a bit. I suppose it's up to me to warn her about him before she takes it too far."

I tried to imagine *what taking it too* far would mean for a woman in her late seventies. "Better you than me."

Douglas scoffed. "Have you solved the other two murders?"

I shook my head. "But we're getting closer. And those missing books on magic are lining Carl's shelves."

"Ah. Now that's interesting. I assume the tunnels were used to transport them?"

"I think so. But why did he take them? And did Carl kill Daniel Booker? And what about Daniel's wife?"

Douglas threw his hands up in the air. "I'm no detective—I leave that part up to you and Jerry. And Summer—if I were you, I'd steer clear of Carl."

"Jerry's already forbidden me to sleuth."

Douglas chuckled. "And of course you're obeying him."

I lifted my brows. "What do *you* think?"

Jerry met me at the door when I got home, his arms going tight around me. "I've been worried about you."

"I've been at work—what could possibly happen?"

"There've been too many deaths—first Booker and then Isabel and now that woman from the past. And this dude is bad news."

"I assume you're talking about Carl," I said, hanging up my coat. I pulled off my mukluks and headed to the kitchen to feed Cutty.

"If he's really the same guy who lived back then, he's a scumbag. I did some more digging today, and not only was he involved in bootlegging, he was also responsible for the deaths of several black musicians. He was running a gambling den after hours and they happened to rack up some pretty hefty debts."

"So gambling and a speak-easy. Mrs. Browning's in love with him. I thought she was smarter than that."

"Love puts blinders on."

When I poured kibbles into Cutty's bowl he came running, his stubby tail wagging in happiness. I patted him and rubbed his ears before straightening to face Jerry. "According to Douglas, Emilia Browning aided and abetted Carl's dirty dealings."

Jerry took my arm and led me into the living room, depositing me on the couch. "Beer or wine, or would you rather a cup of tea?"

"Wine please," I murmured, pulling my legs up under me. I heard the pop of the cork and the sound of liquid being poured.

A minute later he handed me a glass of red wine and sat next to me. "What do those books mean to Carl—why would he steal them?"

I savored the flavors of plum and prune on my tongue before I swallowed. "They must have some intrinsic value we don't know about."

"Did you take a look at them?"

"I examined one of them..." I glanced at him, wondering how he would take what I was about to say, "but when I tried to look further than the copyright page it slammed shut."

Jerry turned to stare at me. "Slammed shut on its own?"

I nodded and took another sip from my glass. "I know magic isn't your favorite subject, but I think the book is spellbound."

Jerry's brows pulled together, his elbows going to his knees. "We need that book."

I nodded, glad he hadn't told me I was making things up. It was an indication of how far we'd come. I was suddenly exhausted, my mind wandering to the feel of his leg against mine, and the heat that always came off him. He had a special scent that reminded me of the outdoors and wood fires. "I wish we could do something besides talk about this damn case."

Jerry frowned. "If you're thinking what I think you're thinking, there's no way."

I sighed and sat back. "Are you still having trouble? I mean with…"

He slammed his beer down. "I know what you mean. And I'm not an invalid."

"I didn't say you were, Jer. It's just that normally if I give any indication of wanting to…"

"There's no more normal for us," he said, his voice gravelly with emotion. "I stopped smoking dope so we could make a baby, but I haven't been back to the doc to have my sperm count checked." He swiveled to meet my gaze, his dark eyes boring into mine. "But you don't want a baby."

"You…you want a baby—now?"

"I told you that weeks ago. Don't you listen?"

"I thought you meant in the future sometime. I'm still on the pill."

"I'm well aware of that, Summer!" he spat. He stood and lurched toward the guest bedroom. The door closed behind him and a minute later I heard the sound of some program or other on the TV.

I sat there, overcome with shock, unable to process this new Jerry. He'd been so sweet and caring lately. Maybe the possibility of having prostate cancer had made him super aware of what he wanted from life. Or maybe it was the stress of the deaths or me traveling back in time. Whatever it was, he seemed spring loaded.

He'd thrown himself into this case like a drowning man, trying to keep busy so he didn't have to think. We hadn't made love in weeks, but I'd thought it was due to the case and his new job and how tiring it all was. I knew now it was at least partially about me and us and our future together. He wanted a baby—but did I?

When I made dinner and called to him, he ignored me. I ate and cleaned up, waiting for him to come out. At eleven I headed into our bedroom alone. He never came to bed. I knew because I hardly slept a wink.

11

At six a.m. I finally dragged myself out of bed and went to take a shower. The night had gone by in slow motion, my thoughts taking me to my early days with Jerry and working their way forward to the present. All I'd discovered was how many times we'd broken up and gotten back together. The baby thing seemed to be the main obstacle between us now, his need for a family taking precedence over what we had together.

When I finished showering I realized that while I was in the bathroom Jerry had come into the bedroom, dressed, and taken off. My pills taunted me, the pristine round container waiting calmly for me to take one. I stared at my face in the mirror, noticing the haunted and confused look. I had crow's feet around my eyes and I could see other wrinkles forming. My mother was eighteen when I was born—I was thirty and the idea of a baby terrified me. I let out a scream, threw the container in the trash and burst into tears.

⁓

After my minor breakdown I made coffee and called Agnes, hoping that talking to her would help my frazzled nerves.

"Calm down, Summer. I can't even understand you."

"Jerry wants a baby," I muttered into my cell phone, trying to control my tears. "He says he made this clear, but I don't remember it. We haven't been intimate in an age, and I thought it was because of his job, or that he was still recovering from…"

"From what?" Agnes interrupted. "There wasn't anything wrong with him."

"He said he was impotent, but I told him I thought it was stress. The last time we did it he had no problem."

"Lalalalala—too much information."

"Really, Agnes? This from the woman who had to get advice on how to seduce her husband?"

Agnes let out a sigh. "I know—it's just that Jerry's already told me too much and expected my advice."

"Recently?"

"No, not recently."

"Well, that's good, I guess." I wiped my eyes with my sleeve and sniffed. "What do I do?"

"Do you want a baby right now?"

"I have no idea! I think he's jumping the gun because he thought he was dying."

"That's my take on it too. But didn't you tell me he had some number of children in mind? You may be too old to pop out the five kids he wants."

I let out a snort. "Yes, he surprised me with that. One sounds doable, I suppose, but five? Ye gods! I wouldn't have time for anything! And we'd have to move into a giant house and…"

"Let's just concentrate on the one, shall we? How do you feel about that?"

"I threw my birth control pills away this morning."

"Because you don't want to lose him."

"True. I have no idea how I feel about it. Do you like being a mom?"

"Are you kidding? I love Sammie and I've loved every minute of it—except the birthing part, that is. And seeing Sam with his son brings me so much joy."

I heard her sniff. "Are you crying?"

"Yes…no. I just had a moment. I'd say if you threw your pills away you're saying yes. You know it could take months before you conceive."

"Especially if we never have sex."

Agnes laughed. "Passionate Jerry can't stay away for long. It's not in his nature."

"He's changed since his scare."

"He's grown up."

"Maybe, but I like the other version better. He was funny and fun and sexy, and always dragging me into the bedroom to ravish me."

"Sam says he's more serious at work too. This case is getting to him. According to Sam they have three murders to solve?"

"I think the new bookstore owner, Carl Pederson, is involved. He might be a ghost."

She gasped. "A ghost can kill?"

"Apparently so. Or maybe he's not a ghost at all, more like the walking dead."

"Yuck! Does my father know him?"

"Yes, and so does Mrs. Browning. She's in love with him."

"Okay—this is getting weirder and weirder. No wonder Jerry's so preoccupied."

"Preoccupied isn't the word I'd use—more like angry and remote."

"Make a nice dinner tonight and talk to him, Summer."

"I'll try. Got to leave for work now. Thanks for listening."

I threw water on my face and stared at myself for a long time, trying to imagine a baby in my arms. I could see Cutty in my arms and I could visualize one of the cats in my arms, but a baby? I shook my head, watching my mouth narrow—was that an expression of distaste or terror?

∽

I was in Tarot and Tea going over bills for the umpteenth time when Valerie walked in, her face as pale as ash. "There's been another murder," she whispered, glancing around my empty store.

My heart skipped a beat. "What now?"

She came close, her eyes wider than usual. "I see it happening," she intoned. Valerie seemed to come back to herself, her forehead puckering. "What was I saying?"

"You said another murder—are you talking about someone other than Isabel, Daniel Booker, and Louise?"

Valerie stared into the distance before bringing her surprised gaze back to mine. "It hasn't happened yet."

"So who is it?"

Her mouth opened, her eyes going wide. "It's you, Summer."

Adrenaline shot through me. "Me? Do you see details?"

Valerie shook her head no. "I'm sorry," she said. "This happens sometime and I can't control it."

"What should I do?"

"Don't put yourself in dangerous situations? If I get more details I'll let you know, but for now I'd say steer clear of tunnels or other dark places."

She left soon after that, leaving me feeling vulnerable and afraid. Dark places could be just about anywhere. I was so shook up that I found myself punching in Jerry's numbers.

"Don't buy into this, Summer," he warned after I told him what she said. "It's just like horoscopes—they may point to certain outcomes but you can always follow another path."

"She gets visions and they're usually right on."

"Like seeing Booker before the police even found him? I've already discussed this with Sam—she's going to be picked up for questioning."

"She didn't do anything, Jerry!"

There was a long silence before he said, "Valerie doesn't know what she's talking about. But just in case she's on to something, please don't do anything stupid."

"Since when do I do...?" I began. But he'd already hung up.

I stuck my Donovan Cd in the player, listening to one of his very early songs, and thinking how apt the words were:

In the chilly hours and minutes
Of uncertainty
I want to be
In the warm hold of your loving mind
To feel you all around me
And to take your hand
Along the sand
Ah, but I may as well try and catch the wind

Three more days went by in which Jerry hardly spoke to me, leaving in the morning before I woke up. He spent every night in the guest room, heading off as soon as we'd had dinner. I'd tried to talk to him but the dark looks he gave me stopped me in my tracks. I had no idea what was going on with the murder investigation or his new job or anything else. Was this anger really all about whether or not I wanted a baby? It was time I followed through with Agnes's suggestion.

ce∞ɔ

The next day I left work early and stopped by the market to buy ingredients for pasta puttanesca, one of Jerry's favorites. I already had spaghetti noodles and garlic and oregano, but I needed olives, anchovies, capers, red pepper flakes and canned tomatoes. I bought a loaf of freshly baked Italian bread and a bottle of red I knew he liked and headed to the front to check out.

"Summer! Good to see you! I'd hoped you'd come to more meetings," she added, whispering.

I turned from where I was unloading my cart, surprised to see Marguerite Powers wearing a fitted bottle green dress. Dark boots disappeared under the full skirt, heels clicking as she moved toward me. Since she was the high priestess of the coven I wasn't used to seeing her wearing anything but her shapeless robes—aside from today and Carl's store I wasn't sure I'd ever seen her dressed in normal clothes. "I…I've been busy with the store and…"

"It's a good thing you weren't at the last one with all that ruckus," she interrupted. "One woman dead and I heard there's been another murder in town?"

I nodded, watching the young gal who was checking me out. "Can we talk outside when I'm finished here?"

She smiled. "Of course, dear."

She met me at one of the small café tables, several packages in her hands. "How is your magic, Summer?" she whispered, gesturing for me to sit next to her.

"Talking to ghosts, you mean?"

"Your mother told me years ago that your real power wouldn't show itself until you turned thirty. You are thirty, are you not?"

"I'm not a witch."

Marguerite stared at me. "Of course you're a witch."

"I can talk to ghosts—that's all."

Marguerite laughed. "You were born a witch, Summer. Your mother was a witch, your grandmother as well." She peered at me. "Nothing new has shown itself this year?"

"I went into the past."

"You time-traveled?"

"Not exactly. I was here and then I was there."

"And where is there?"

"Tunnels under Tarot and Tea used during prohibition," I whispered.

"Ah, yes. I've been seeing that timeline in my meditations— it must have something to do with the murders."

I leaned forward, throwing caution to the wind. "Carl Pederson, the new bookstore owner? He was a bootlegger back then—I saw him in the tunnels in the past."

"Are you saying he's a ghost?"

"I don't know what he is, but I know he's dangerous. I think he's the murderer."

Marguerite frowned. "If not a ghost, then…what?"

110

I shook my head, wondering if I'd revealed too much. The avid expression on her face said I had. "Mrs. Browning knows him from the past. Maybe she can tell us."

Marguerite rose gracefully and picked up her packages, her gaze turning remote. "The next meeting is Samhain. I hope to see you there."

"You're going ahead, even with Isabel's murder?"

"Why yes, of course we are. It's important to respect and uphold the traditions, Summer. Your mother would not be happy to know that you're denying what you are."

"Lots of normal people see ghosts. I'm just..."

"A witch," she finished for me. "Have you even tried casting a spell, or..."

"Why would I?"

Marguerite let out a long sigh. "Your mother died before she could explain things to you, dear. Perhaps I can help. Come to the next meeting and we can talk."

"Where are the meetings being held now?"

"Close to the river." She noticed the stunned look on my face, her hand touching my shoulder. "Not where Daniel Booker died. We are further down river where it takes that sharp turn—the clearing is on the other side—there's a log that lies across at the narrowest point. It's quite hidden from prying eyes."

I did know the place and I didn't want to ever be there again. It was the spot where detritus gathered and caught, and where my mother's twin sister, Vivienne, and Frank, my father, had drowned. Their bodies had been in the water for days before they were discovered.

The past was intruding on the present, bringing ghosts along with it—ghosts I hoped I'd never have to face again.

"I was in the back the other day when you came into Carl's store—the day he was pretending to be a vampire?"

She chuckled. "Look what he did to me." She pulled her collar down, showing me the blue bruising around her neck. "And he pinched me too," she added, showing me another bruise on her wrist. "I didn't get a bad feeling about him, only that he was a flirt and rather fresh." Her eyes widened. "I'd never met him before that day—can you imagine?"

"I think Mrs. B was jealous."

"Oh dear. I certainly didn't intend to step on anyone's toes. I was only looking for a certain book on magic."

"Did he have it?"

She stared into the distance. "As soon as I mentioned it he went into his vampire act. And then Emilia wanted my help with some silly thing. I never got a chance to look."

"What was the book?"

Her clear gray eyes met mine. *"Black Magic and the Occult."*

⁂

Jerry wasn't home when I arrived with my groceries. I opened the bottle of wine and poured myself a glass, determined not to worry about anything but Jerry's and my relationship. The sauce was simmering on the stove, the noodle water nearly boiling when Jerry walked in. He threw his Jacket on the couch, frowned at me and headed toward the guest room.

"I'm making puttanesca."

He turned, his hand on the doorknob. "I'm not hungry."

All my anger and frustration rose to the surface all at

once, my pulse beating in my ears. The spoon covered in sauce went flying as I ran toward him, slamming him against the door just as he opened it. We both tumbled inside, landing in a heap on the floor.

"What the hell?" he shouted.

"You bastard!" I yelled, pummeling him with my fists.

He caught my hands and held me, his frown deepening. "Why am I a bastard?"

"Because you spring stuff on me, you won't talk to me about anything, you...you ignore me and give me the cold shoulder...you sleep in the guest room..." I couldn't go on as tears spilled down my cheeks.

"Jesus, Summer! What in hell has got into you?"

"I made your favorite meal," I cried out, "and you couldn't care less—ready to go into your little cave and leave me alone—again. I threw away my pills, and..." By now I was crying so hard I couldn't form words.

Jerry rose to his feet and helped me up, leading me to the couch. "When did you throw away your pills?"

"A few weeks ago. Isn't that what you wanted?"

"Your dinner is burning," he muttered, hurrying into the kitchen.

I watched him from where I'd curled into myself, realizing how much I missed our intimacy. I missed *him*. Once he'd turned the burner off and stirred the sauce he dropped the pasta into the boiling water. "Saved," he said, pouring himself a glass of wine from the bottle I'd opened.

He sat next to me, his calm gaze on my swollen face. "I thought you weren't sure."

"I'm not sure about anything. But I don't want to lose you. I love you."

He picked up my hand and held it between his. "I love you too. This thing scared the crap out of me, and I…"

"You felt like we should get a move on because your life might end at any minute?"

Jerry smiled for the first time. "Approximately. If you need to I can wait. I just want to know that you're with me on this. You haven't ever said."

"I want a baby with you. The thought of it is…well…to tell you the truth it turns me on. But you're so different lately—like you don't even want to have sex, when before you were all over me. I like the passionate Jerry better."

He stared into the distance. "The possibility of having prostate cancer kinda threw me. I don't think I've recovered yet."

"Do I still turn you on?"

He faced me, his brown eyes soft. "Yup, you do. I've been holding back because I've been afraid that I'll…"

"Fail me in some way? Impossible, Jer."

He let out a sigh. "If I can't get it up it's failing you, Summer."

"Since when can't you get it up?"

"Since…well, recently."

"You haven't approached me, so I'm figuring you're talking about masturbating?"

Jerry let out an embarrassed chuckle. "Well…yeah."

"I guess you don't turn yourself on as much as I turn you on," I murmured, my fingers moving to his zipper.

He grabbed my hand. "If you stopped the pill you could get pregnant."

I scoffed. "It could take six months to a year for me to conceive. I've been on the pill for a long time."

He gazed at me, his expression becoming the one I so fondly remembered. When he reached for my buttons I helped him take my shirt off, my breath catching when his warm lips found my skin. A few moments later we were naked and stretched out together on the couch, our mouths and fingers bringing us to the brink. "Are you sure?" he whispered, moving into position on top of me.

"I'm very sure." His moan was followed by my gasp as we connected fully.

The pasta cooked on. Luckily the water didn't all boil away.

12

After that night of reconnection Jerry made sure that I had no more worries about whether or not he was attracted to me. As far as his problems went, they were nonexistent. I worried that he might be trying for a baby, a thought that filled me with several conflicting emotions. I loved the idea of him wanting to make a baby, and I also loved the thought of carrying his baby inside me, the picture in my mind quite different from what I knew the reality would be. The truth would be me on my knees over the toilet heaving with morning sickness, wearing horrible voluminous clothes, and Jerry disgusted with the size of my breasts and belly and avoiding me at all costs.

But instead of talking to him about my uncertainty I succumbed to his attentions as he undressed me every night, applying his special brand of foreplay that I couldn't resist. I fell under his spell, unable to say no, even though something in the back of my mind said I should. But then again I'd read a hundred articles about going off the pill. It took months for the body to reclaim its natural cycles. I had nothing to worry about.

Agnes called early as I was stepping out of the shower. Of course the first thing out of my mouth was how great our sex was now. "He's the old Jerry again," I gushed.

"Didn't you tell me you stopped the pill a while back? What if you're pregnant?"

"I'm not," I said, hitting speaker as I washed my face.

"What will you do if you are?"

I thought about that for a second, dismissing it just as quickly. "I can't get pregnant that fast. Not after how long I've been on the pill."

Agnes let out a sigh. "Summer, you can be so exasperating. I'm glad you're back together in this way; Jerry seemed so out of sorts. But don't you think you should consider this more seriously?"

"So you *have* seen him."

"Only in passing."

"I won't even ask what that means," I said, splashing cold water on my face. "I hope he doesn't revert to the serious Jerry again. I can't relate to that version at all."

"You may have to. He's not the light-hearted man he once was."

"Only because of the prostate scare. It takes a while to let go of stress."

"And he wants a family. That's a big change for someone like him."

I patted my face dry and stared into the mirror. "I think you might know him better than I do."

Agnes chuckled. "I have a different perspective."

I put some moisturizer on my face and found my

lipstick. "If he confides in you first again, I'll kill him."

"But how would you know?" she asked sweetly.

"Because my best friend would tell me? Listen, Ags, I've got to go to work." I said goodbye and hit end, filled my lips in with pale pink, grabbed my coat and hurried to the car.

❧

At work I couldn't focus on much of anything, my body still tingling from what Jerry had subjected it to early this very morning before he left for work—so much for his erection problems.

"You seem rather dreamy today," Valerie commented, coming up to the desk.

I removed my hand from under my chin and brought my mind back to the present. "Sorry, I…"

Valerie smirked. "I take it things are better between you and Jerry?"

"Does a girl get to have any secrets around here?" I asked grumpily.

"Not when you're talking to a witch or a psychic." She glanced around the store and leaned closer. "The police came by my house early this morning. They took me in for questioning."

I gasped. "About Daniel Booker?"

She nodded. "I guess I saw him before the police did, but I was sure they'd been there. There were footprints all around his body and I was positive they'd checked him out and were calling for the ME."

"Did you see police cars?"

"No. I called it in just in case."

"And left your name?"

"Well, no. I just told the switchboard that there was a dead man out by the river and told them where to find him."

"Not exactly the actions of a murderer."

"That's what I told them, but they wanted to know why I didn't tell the 911 operator who it was." She glanced into the back of the store where a young couple was poring over a shelf of essential oils. "I told them because she didn't ask! They made me promise not to leave town."

"I hope they arrest Carl Pederson. I'm sure he did it."

"Apparently Daniel's death is a complete mystery. All they found was some bruising on him, but nothing bad enough to kill him. As to this Pederson fellow, have you spoken to Emilia about him?"

I shook my head, looking up as Mrs. Browning entered the shop. "Speak of the devil."

"Hello, dears," she said, heading toward us. I was sure she looked younger than she had the last time I'd seen her.

"Hello, Emilia," Valerie whispered. "Summer tells me you're stepping out with the new bookstore owner."

Emilia glanced at me before smiling at Valerie. "He's an old friend of mine. We've known each other for..." She looked up, her eyes glazing. "Well...a very long time." She fiddled with the neck of her dress, pulling it up to hide a bruise-like mark.

"Summer thinks he might be dangerous," Valerie whispered.

"Dangerous? Carl is a sweetheart—always has been."

I leaned forward to examine her neck, afraid of something I couldn't name. She saw me and quickly turned away.

"He threatened me," I said quietly.

Mrs. Browning let out a girlish laugh. "Nonsense. You imagined it."

A shiver went down my spine as the energy shifted around us. "I think he killed his manager, Louise. It was her skeleton we found in the tunnels."

Emilia shook her head, her eyes closing. "Louise worked for him years ago. He counted on her—he would never harm her."

I watched her hand go up to her neck again, her fingers tracing the mark before she turned away and went into the stacks.

"Are vampires real?" I whispered.

Valerie's eyes went wide. "I've never encountered one…" her voice trailed off as she watched Mrs. Browning. "You don't think that Carl…"

"Mrs. B has a suspicious mark on her neck and that man doesn't seem like a ghost to me."

"But Emilia's a ghost—if he bit her what good would it do him?"

"I don't know, but if it's true, I'm scared." I scanned into the back, realizing that Emilia Browning was no longer there. "Where'd she go?"

Valerie paled. "I don't know. What if you're right about Carl? We have to warn Emilia off!"

We stared at each other, neither of us speaking until the couple emerged from the stacks with some essential oils to buy. "Did you happen to notice an older woman back there?" I asked casually.

The fortyish blonde haired woman looked up. "She went into the back, I think—to the bathroom perhaps?"

Valerie and I exchanged a glance before I rang them up. Once they left I turned to her. "She went into the tunnels."

Valerie nodded. "I suggest you nail that trapdoor shut."

"She's a ghost, Valerie—she can come and go as she pleases."

"I wouldn't be so sure," she intoned, her gaze on the far distance. A moment later she came back to herself. "I need to get to the bakery before my daughter leaves."

"How is Becky? I don't see much of her these days."

"She finally has a new beau."

"Really? She hasn't mentioned it."

Valerie smiled and turned toward the door. "She's afraid of jinxing it."

I watched her leave, uneasy with the idea of being alone in my store. I knew Mrs. Browning was with Carl. And I also knew she was telling him all about my suspicions. In the back I searched for a hammer and nails and bent to the task of nailing the trapdoor shut for good. Even if she was only a ghost it still made me feel better to close the entrance off. But when I thought back I realized I'd never seen her go through a door or a wall like Douglas. Something snaked up my spine, my pulse racing for a second as ghouls and monsters marched across my vision. *Stop it!* I told myself sternly.

A meow caught my attention, a black cat strolling casually across the floor with its tail in the air. "Mischief, is that you?" I whispered, running after it. But it seemed to fade into the shadows toward the back of the store. "Where are you? There's nowhere you could go back here," I muttered, looking around. The door to the kitchen was closed and there was no other escape route.

By the time I was sitting at my desk again I realized my uneasiness had evaporated, the search for the phantom cat grounding me and bringing me back to myself.

13

It was two weeks later and I was just closing up for the night when Agnes called my cell, asking if I wanted to have a glass of wine with her. The day had been long with little to no business, any hope of making my September payroll already gone. I was feeling sorry for myself and angry about Carl's new bookstore. "I'd love to," I told her, the idea of an enormous glass of wine helping to assuage my bad mood.

"It isn't any big deal, but I need to talk to a friend."

"Meet you at Grub and Grins at five-thirty."

"Perfect. Thanks, Summer."

This wasn't like Agnes, who wanted to be home when Sam arrived and rarely left her baby boy with a sitter. I locked up and drove toward the bar, musing about my lack of customers. I wondered again if there was something supernatural happening—that man had threatened me and there was something about him...

I let the dark thoughts go when I drew close to the bar, my mind on finding a close parking place to avoid the rain that I knew was coming. I looked up at the sky, surprised to see it clear, with no clouds on the horizon. Why did I have the sense that it was going to rain? I shrugged it off and pulled into a parking spot right out front and hurried inside.

Agnes called out when she saw me, waving me over to her stool at the end of the bar. As usual she was dressed in black, her severe roaring twenties haircut emphasizing her sharp cheekbones. She looked ethereal and gorgeous with her pale skin and the dark kohl around her eyes. I felt dowdy and fat next to her, despite the fact that I was several inches taller and the perfect weight for my height. I slid onto the stool next to her.

"I ordered you a glass of white wine," she said, pointing to the chilled glass filled with pale liquid sitting on the bar.

"Thanks."

"It's Sauvignon Blanc. I thought you liked that."

"I do—are you in a hurry or something?" I asked watching her flip her hair behind her ears and uncross and cross her legs.

"Sam will wonder…but…never mind that. I needed to talk to someone," she whispered, looking around.

I picked up my glass and took a sip, watching her fidget. "What's wrong?"

She leaned close. "I may be pregnant again."

"I thought that breast-feeding…"

"I stopped that nearly six months ago."

"So no birth control? You were all over me about that a few weeks ago."

Agnes glanced at the mirror behind the bar where bottles were lined up, fiddling with her perfect hair. The bartender was young and good-looking and came by to see if she needed anything, his gaze appraising.

She smiled at him winningly. "No thanks, Bart. But maybe in a bit?"

"You're making me nervous," I hissed as soon as he was out of earshot.

"I told Sam I was on the pill so he wouldn't have to use…well…you know."

"A condom?"

Agnes winced and glanced around. "He doesn't like how they feel, and…"

"So what's the big deal? You'll have another baby. I'm sure Sam will be…"

"No, he won't. He made it clear he wanted to wait until Sammie's in pre-school. I have to get an abortion."

I stared at her. "You can't be serious. This is Sam's baby, Agnes. He'll understand."

Tears welled and rolled down her porcelain cheeks. She shook her head and wiped them with her sleeve. "He's not the easygoing guy everyone thinks he is. He gets angry over the tiniest things now. We hardly ever have sex."

"Sounds familiar. Is something going on at work?"

"You mean besides three unsolved murders?"

I took a gulp of wine and glanced around at the early-bird crowd of young office workers out for a drink. *'And these murders are like, surreal—you know what I mean?'* I heard a young man say. *'Halloween's just over a month away and it seems like we have a vampire in our midst.'* There was loud laughter after that.

I turned back to Agnes who had said something I missed. "…and he isn't even home most nights now…he…"

"Where's he going? Is it work related?"

Agnes turned her liquid eyes to mine. "Do you think he's having an affair?"

125

"Why would he be having an affair? He loves you and you have a baby."

"I wish I was sure of that."

"Agnes, you were the one who told me to make a special dinner and talk to my husband—I'm giving you the same advice right now. You need to tell him you're pregnant and ask him why he's away so much."

"I think I should just get an abortion. It's early days."

"You don't want the baby."

"Did I say that?" She let out a sob. "Maybe I don't want it. Sammie demands all of my time, I'm not ready to get fat again so soon, and Sam isn't around. I'd have twice as much work to do and no support."

After finishing our drinks I changed the subject, hoping to divert Agnes. "Coven meeting is coming up next month. Want to go with me?"

Agnes looked over, a new expression coming into her eyes. "I think I would. Might be really good for me."

I smiled. "I agree."

When I left the bar it was pouring rain, the evening sky dark and thick with cloud. Driving home I thought about being pregnant and how I might deal with it, if and when it happened. I still didn't know what I wanted, the vision of myself enormous and trying to run the store, making me feel weak all over. We were now playing the odds, throwing caution to the wind. I'd blithely told him it wasn't possible this soon, but what did I know? Some couples conceived within a month of quitting their birth control regimen. I'd stopped mine in late August and now it was nearing the end of

September. I had to get clear on this before I was forced into a decision.

"Why didn't you call to say you'd be late?" Jerry grumped when I walked into the house.

"I had a glass of wine with Agnes. I wasn't even sure you'd be back this early," I said, pulling off my wet coat and hanging it up. "Thought you and Sam might have a beer of something."

Jerry ran his fingers through his hair, his gaze still troubled. "I have no idea what Sam's doing. He takes off early nearly every night."

"He does? Agnes is worried he's having an affair."

Jerry scoffed. "More like he's taking a class to help him move up in his career. He wants to make lieutenant this next year."

"Do you know that, or are you surmising?"

"He hasn't confided in me recently, but I know that's what he wants."

I moved into the kitchen and began to prepare a meal, my mind on babies. "Agnes is pregnant, "I told him when he came up behind me to pour wine.

"Wow—another baby," he said wistfully.

"She's thinking of having an abortion."

Jerry stared at me. "That's a mortal sin."

"What? You really think that?"

He looked away, a frown appearing. "It is to a Catholic. You do know that's how I was raised."

"Jerry, I...I always thought we were on the same page about the right to choose."

"I don't consider myself Catholic anymore—too much

weird crap going on within the church. But I can tell you this—Sam's Catholic and would not be happy about it."

"If he knew."

"She'd keep it from him? Jesus, Summer. That's a shitty thing to do."

"I told her to talk to him. I agree with you. It sounds like…"

"Like us a month ago? Yeah. Sam's been kind of secretive with me. I think he's ashamed of taking classes."

"Why? Didn't you take classes?"

Jerry shook his head. "My dad was chief, remember?"

"Speaking of that—any news on the murders?"

"The ME is completely stumped. She's sent out queries to the most renowned medical examiners in the state trying to come up with something that makes sense."

I flipped the chicken breasts and added tarragon, sea salt and pepper. "I'm planning to go to the coven meeting on Halloween. It's full moon."

"You're not going anywhere near the coven meeting," Jerry said, a deep frown appearing on his face.

I just stared at him for a few seconds until my voice came back. "You can't *forbid* me, Jerry. I'm a grown woman with a life separate from yours."

"Marguerite Powers is dead. Wasn't she the head priestess or something?"

I couldn't breathe for a second, my mind going in circles. "I talked to her at the market the day I made puttanesca!"

"She was discovered late last night by some kid messing around near the river. She had blue bruises on her neck and her skin was sunken—just like the others. Her body was found where the coven has its meetings. The police are combing the area for clues."

"She had those bruises the last time I saw her," I muttered, remembering. "Carl bit her, Jerry. I saw him do it."

Jerry looked down, his dark brows pulling together. "When did he bite her?"

"Couple of weeks ago? Can't remember now." I shoveled food onto two plates and carried them to the table, but I'd totally lost my appetite. Who would take over for her? I couldn't imagine the coven meetings without Marguerite and Byron Forsyth. He was her life partner—her lover. I tried to eat and finally ended up throwing mine away.

"You're not hungry?" Jerry asked.

"Not since I heard about Marguerite."

I heard a thump and saw Mischief making his way off the countertop. His green eyes met mine for a second before he jumped to the floor and headed to the table by the washer where I kept his food dish.

14

When Douglas entered Tarot and Tea the next day I was so relieved I nearly hugged him. My customers had dwindled down to next to nothing. I'd read in the morning papers how popular Carl Pederson's store was and how the lines stretched down the block. What did he have that I didn't, besides the novelty of being new? But dark thoughts lurked at the back of my mind. These deaths were his doing and I wanted to know how and why before he killed again.

Douglas walked toward the counter his usual smile conspicuously absent. "Have you seen Emilia?"

"The last time I saw her she disappeared from the back of my store—I assumed she went into the tunnels to meet Carl."

Douglas frowned, releasing the buttons that held his tweed jacket closed. Under it he wore a matching vest over an ivory button down linen shirt. "When was that?"

I shrugged, wondering why time seemed to be doubling back on itself, weeks seeming like months and days going by so fast I forgot about them in the next instance. "Not sure now—maybe two weeks?"

He stared at the floor. "She hasn't been home in a long while."

"You're worried."

"Yes, I'm worried. She's a close friend of mine."

I felt a chill. "But she's a ghost, Douglas. What could happen to her?"

"I don't know, but something is not right."

"I'm sure she's with Carl Pederson. There's no other reason for her to sneak into the tunnels the way she did. Did you hear about Marguerite?"

Douglas nodded, his expression darkening. "I was very saddened by the news."

"Carl bit her, Douglas. What is he?"

"I knew him long ago so I assumed he was a ghost, but from what you've witnessed I'm no longer sure. There are creatures…" His voice trailed off, his gaze in the distance.

"Vampires?"

"No, not vampires—the dead who long to live again."

"What are they called? We have to expose him as the murderer."

Douglas shrugged. "I don't know what they're called. You have access to the Internet. Perhaps you should look it up." He straightened his impeccable vest and re-buttoned his jacket. "Samhain is coming," he said brightly, shaking off the dark mood. "Will you be there?"

"Jerry says the police are out by the river searching for clues. Not sure they'll be done by then. Maybe we could have the meeting at the Victorian—it's certainly warmer," I added, glancing out the window at the rain. "Will Byron lead it now? And what about some sort of ritual for Marguerite's death?"

"Yes," he said, his eyes going dark again. "We should plan a ritual for the night of Samhain—that gives us over a month to contact everyone. Please spread the word and I'll do the same." He came close and pulled me into a hug.

"I'm bringing Agnes," I told him after he released me.

He let out a sigh. "Good. Haven't seen my daughter in weeks."

I almost mentioned the pregnancy before I thought better of it. Douglas would not support her if she opted for an abortion. But I was fairly certain that when it came down to it she would decide to keep it.

The rest of the day went by slowly as I grappled with the possibility that I might have to close up shop. I simply wasn't making enough money to justify keeping it open. I scanned the shelves filled with all the merchandise I'd chosen, wondering what on earth I would do with myself if I didn't have Tarot and Tea. I could feel a panic attack hiding right under the surface.

Since there was no one in the store I decided to take Douglas's advice to search for supernatural beings on the web. Gamelan music played in the background as I searched, coming up with only one entry that made any sense. It was called a Gjenganger, a creature out of Scandinavian lore that returned from the dead because of something he or she had left undone. The person who turned into one could be a murderer or a victim of murder, or even a person who committed suicide. This creature committed violence against the living by pinching or biting, which eventually caused death. They were entirely corporeal and their pinches or bites left blue marks, the skin underneath like a deflated balloon. I thought about the murders so far—they all fit this description. Wasn't Pederson a Scandinavian name?

I was suddenly filled with adrenaline. When I called Jerry there was no answer and I was too much in a hurry to leave a message. I locked up and drove like a maniac along the flooded streets, my bald tires sliding dangerously. At the cottage I pulled up too fast, my front tire riding up over the curb. I backed into the gravel driveway, knocking over a trashcan before I cut the engine and hurled myself out of the car. I let go my held breath when I saw Jerry's motorcycle parked up under the eaves.

Rushing through the door I began babbling, trying to get the story out before I forgot the details.

"Summer, slow down!" Jerry shouted, grabbing hold of my forearms. "You aren't making sense!"

"It's a supernatural being, Jerry. And I think Carl is one."

"You said these bruises can kill—how long does it take?"

"I have no idea, but Mrs. Browning had one on her neck and so did Marguerite!"

Jerry scoffed. "Isn't Mrs. Browning already dead?"

"Yes, I think so. But she's involved with him...she disappeared weeks ago and hasn't been seen since."

"Sit down by the fire and take a couple of deep breaths. I'm going to make you a hot toddy—you're shivering."

"It's only nerves." I glanced up at him. "I used to be calmer—when did I start reacting like this?"

"After being kidnapped by a bunch of slavers in Mexico?"

"Maybe so," I muttered, trying not to remember the stench of the closed up van, or the...

I pulled my mind back from the past, trying to

concentrate on what was happening in the present. I breathed as he'd told me to do, my arms around my body as I watched the flames in the fireplace flicker upward, various creatures taking shape within the curling yellow and blue and turning into something else in the next instant. There were monsters there, creatures with horns, and others with scales, some with tails that slapped and curled. I heard Jerry squeezing lemons, the sound of the kettle whistling as the water heated, the squeak of the refrigerator door as he looked for what he needed.

"Honey or maple syrup?" he called out.

"Maple syrup, please."

A few minutes later he was in front of me holding out a mug. "The ME thought Isabel's bruise was due to a puncture wound. But she never found poison in her system. Nobody on the force will believe what you just told me—you get that, right?" He lowered himself to the carpeted floor next to me.

I took a tentative sip, relaxing as the whiskey and the mixture of flavors soothed my overwrought nerves. "So what do we do? I know it's Carl—I can feel it."

"Are you psychic now?"

I glanced at him. "According to Marguerite I'm a real witch and coming into new powers this year. I traveled back in time—that's new."

Jerry let out a low chuckle. "And you've also talked to a jaguar and been with the jaguar king—all dreams, Summer. Will our baby have these so called powers?"

"So-called? Are you saying you don't believe me? As to our baby—I have no idea." The mention of a baby shattered my peace, my nerves ratcheting up again. I took another sip and closed my eyes, feeling the heat of the flames against my face and chest. "Since this case involves the supernatural I guess it's up to me to solve it."

"You may be the brains but I'm the brawn," he whispered, taking the mug out of my hands. "But right now you need some TLC."

He nuzzled my neck and moved his lips downward, unbuttoning my blouse as he went. I wasn't really in the mood but when his fingers went under my long wool skirt to trace a meandering line along the inside of my thigh my mind switched off. I went from cold to hot in an instant. "What if someone looks through the window or comes to the door?" I whispered.

"It's dark outside."

"But it's light in here."

Jerry got up and turned the lamp off before resuming what he was doing. A few minutes later we were naked on the floor, my mind emptied of everything except the feel of his fingers, his mouth, the warmth of his body and my increasing desire. I helped him along, my hands tracing along his slim hipbones, my fingers finding the parts of him that needed attention.

"Jesus," he moaned, his hands going to my hips as I climbed on top. We were very near the point of no return when the doorbell rang, followed by loud knocking and the creak of the door as it opened.

"Jerry? Are you guys here?"

Before either of us could react the overhead light went on. I blinked in the brightness to see Sam staring at us like he'd seen a ghost. He muttered an oath, backed out and closed the door.

I giggled. "This is the second time Sam's seen us screwing," I whispered. "And both times I was on top."

Jerry grimaced, his eyes narrowed in pain. "You familiar with the term blueballs?" He rose awkwardly, pulled his jeans on and headed toward the door while I grabbed my clothes and fled to the bedroom, laughing all the way.

But I wasn't laughing later when Jerry came into the bedroom with a grim expression on his face. "There's been another murder," he announced. "Same MO and no way to determine cause of death."

"Who is it this time?" I asked, dreading the answer.

"You're not going to believe this, but from what the police have determined, it's Philippa Booker."

"She was alive?"

"Yes. But now she's dead. Blue bruising all along her neck, and the skin under it was caved in."

"It's Carl, and it has to be connected to that book on black magic. Everyone dead was linked to it in some way."

"We have no reason to arrest him nor can we question him without cause."

"But he did it, Jerry."

"How can we solve murders that don't make any sense? How are the bruises killing them? Who is this dude?"

"I told you. He's a Gjenganger—he's not human. He died and came back to do harm."

"You're saying that this book on black magic is the cause. Why?"

"It wouldn't let me open it to find out why."

Jerry made a face. "The book wouldn't let you open it?"

"That's right, Jerry—I told you that weeks ago. Perhaps

you and Sam need to go and have a look around Carl's store."

"On what grounds?"

I shrugged. "Interest in the occult?"

"Are you still feeling…hmm…blocked up?" I asked later when we were in bed.

He turned. "You feel like unblocking me?"

"I do."

He smiled, tugging down my pajama bottoms as his mouth found mine. The 'unblocking' didn't take long.

15

It was two days later around eleven in the morning when Jerry called me at the store. "Sam and I checked out Carl Pederson's book store. Nothing seemed amiss and the guy was perfectly pleasant, laughing about the way the newspapers are covering these murders. Have you seen the headlines? They've been calling the murders supernatural, and one column mentioned vampires. The residents are getting worked up and nervous. I don't like this, Summer."

"Are you saying you believe him over me?"

"I'm not saying anything. The jury's out until the ME comes up with a cause of death."

"Jerry, I..."

"Got to go—talk to you later."

A half-hour later Valerie came through the door, slamming it shut behind her. "Have you seen Emilia?" she asked worriedly.

"No, not since that day..." I glanced around the store. "You know the one. Are you saying she isn't back yet? It's been like a month!"

"She isn't at the Victorian and I haven't seen her at our

usual haunts. I even went to Pederson's store and asked if he'd seen her."

"What did he say?"

"He said, no, of course. But I could tell he was lying."

I let out a heavy sigh. "Finally someone on my side."

"What side are we talking about? I'm searching for Emilia, not handing out a murder charge."

"So why would he lie? What if he's hurt her?"

"How could he?"

"I don't know, but I can tell you're worried." I glanced into the back of the store, checking on two customers immersed in a couple of goddess books. I certainly did not want to scare them away—I needed the sales. "There's been another victim and the police think it's Philippa Booker."

"Philippa? Oh my goodness! Why on earth would he kill her?"

"I think the book is the link. *Black magic and the Occult* wouldn't let me open it," I continued, whispering.

"That's one of Philippa's purchases from back when we were having meetings at Bookers. Apparently it contains spells to bring back the dead."

Something stirred in the back of my mind. "Who would Carl want to bring back?"

Valerie gazed at me, her eyes narrowing. "If he's a ghost maybe himself?"

"Or...Mrs. Browning?"

"Why would he bother with that? She may be a ghost but she's solid."

"Maybe he wants the younger version."

Valerie smiled. "From pictures I've seen she was very pretty back then." Her face dropped. "If he tries and fails she could disappear forever."

"And why did he kill Daniel Booker, Isabel and Marguerite?"

"You seem certain that he did."

"I am certain. I told you about the Gjenganger, right?"

"The what?"

I proceeded to explain what it was and why I suspected Carl of being one.

Valerie didn't say anything for a while, her eyes downcast. "The bruising sounds like the clincher. Why can't I see any of this with my third eye?"

"Maybe's he blocked you. He certainly had Marguerite fooled."

"If it takes a week or more for the victims to die it would explain why no one saw Isabel's killer." She gazed at me. "Maybe you're right about the book being the key. Philippa bought it for Bookers, it was stolen from Daniel, and Marguerite was a very powerful witch who would have figured it out sooner or later. That leaves Isabel. Why did he kill her?"

"She and Henry were in the market for books on black magic—they had two on hold here. Possibly they saw the book at Carl's and wanted to buy it?"

"But all of this just to bring Emilia back sounds over the top."

"Don't forget that he might want to come back too. Maybe there are others…" I glanced toward the door as Carl entered, his dark eyes narrowed in anger as he walked toward my desk. "What did you do to my book?" he demanded nastily.

"What book?"

"My book on black magic. It refuses to open."

"I admit I tried to open it, but all it revealed was the copyright date before it slammed shut."

"Liar. That book is my future. You'd better come along to my store and fix it or you'll go the same way your friends went."

I glanced at Valerie who had moved back a step, her eyes wide. "Are you admitting you killed them?" I whispered, worried about my two customers.

He frowned and took hold of my upper arm. "You know what I am."

"And if I do, what would keep me from turning you in?"

He laughed. "Who would believe you?" He jerked me forward toward the door. When I looked back Valerie mouthed something I couldn't understand. Once we were outside it seemed as though we flew to his car, my feet barely touching the ground before I was flung into the back seat. When we reached his store he dragged me into the back where the books on magic were shelved. "Fix it," he hissed in my ear.

I picked up the book, feeling the tingle in my fingers. When I tried to pry it open it refused to budge. "It's magically bound."

"Who bound it if not you?"

I shrugged. "I'm not a real witch but there are others in this town who could have. You didn't kill them all."

"Who are they?"

"Do you really think I'd give you their names? What's so important about this book?"

He shook his head, staring at it malevolently. "It's my future," he muttered. He grabbed me roughly and dragged me toward the trapdoor. "Let's see how a night down there might change your mind about things."

"I'm not afraid of the tunnels or the dark."

"You will be now," he said, an evil smile on his face as he held me with one hand and pulled open the trapdoor with the other. It was at that moment I heard Jerry shout my name.

"I'm here!" I yelled, jerking away from Carl.

It took only a second before Jerry appeared, gun drawn. "What in hell is going on here?"

A smile curled at the corners of Carl's thin mouth. "Your wife was just about to tell me the secrets that lie inside these books I seem to have acquired."

Jerry's eyes glazed over, the hand holding the gun lowering to his side as he stared into space. A buzz filled my ears, getting louder and louder until I could barely stand it. I had my hands over my ears when the room tilted, Jerry's eyes meeting mine before I fell, landing heavily on my hip. I heard the gun go off and an inhuman yell before the room was plunged into darkness.

"Summer, are you all right?"

I opened my eyes to soft light, Jerry bent over me. "I...what happened? Did you get him?"

Jerry pulled me up to sitting. "I think I nicked him, but he got away before I had the chance to cuff him."

My gaze travelled to the open trapdoor. "Why didn't you go after him?"

"And leave you up here unconscious?"

I put my hand up to my head where a bump had formed. "How did you know I was here?"

"Valerie called me." He knelt next to me and pulled me

into his arms. "I told you to be careful, and here you are again, nearly getting yourself killed." He drew back to gaze at me worriedly. "You could be carrying our child, Summer. This is no time to be…"

"Carl came into Tarot and Tea and grabbed me. It isn't like I went with him willingly. And there's no way I'm pregnant yet, so don't use that argument to bend me to your will."

"Bend you to my will? I'm just…"

"I know what you're doing, and I know you love and worry about me, but I can take care of myself."

When Jerry reached for the book on black magic he let out a yelp of pain. He glanced at me."Can you pick it up? It's evidence."

I reached for it, feeling the painful tingle that went into my fingers and up my arm. I suppressed a cry and steeled myself, following Jerry toward the front of the store and out. What had happened during those minutes was a puzzle, but I was pretty sure it was my doing that the floor had tilted, upsetting my balance and knocking me out for a few seconds. Carl had put some sort of a spell on Jerry before I'd unwittingly helped him escape. After securing the book in one of the saddlebags I climbed on the back of the bike, wondering who had bound it and why.

"I'm taking you home," he said, starting his bike.

"But my car and…"

"We can pick up your car, Summer, but that bump on your head should be seen."

"No, Jerry—it's nothing, but I do feel rather shaken. Maybe Valerie can watch the store for a few more hours."

Jerry drove me back to Tarot and Tea on his motorcycle and waited while I talked to Valerie and gave her the key to lock up.

"Did Jerry catch him?"

I shook my head no. "Carl went into the tunnels."

Valerie's gaze met mine. "I taped him on my phone—not sure it's crystal clear, but I did it."

"A cell phone? Since when…"

"Becky made me get one. Guess she doesn't want to worry about me in my doddering old age." She let out a mirthless laugh.

"You are far from doddering, Valerie. Maybe Becky just wants to be able to reach you."

Valerie shrugged. "In any case, take it and see if Jerry can decipher it." She held it out.

I glanced out the open door watching Jerry pace beside my car. "I should go, but remind me to tell you something tomorrow."

"Something…about Carl?"

"No. About me."

She gazed at me quizzically before asking, "What should I do with the key when I leave?"

"Stick it under the mat. I'm not worried about a break-in between now and early tomorrow."

16

It was barely four in the afternoon but the sky had gone completely dark, our trip home feeling spooky as we passed skeletal trees and heard the scream of the wind. I saw my cat again, his dark form racing in front of the car before he disappeared into the shadows on the other side of the road. "Did you see that?" I asked Jerry.

"See what?"

"A black cat just ran right in front of the car."

He turned for a second. "Bad luck, right? Seems like bad luck follows you, Summer."

"I don't believe in that."

Jerry laughed. "You believe in supernatural beings but you don't believe in black cats being a harbinger of bad luck?"

"That's right. Black cats are lucky, not unlucky. I should know—I have one."

Jerry made a derisive sound in the back of his throat.

I glanced at his dark profile. "Carl put a spell on you, Jerry."

He glanced at me. "What are you talking about?"

"Just before the room tilted you lowered the gun."

"Bullshit—I shot at the dude!"

"But before that there was a moment when you were just standing there staring into space."

"If that's true why don't I remember it?"

"Because you were under a spell."

"And what do you mean the room tilted?"

I shrugged and turned to stare out the window. After that he didn't say anything and neither did I, the rest of the trip made in uncomfortable silence. I thought about a baby, vowing to start my pills again. With everything going on at the moment an accidental pregnancy was just too overwhelming to even contemplate.

"Can you keep that damn book from burning me?" Jerry asked once we got inside the cottage. "I have to take it to the station tomorrow morning."

"I'll put it in a grocery bag."

Jerry headed off to the bedroom as I stared out the window into the darkness. When Cutty gave a sharp yip I came back to the present, obeying his orders to feed him. "Sorry little guy, I'm kind of preoccupied." His response to that was to gobble from the food dish I put down. Mischief suddenly appeared in front of me, her green eyes like marbles. "Was that you on the road?" I whispered, reaching down to pick her up. She let me cradle her for a moment before she wriggled free and ran for the counter, where she jumped up to climb inside a basket. A second later Tabby meowed for his dinner and I walked over to his food dispenser on the table by the washer and dryer. It was totally empty. I grabbed the bag of cat kibbles and filled it before following Jerry into the bedroom.

"Are you hungry?" I asked, my gaze going to where he was stretched out on the bed.

He looked at me, a frown on his face. "Not really—too concentrated on what just happened."

I handed him Valerie's phone. "Valerie recorded him, which means you'll have his confession."

He glanced down and fiddled with it until he found what he was looking for and held it up to his ear. "Garbled, but possibly the expert at the station can decipher it." His worried gaze met mine. "I can't deal with the possibility of you getting hurt."

I sat on the bed next to him. "This isn't any different than anything else we've gone through. Why are you freaking out?"

"What if you're pregnant?"

"If you plan to worry like this maybe I should go back on the pill."

"Don't say that."

"I'm not ready for this, Jerry. I can't be curtailing everything I do just to satisfy your irrational fears."

He watched me, his eyes going dark. "Until we catch this guy I'm asking Sam to assign a detail to your store."

"How will that look to my customers? I'm already selling next to nothing. Can you imagine how they'll feel if there's a cop hanging around?"

"He'll be in plain clothes. And I also want you to see a doctor."

"For what reason? I haven't missed a period yet."

"Are you sure? From my calculations…"

"Your calculations? Are you keeping tabs on my cycle now?"

Jerry let out a huff of annoyance. "Yes, Summer, I am. And you *have* missed a period."

"But…what about your sperm count?"

"I had it checked and it's back to normal."

I was suddenly hot all over, the likelihood that I was already pregnant sending adrenaline shooting through my veins. Jerry had never paid one iota of attention to my cycle, the idea of him actually *knowing* that I'd missed a period bringing all sorts of strange emotions to the surface of my mind. Agnes was right—this was not the Jerry I knew. This man was serious about a family and his main motivation for having sex was making a baby. Meanwhile I'd been so enamored with the attention I'd forgotten all about the risk we were taking, not even noticing what was right in front of my eyes.

He thought I was on the same page with him—why else would I throw my pills away? "I'm going to make dinner," I said, hurrying out of the bedroom. The muddle I'd created for myself sent my rational thoughts scurrying, a tornado of unfettered fears filling my brain as I tried to chop vegetables without slicing off a finger.

When Jerry appeared I shrank away from him, an overwhelming urge to run out of the house coming over me. Dinner was eaten in silence, Jerry's gaze seeking mine several times, an expression of bewilderment in his eyes.

"What's wrong?" he finally asked when I got up to clear the table.

I turned to him, trying to find the right words. But before I could form them my eyes filled with tears.

"You don't want a baby," he said, his gaze going dark.

"I…I don't know what I want or what I was thinking."

"When will you know? Because I thought we discussed it and came to a mutual decision."

"Did we? I can't remember if we did. I'm scared, Jerry."

Jerry got up from the table and pulled me close. "It will be a big responsibility and a big change, Summer. But there are two of us here, and I plan to be a hands on dad."

"Can you carry it to term too?"

Jerry laughed. "Sorry, but I can't help you there. First thing in the morning I want you to call your gynecologist and have a test."

"Couldn't I just use one of those early pregnancy test kits?"

"I'd rather you went to a doctor. That way if anything weird is going on you'll know right away."

"Weird? Like what?"

He shrugged and raised his hands. "I don't know—things that happen when you're older?"

"I'm only thirty."

He let out a heavy sigh. "Do what you want then. Just please find out if you are or you aren't."

"And if I am…what if I don't want it?"

Jerry's eyes widened. "You've got to be kidding."

"I told you I don't know what I want."

He took hold of my forearms, his eyes pleading. "If there's a baby I want it. I'm not sure I could live with you, if you…"

"If I got an abortion because I don't feel ready to have a baby? What about *my* feelings?"

"I get that you're afraid, but we love each other. If you're carrying our child it's because of that love."

"I can't talk about this anymore. Please sleep in the guest

room tonight." I ran for the bedroom and closed and locked the door, ignoring him when he pounded on it and shouted for me to open it. He finally quit and I heard the guest bedroom door close, the loud sound of a football game coming on. I put my pillow over my ears and tried to sleep.

A baby was crying somewhere but I couldn't find it, my fears mounting as I searched through empty rooms. When Jerry appeared carrying a swaddled bundle I breathed a sigh of relief, but when he handed me the baby and I looked down, the face that looked back at me was Mischief's. I let out a shriek and dropped the bundle, watching Mischief disentangle herself and run off.

17

The next morning I lay in bed until after I heard the rumble of Jerry's motorcycle heading away. Rain pelted the window behind my headboard—another cold and miserable day. My usual urge to call Agnes wasn't even there, the decision I had to make taking up all my headspace. *Jerry will divorce me if I have an abortion* kept running through my head like some sick mantra, the finality of it making me feel ill. Even if I found out I wasn't pregnant, that attitude had changed things between us forever.

After a quick cup of coffee made in my simple but easy French press, I fed the animals and hurried out to my car. On the trip to the drugstore to get the early pregnancy test, I realized that not only did I need new tires, but I also needed new windshield wipers. They were barely managing to do the job. The weather worsened as I went along, thunder rumbling across the slate colored sky. It almost seemed like my black mood was affecting it somehow.

Samhain was fast approaching and so far Jerry had not given the green light for the spot by the river. The rain had slowed the investigation down and probably washed away any evidence. I hoped that by now Douglas had secured the Victorian for that night, the idea of standing outside in the freezing rain sending goosebumps up my arms.

When I reached Tarot and Tea it was still early enough to have a cup of tea and take the pregnancy test before I opened. I found the key under the mat and unlocked the door, leaving the shut sign up as I hurried into the back. In the bathroom I read the instructions, my heart in my throat. Either way I figured it was the end of Jerry and me.

When the results showed negative I had a sudden sadness that made no sense. Why wasn't I happy? But then I remembered that Jerry was no longer there for me. He'd decided that having a baby was more important than my feelings. I made tea and sobbed.

My first customer was Valerie, her warm smile a balm to my shattered nerves. When she got close and noticed my red eyes her smile faded. "What is it?"

I explained as best I could, trying not to burst into tears again. "I'm sure we'll be getting a divorce," I finished, turning away to blow my nose.

"He'll come around."

"Do you think I'm wrong?"

"I think you're not ready. This could change in a week, a month, or a year, or possibly you'll never be ready. But don't beat yourself up about it. At least you aren't pregnant and don't have to go through some horrible procedure to get rid of it."

"What about my marriage?"

"I suggest speaking to someone about it—this is a big issue between you two that won't be solved without some expert help."

"I didn't know you believed in therapy."

"Normally I don't, but this is a special case. Didn't you see a woman a year or so ago that you connected with? Why don't you call her?"

"Corinne Samuels. She helped me when we got back from Mexico." I looked up. "Jerry was on about a baby then too. But that time I was able to tell him I wasn't ready."

"I suggest giving her a call."

I glanced at the clock. "May as well do it now—maybe she can see me today." I pulled my cell phone out of my purse and Googled her name. "I can't face him, Valerie. I may have to get a hotel room until I can sort things out."

"You can't face him because you feel guilty." She nodded at the phone. "Call."

While I punched in the numbers she wandered off to look at some new books I'd recently acquired on Celtic myths and the magical properties of trees. Corrine answered after the first ring, something metallic clattering in the background.

"Corinne? This is Summer McCloud. I need to make an appointment."

"Good to hear from you, Summer," she said breathlessly. "Can you come now? I just had a cancelation." Another crash sounded, followed by her muffled oath.

"I'll be there as soon as I can. Thank you so much." I clicked off and put my phone in my purse.

"Did you get her?" Valerie asked, appearing with a small book in her hands.

"I have to go right now. If you can't stay I'll lock up— it's not like customers are banging on my door."

She patted my arm. "I can stay for an hour or two. If you're not back by then I'll lock up and leave the key under the mat."

"Thanks, Valerie." *I should be paying her*, I thought as I hurried out the door toward my car. Valerie was in the store nearly as much as I was and I'd come to rely on her like an assistant.

The rain had changed into a combination of ice and water, the slush gathering on my walkway and and along the street. Wind added to the general sense of chaos, as trash whirled into the air, plastic bottles and coffee cups scattering. I turned on the wipers, wishing I'd bought new ones the last time I had the chance. The bare arms of the trees lifted to the sky, beseeching a non—existent sun. I couldn't remember the last time we'd had such terrible weather this early in the year, or for this long.

Corinne lived in a turn of the century cottage, the casement windows closed against the weather. Window boxes were filled with the last of the pansies, their bright lion faces a spot of color in an otherwise dismal day. I knocked and waited, gazing around her tiny garden of herbs and fall vegetables that were on their last legs. By tomorrow they'd be gone, dead from freezing.

The door swung open, Corinne's smiling face looking out at me. "Come in, my dear!" she invited, helping me off with my coat.

I pulled off my Mukluks, adding them to the jumble of shoes, raingear, umbrellas and other detritus that filled her entrance.

She kicked some things out of the way, giving me a

sheepish smile. "I can no longer use the excuse that I just moved in, can I?" She let out a cackle and led the way into her office, gesturing toward a chair covered in several paintings, moving ahead of me to remove them. "Sorry. Doing a bit of redecorating."

I glanced at the stacks of books on a shelf, the pile of papers on her desk. Two abandoned mugs sat precariously near the edge. On a side table there were several framed pictures lying face down, others on a chair next to them. The walls were covered in art of every description, from animal sketches to wild abstracts in bright colors.

She noticed me looking at them. "I'm a collector," she admitted. "And I tend to like things that don't necessarily go together." She moved the two coffee cups off her desk to the window ledge behind her, making room for them by shoving aside a ball of red wool, knitting needles and several magazines. Instead of sitting behind her desk she turned an antique chair to face me, sat down and clasped her hands together in her lap. "Now tell me what brings you in? I noticed a certain desperation in your voice on the phone."

"I am desperate," I admitted. "Jerry and I are about to split up."

"Well, let's begin there, shall we?"

After I finished explaining about stopping the pill and Jerry's prostate cancer scare and low sperm count, she held up her hand. "Every one of these things you've mentioned are extremely stress producing. Is it your belief that Jerry is pushing the baby thing because he's facing his own mortality? As I remember this was one of the issues we spoke about the last time you were in."

"That was after our honeymoon when I nearly got killed—at least I was honest about not being ready. But this time I let him think I was on the same page, even though I wasn't."

"And when you finally came clean, his reaction was not what you'd hoped."

"I can't win either way. The fact that I'm not pregnant doesn't help anything. Just the mention of an abortion set him off."

"Is he a religious man?"

"Well…I didn't think so, but he *was* raised Catholic. He has a zillion brothers and sisters."

"I'd say the Catholic thing is rearing it's ugly head— sorry to be so blunt."

I laughed. "I don't believe in any of that stuff, and finding out that he does has changed things for me too."

"From what you've told me, two things are going on for him. 1. He had a very serious health scare. 2. He's reacting from a place that has nothing to do with now and he may not even realize it." She peered at me, her hazel eyes inquiring. "Do you feel guilty?"

I nodded. "Very guilty. I should have told him I wasn't ready. I was afraid of losing him, and that's why…"

"Understandable, Summer. What I have to suggest may not be to your liking, but I think it has to be done if you're to mend your marriage."

I waited, afraid of what she was about to say.

"You will need to face each other and talk this out. I know that sounds impossible right now, but it's the only way. If you feel he needs help, tell him so. If you feel that he's treating you unfairly, tell him so. Explain your position honestly and without guilt. You made a mistake and you're sorry that it affected things so badly."

"But I don't even know how I feel about having a baby—that's the most confusing part."

She shook her head, pushing a wayward strand of hair behind her ear. "Confusion is not an excuse. Close your eyes and breath deeply."

I did as she asked, feeling my shoulders drop.

"Now imagine yourself holding a tiny baby—your newborn. How does it make you feel?"

I imagined the swaddled bundle—instead of Mischief a wizened baby face peered up at me. "I'm scared and elated at the same time."

"Look at the baby, Jerry's and your baby, and let your feelings rise to the surface."

"He's so fragile. He has dark hair like Jerry's and his eyes are dark too. His little fingers…" I began to cry.

"And how do you feel?"

"I love him and I love Jerry and I love that he's Jerry's and my baby."

"It's something new between you, something wonderful—something you share that's not like anything else."

I opened my eyes and wiped them with the tissue she handed me.

"You do want a baby, Summer. Now I'm not saying you want one today, or even tomorrow, but from this exercise I'm certain that you will be a willing partner when the time comes. Your fear has eclipsed your real feelings. Can you tell me what this fear is all about?"

"Responsibility mostly—and our house is too small, and

Jerry will be so involved with the baby that I'll be pushed aside."

"Ah ha. I think we've come to the crux of the matter. You're afraid of what a child will do to your relationship. Can you expand on that?"

My face heated up as a blush rose to the surface. "We have really good sex."

Corinne chuckled. "And a baby will affect this, how?"

"Crying, needing to be fed—basically interrupting us at every turn."

Corinne laughed. "A baby does change things, but if your sex life is as good as you say it is, I'm sure you two can work around it. Let our session settle in for a few days and see how you feel about things." She rose from her chair. "We covered a lot of ground today—I think it's best to stop here."

"But what about Jerry?"

"Meet him for drinks and dinner and tell him what we talked about today."

She gave me a hug and shepherded me out, leading the way through the mess in the front hall. I pulled on my boots and handed her a wad of cash. "Shall I make anther appointment?"

"See how things go and call if you need me." She opened the door and pulled her sweater tighter around her thin frame, peering at the accumulating sleet. "Be careful driving home."

The drive back to Tarot and Tea sent me skidding several times. By the time I reached my shop, my nerves were completely frayed.

"Well?" Valerie said as soon as I had my boots off inside the door.

"I have to call Jerry and invite him out for dinner."

Valerie glanced out the front window. "In this weather?"

"And he's riding his bike today."

She let out an amused sound, the idea of my husband wet and miserable seeming to bring a smile to her lips. "You certainly seem lighter, Summer. That woman is a miracle worker."

I nodded and used the landline to call Jerry's cell. "Can we meet for drinks and dinner tonight?" I asked, cutting him off before he could say anything.

"Tonight? Have you looked outside? There's a major storm on the way."

"I don't care. We have to talk."

"I get that, but how about talking at home?"

"I figured we wouldn't be sleeping in the same house after last night."

He let out a low sound. "Yeah. I already booked a motel room."

I ignored the sinking sensation in my stomach. "Let's meet early—say five?"

"All right, but don't expect anything."

He'd already booked a room? And he sounded seriously pissed. Dinner would definitely be interesting, but I was determined to tell him the truth and try to come to some understanding.

∞

After Valerie left I spent the rest of the day trying to plan what to say to Jerry and wondering why I had no customers. During a lull in the weather I locked up and drove my car by Pederson's Books to see if my customers were all flocking to him. Indeed they were, with a line out his door and several groups huddled together talking as they waited. *In this weather?* I was shocked and dismayed to recognize a lot of my regulars. At least Mrs. Browning was not among them, nor was Douglas or Lucia. And then I remembered that Mrs. B hadn't been seen in weeks. As I drove slowly past, Carl peered out the door, his pale eyes following me. He knew I was there, had come to the door because of it. Creepy! Why wasn't he being arrested? Valerie's recording must have been deciphered by now.

When I got back there was a note on my door from Becky, irritated that the store was locked up. I let out a huff of impatience, thinking about how unfair it was that she'd arrived within the short fifteen minutes I'd been gone.

I unlocked my door and hurried inside just as the sleet turned to snow. The sky was a yellowish gray that didn't bode well. I hurried into the back and applied lipstick, adding rouge to my pale cheeks. I fluffed my bedraggled hair, finally deciding to twist it up and secure it with a clip. I pulled off the heavy shirt I wore over my skirt, leaving on my pale lacy camisole that was not all suited to the weather, and fiddling with the straps until some cleavage showed. I stared at my reflection in the mirror, wondering if I was going a little overboard. This man was my husband, after all—he'd seen me naked a million times. But I left the camisole the way it was, slipping on my heavy down coat and Mukluks before I locked up and hurried to the snow-covered car. If I got stuck between my store and Grub and Grins I wasn't sure what I would do. Two inches had fallen and it showed no sign of letting up.

18

I was completely unnerved by the time I reached the bar, my skidding and sliding trip nearly taking me off the road several times. The Mukluks were warm, but the soles didn't have enough tread to keep me from nearly falling on the way inside. I felt like I was meeting Jerry for the first time.

He was in a booth, his brooding gaze on the glass of dark liquid on the table in front of him. I slid in across from him and pulled off my coat, flinging it onto the seat next to me. "I nearly died on the way here," I muttered.

He stared at me. "I was on my bike—think how much much fun that was."

A laugh rose up my throat when I noticed his hair in unruly wet tufts and the soaked leather jacket hanging on a hook, but my amusement died when I saw his hollow, red-rimmed eyes, the exhaustion that was obvious in the hunch of his shoulders. "Sorry for suggesting this meeting, but…"

"We just *had* to hash out our differences in a public place on a night when no one is stupid enough to venture out?"

I grimaced and signaled to the woman wearing black behind the bar, ordering a glass of wine before bringing my attention back to him. "If we don't want to end our marriage, yes."

"Maybe we do want to end it," he muttered, picking up his glass of straight whiskey.

"If you've already decided to file for a divorce I guess there's no point to this, but I…"

His bleak gaze met mine. "I haven't decided anything, Summer."

That was good at least. When the waitperson returned with my wine I took a sip, placing my glass down carefully and wondering why I was wearing a sexy camisole and makeup. Goosebumps had risen on my arms and so far Jerry didn't seem at all interested in anything but his whiskey. "I went to see Corrine this morning," I began, trying to get things started.

He glanced up. "Who the hell is Corinne?"

"The therapist I went to after my experience in Mexico?"

"Oh yeah. I remember now. Go on."

I gazed at the empty booths and tables, glad that I could speak freely. "She thinks it's fear that's keeping me from seeing the truth."

His eyes narrowed. "What's the truth?"

"I do want a baby. I'm just scared of what it will mean for us."

His expression changed into one of confusion. "Us?"

"Yes, the changes it will bring. Like for instance, to our sex life?" I whispered, leaning close.

"Why would it affect that?"

I scoffed. "What do you think? Diapers, crying, lack of sleep, feeding schedules."

"Only at the beginning, and from what I've heard you can't have sex for a while anyway."

How much reading had he done? "She had some insights about you too, Jerry. She thinks your reactions to me are from being raised Catholic; she also mentioned your health scare. We both knew that was part of it, but the way you reacted to my feelings made me feel dismissed and cut-off, as though…"

"As though you didn't count?" he asked, glaring at me.

"But…it's my body. I have a right to…"

"What upset me most was thinking you and I were together on this, and then when it came down to it you weren't anywhere near. It hurt me and I felt dismissed, just as you did."

I took another sip of wine and sat back. At least he hadn't stormed out yet. "FYI I took the test this morning and it came up negative."

Jerry didn't say anything, his gaze on his glass. "I still think you're pregnant," he finally said. "There's something different about you."

"Like what?"

He shrugged. "I can't put my finger on it. Maybe it's a smell or something off the wall like that. I just have a feeling."

"Jerry Brady has an intuition?" I asked, smirking.

"Go to a doctor before you make fun of me. Now tell me this—after your talk with Corinne, if you are pregnant, will you keep it or get rid of it?" His gaze bored into me, his brows pulling together.

I thought of the dark-haired baby that looked like him, the tiny fingers that clung to mine and the love that filled my heart. "I won't get rid of it, but we do need to discuss what happens if I am."

His expression finally relaxed. "Then divorce is off the table."

"Was it ever on?"

He grinned. "Well, sort of. I was pretty pissed at you—you betrayed my trust."

"And I had the same exact feeling. I still don't get why you're so sure I'm pregnant. Maybe it's just wishful thinking."

He cocked his head to one side. "Maybe, maybe not."

Jerry left his bike at the bar and drove me home in my car. "You need to get new tires," he muttered when the car slid on a patch of ice.

"I know, but my shop isn't doing well, and…"

"For god's sake, Summer. I can pay for them. I have a consulting job now. We are married, you know."

"Not to mention your inheritance."

"Yeah, that too."

"Speaking of your job, what did you find out from Valerie's recording?"

He pulled up to the cottage and shut off the engine, watching the windshield fill up with snow. "Not a damned thing. It was blank."

"Blank? But she said she listened to it herself. And you heard it too, remember? You said you thought the experts could decipher it."

He shrugged. "Can't help that," he said, sliding out and heading around the car.

When he opened my door I grabbed his arm and we

navigated the slippery flagstones to the door. "Carl is stealing my customers."

He opened the front door. "Stealing?"

I followed him inside. "I had zero customers today, Jerry, and when I drove by his bookstore I recognized a bunch of my regulars. He's a supernatural being—he could very well be using his powers to lure them away from me."

"Or maybe it's just a novelty for them. Try not to read too much into it."

"After four deaths? It's hard not to think about it. What do we do now?"

He closed and locked the door, turning when Cutty ran up to him. "Are you hungry, little guy?" When he picked him up and nuzzled him, carrying him into the kitchen, I knew exactly how he'd be with our child. A warm feeling stole through me.

"What?" he asked, noticing me watching.

I smiled. "Nothing."

In bed later we touched on the subject of Carl again. "He's gotten away with four murders. How do we stop him?"

Jerry's mouth tightened. "I thought the book might help, but it won't open for anyone."

"I told you, it's spellbound."

"How do you unbind it?"

"Find the spell that bound it in the first place. Maybe that's why he killed Philippa—because she wouldn't give him the spell."

"And you think he needs this book, why?"

"To bring himself back from the dead, and maybe Mrs. B as well."

Jerry gave me a skeptical look. "I know you believe in all this, but I'm struggling here. I have a cop's mind and I deal in facts, not superstition or spells, or the undead."

I grinned and moved close, snuggling against his warm body. "That's where I come in."

Jerry pulled away and stared at me. "Sam's detail will be at your store tomorrow—I already arranged it. And before you start snooping around again I want you to see a doctor."

"And what if I am? Do you expect me to sit around for nine months like an invalid?"

"No, but I also don't want you putting your life at risk."

"And if I'm not, is it okay for me to 'snoop around', as you call it?"

Jerry pinned me with his gaze. "I don't want you doing it either way, but if you are, the first trimester is the most precarious. If someone threw you against a wall for instance, you could lose the baby."

"You're a fount of information."

He gave me a sheepish smile. "I've read a couple of articles. I figured I should in case we…"

"Managed to conceive?"

"Come here," he ordered, pulling me to him. "I'm glad we talked, but now it's time for a different communication." When his mouth found mine I relaxed against him, glad to have our troubles behind us. At least our bodies knew what to do.

But afterward when I brought up the case we argued again. And when I persisted he was off like lightning into the guest bedroom, making me wish I'd never bought the TV.

19

Halloween and the full moon passed by, the coven meeting scrapped in the wake of the murders and bad weather. Marguerites ritual had been put off, moods dark as the weather persisted. Trick or treaters were sparse, huddled inside heavy coats instead of dressed in costumes. Jerry and I handed out candy to a few unhappy looking children, their parents idling in their cars waiting to drive them to the next house.

⁓

When Valerie arrived at the store the next morning, breathless and covered in snow, I had an immediate adrenaline rush. "What happened?" I asked, my voice going up an octave.

"I had a terrible dream about Emilia last night—she was calling to me and asking for help."

"Where was she?"

"I don't know. I only heard her voice. It's been weeks now—we have to find her."

"Jerry said the recording you made was blank."

"How can that be? I listened to it after you left. I could hear him clearly."

"What about Emilia? Is Carl responsible for her disappearance?"

"Other than my dreams I can't see her—I've done the Tarot and meditated on my third eye and I get nothing."

A well-built man walked in, shook the snow off his leather jacket and removed his mirrored sunglasses to reveal startling blue eyes. He nodded to me and went to stand by the door. "My detail," I whispered.

Valerie glanced at him. "Handsome," she murmured. "I have to run. Becky's waiting."

"Waiting where?"

She smiled. "At the bakery. Shawn's with her and I get to meet him for the first time."

"Give her my love."

At eleven I made my detail a cup of tea, carrying it from the kitchen and handing him the steaming mug where he leaned against the wall by the door. "What's your name?"

"Bill, ma'am. Bill Harris."

"I've had no customers all day, Bill. Perhaps it's time for you to head back to the precinct."

He shook his head, his gaze on the mug in his hands. "Can't leave until you do—strict orders."

"Did Jerry tell you that?"

"No, ma'am. Detective Anderson is my boss."

"I hate to have you wasting your time here when you could be investigating murders."

He grinned. "Murders would be my choice too, but I'm new and the new guy gets the..." He stopped in mid-sentence. "Sorry, ma'am, didn't mean any disrespect."

"None taken, Officer Harris. I'm glad you're here—it

makes me feel safer."

He grinned again and took a sip from the mug. "Good tea, ma'am."

"You can call me Summer," I said over my shoulder, heading back to my desk where a stack of papers waited.

It was barely four when I decided to close up shop. The weather was abominable, and I'd had no customers since the one who'd stopped by early in the morning, leaving without buying anything. After Jerry called to pester me about the doctor's appointment, I made one, but an hour later I changed my mind and canceled it. For one thing the weather was too iffy, and for another, I'd already taken one test that came up negative—why should I pay for a second one? And besides all that, I hated doctors and hated everything associated with them, including the inevitable long wait to get seen.

Bill left with me, his arm welcome as he helped me navigate the accumulated ice between the shop and my car.

"You get to sit in a chair tomorrow," I told him, slipping behind the wheel.

"It won't be me tomorrow."

"Who will it be?"

He shrugged. "Whoever they can spare, I guess."

"I'm sorry you had to do such a boring job."

He gave me a sheepish grin. "I'm a rookie and that's what rookies do."

"Maybe tomorrow you'll have a more interesting assignment." I closed the door and started up my car, relieved when the engine turned over. When I turned on the wipers they scraped across the sheet of ice, barely doing anything. I turned on the heat full blast. I was still waiting for the ice to melt when my cell phone rang. Agnes. "Hi Ags, what's new?"

"You won't believe this—Sam's taking classes to further his career!"

"Really? Jerry thought he might be, but he wasn't sure."

"Why didn't you tell me?"

"Because Jerry was guessing and I didn't want to interfere."

Agnes let out a snort. "*You* didn't want to interfere? The woman who meddles in everything?"

"Very funny. It sounds like things are better between you—did you tell him about...?"

"Oh Summer, I'm so happy! I'm having another baby!"

I let out a chortle. "No abortion then."

"Of course not! Sam wants the baby as much as I do."

"Ags...you did say that..."

"I know what I said, but it was only because I was worried about Sam. He was keeping things from me. When we finally talked and I told him, he was ecstatic."

"I'm glad to hear it. I wish Jerry and I didn't fight every couple of days—it's a strain."

"Why are you fighting?"

"It's the baby thing. He's been keeping tabs on my cycle and telling me about articles he's read—it's really annoying."

"I told you he'd changed."

"I know you did. He's definitely not the free-wheeling man I married."

"Have you decided if you're ready or not?"

"I...I do want one. I'm just not sure that now is the best

time. But I didn't start the pill again."

Agnes laughed. "Russian roulette then."

"I guess," I admitted.

"Got to go. Sam's calling. I'm already showing—can you believe it?"

I laughed and said goodbye, wishing I could feel the way she did. Even after talking with Corinne I was still on the fence, uncertain about it all.

Jerry was just arriving when I drove up to the cottage. I saw Sam driving away in a police car, glad that Jerry wasn't out on his bike in the weather. He waited for me by the door, a newspaper held over his head to keep the snow off.

"What's with this weather?" I asked, hurrying toward him.

"Early winter? I have no idea, but it's caused a bunch of accidents already. Sam has his hands full."

"And what about you? Any news about the murders?"

His lips pressed together. "Even with the expert help there's no clear indication of how they died. It's driving everyone crazy."

I took my key out and unlocked the door, reaching down to pick up Cutty when he appeared. He wriggled and licked my face until I put him back on the floor. "He hates having you gone," I said, turning to Jerry who was hanging up his coat.

"So I'm to stay here all day because of the dog?" he asked in an irritated tone. "I have better things to do with my time."

"What did you do today?"

He glared at me. "I worked on the case—what do you think?"

"Well, I don't know. You aren't on the force—where exactly do you do this work?"

"I use the conference room."

The closed expression on his face kept me from prying any further. I went into the kitchen to feed the animals, trying hard to keep my annoyance at bay.

"Agnes told Sam she's pregnant," I called from the pantry. "And you were right about the classes—he finally fessed up." When he didn't answer I looked into the living room. He wasn't there. And then I heard the voices coming from the guest bedroom. The TV was on and the door was closed. I ignored my irritation as I pulled dishes out of the refrigerator and heated up leftovers.

"Dinners ready," I called later, opening the guest bedroom door.

"Not hungry," he answered, his gaze glued to the screen.

I closed the door and left him to it, wondering if this was to be our life. When I found my book and curled up on the couch to read, Cutty jumped up and snuggled next to me. "At least you love me," I murmured, feeling sorry for myself.

I was in bed when Jerry finally came in, his eyes red-rimmed. I didn't say anything as I watched him head to the bathroom to brush his teeth. "What's wrong?" I finally asked when he came out.

"You know what's wrong," he said, sliding into bed.

"No, I don't. Is this about the baby again?"

He turned on his side and flipped off the lamp. "We can talk about it after you see the doctor."

"I'm not seeing a doctor. There's no point in it."

He turned to look at me over his shoulder. "Fine, Summer. Maybe I should have stuck with my plan."

"What plan is that?"

"The one where I stay in a motel room and file for divorce."

I froze. "Are you kidding?"

He turned his back to me. "I'm sick of your bullshit, Summer. You promised you'd see a doctor. I expected you to keep your word."

"And you won't tell me what you do all day. I'm sick of your bullshit too." I flipped my light off and lay in the dark, my blood boiling. It was less than a minute later that Jerry got up and left the room. I heard the other bedroom door slam closed. So much for thinking things were getting better.

～∞⌒

He was gone when I got up the next morning, his bike missing from where he always parked it. The weather had cleared some, the clouds thin enough to let some weak sunshine through. I tried to eat but ended up throwing my eggs away, but I did manage to feed the dog and the cats and put some laundry in the washing machine. I added detergent and turned it on, determined to keep my mind off our relationship and work to solve the murders. If the police were unable to accept my version of events I would have to do something to prove it.

"I'm going to bait him," I told Valerie when she arrived at Tarot and Tea. "I'll tell Carl I have the book and I know how to open it."

"And how will that help?"

"If I do it right I'm hoping he'll divulge what he has in mind. If I can get him to admit how the bruises work maybe I can figure out how to stop the killing."

"This is the most hair-brained scheme you've ever come up with," Valerie said, staring at me. "For one thing he won't tell you, and for another you don't have the book. What's going on with you?"

My shoulders slumped. "He has Emilia and the police can't figure out how those people died. They never will because it's supernatural, and none of them, including Jerry, believe in the supernatural."

Valerie turned when a young blonde-haired man came in, his gaze going to me before he took off his jacket and slung it over the chair I'd placed by the door. I gave him a nod.

"Why are they all so good-looking?" she whispered.

I shrugged and smiled. "Solving it is up to me now," I continued, whispering. "Maybe if I go into the tunnels I'll have another vision."

Valerie shook her head. "I've thought long and hard about this, Summer. Emilia needs our help, but we're dealing with an entity who seems to be indestructible."

"I'll look up the Gjenganger again and see if I can find more information. There has to be a way." When she walked over to peruse the new essential oils I turned on my computer and Googled Gjenganger. I clicked on Wiki. "Do you think Carl was buried here in Ames?" I called out.

"Could be."

I hurried toward her. "We need to dig up his grave and destroy the bones."

"What?" Valerie's cry brought a startled look from my detail.

"Or we can rebury him and add a bunch of stones."

"Didn't you say these creatures come back because of something left undone? If you can help him solve that, maybe he…"

"He wants to come back to life, Valerie."

"We need that book on black magic—maybe there's a spell in there that will get rid of him."

"It won't open, remember?" I glanced at the man by the door. "Can you stay here while I go into the tunnels?" I whispered.

Valerie let out a huff of impatience. "Not sure what's got into you today." Her eyes went opaque as she stared into the distance. A second later she stared at me. "Are you and Jerry fighting about a baby again? I thought you worked it out."

"I thought so too, but I guess not. I won't be surprised if we get divorced."

"Oh, for goodness sake!" Valerie exclaimed, eliciting another sharp look from the man by the door. "You two love each other—why are you letting this get between you?"

"It's him, Valerie. He's positive I'm pregnant and he won't leave it alone."

"Are you sure you're not?"

"Yes. I took an early pregnancy test," I hissed. I glanced into the back of the store where my trapdoor lay hidden under a rug and nailed shut. "I'm going now. I won't be long."

"Summer…" Valerie whispered, glancing at the cop by the door. "What do I say if he asks where you went?"

I put my finger to my lips and kept going. I used the hammer to pry up the nails, trying to be quiet. But each one squealed in protest, as though the nails themselves were telling me not to do this. Once the trapdoor was open I climbed down the ladder backward, and pulled it shut behind me. The tunnels were very dark and very damp, an odor I couldn't identify wafting by me. I turned on my phone flashlight and worked my way toward Pederson's store, my heart thumping against my ribs. A minute later I felt the air shift around me as I was launched into the past.

The tunnel was lit up like a Christmas tree, strings of bright lights hanging on both sides of the tunnel and lanterns here and there. When I heard voices I plastered myself against the wall, watching Carl carry a woman's limp body by me. Just beyond where I stood he came to an abrupt halt and heaved her roughly into the dirt. "Serves you right, you bitch," he muttered, giving her body a kick. When he turned to a person hurrying to catch up I was horrified to see a younger version of Mrs. Browning. Her hair was brown instead of gray, her body thin and shapely under a fitted gray skirt and matching jacket. Large eyes peered out from an unlined face, her lips full and painted a tasteful pink. But this was no loving conversation, she was angry, tugging on his arm and yelling.

"What have you done to Louise?" she shrieked.

He took hold of her arms. "Emilia, please. This is not my doing. I didn't kill her, but if they find her body I'll be hauled off to jail. You don't want that, do you?"

"I hope to all that's holy that you didn't have anything to do with this, Carl. I've covered for you with the smaller things, but this is too much for me."

"I'm telling you I didn't do it. You know how I feel about you—I'd never lie to you." He pulled her close and kissed her, upsetting her hat, which fell into the dirt.

She pulled away, flustered, and reached for it. "Carl, please. We've discussed this before. We are not married yet and I'm not that sort of woman."

Carl laughed. "You love me, Emilia. Why not let yourself go for once? We'll be married soon enough, but until then I'd like more than a chaste kiss every once in a while."

I was suddenly thrown back into the present. My phone was on the ground, the tiny light glowing. When I reached for it I felt another shift, the earth tilting as I careened into the past once more.

I glanced at the dark and cobwebby tunnels, the tiny light glowing from the small flashlight held in Carl's hands. I shrank back away from him, but he didn't see me, his focus on Mrs. B.

"Give me a chance, Emilia," he pleaded. "All I need is that damn book and then we can have the life we've longed for."

Mrs. B pursed her lips, a hand going to her wiry disheveled hair. Her hat was missing and dirt was streaked across her cheek. She looked exhausted. "I no longer want that, Carl. I'm long dead and the ghost I've become is enough for me."

"You can't mean that! That book can restore your youth and give us back our lives. After these weeks we've spent together I thought... don't you love me?"

"You have now killed four people over that book, several of whom were my friends. I may have loved you once a long time ago, but I can't condone what you've done. Please let me go back."

Carl's expression changed, his pale eyes turning nearly black. He grabbed Emilia by her wrists, twisting her around to face away from him. "Who put a spell on that book?" he growled.

Emilia grimaced in pain as she attempted to pull away. "I don't know who did it. I think it was probably Philippa—but you've killed her now."

He bent her head back, his mouth coming close to her neck. "I tortured that bitch before I bit her. If that spell was her doing she would have told me."

Emilia seemed to calm, her rigid body relaxing against him. "You do know that biting me will not accomplish anything—I'm a ghost."

He scoffed. "Ghosts can be bitten too, Emilia. And if I choose to do so, you will disappear forever. If you won't help me with that spell then you get what you deserve."

"And you don't think you've lived long enough? Remember when I died, Carl? You were heartbroken. But you lived on, didn't you? You've been around for a century now, trying to gain immortality. What year was it that you died and became the creature you are now?"

"I was murdered, you hag. It's why I had to come back and get the bastard who killed me."

"And have you done that? Who was it who killed you, Carl?"

"You know damn well who it was—that fucking copper who took down the entire bootlegging operation. Brady was under cover at the time pretending to work for me when all the while he was gathering information to bring me down. Bastard! A relative of his is here now and I plan to…"

Why, Carl? Why are you so vindictive? It's been nearly a hundred years now. What does the current Brady know about all that? And as to bringing me back—why would you care to?"

"What do you think? Did you actually believe I'm attracted to the version of you that's standing in front of me?"

"You've aged too, Carl."

He let out a low laugh. "Not for long. The spell in that book will restore me."

"Too bad you can't open it," Mrs. B said—goddess bless her. A resounding slap echoed down the tunnels. "So why don't you bite me?" she asked a second later. "What are you waiting for?"

"I think you know how to open it."

"Even if I did it's not in your store anymore, or had you forgotten?"

"God damn it, old woman! Where is it?"

"It's at the police station where it belongs. Have you actually seen the spells inside that book? I doubt if any of them can help you."

"I know it can—Isabel said it could before I bit her. She looked inside it years ago."

"Before it was spellbound."

"Did you bind it?"

"No, Carl. I'm not able to do that sort of thing. Why would you kill Isabel after she revealed the information you wanted?"

He laughed, an ugly sound. "She mocked me, just as Marguerite mocked me. They didn't take me seriously." He twisted her arm again, a look of hatred on his features. "Tell me who bound it."

"All right, all right," she cried out, tears of pain filling her eyes. "Will you let me go if I tell you?"

When he released her she rubbed her wrists, her gaze settling on where I hid in the shadows. She could see me. "It was Summer, Summer McCloud."

One second later I was standing in the tunnel alone, my cell phone on the ground next to me. I picked it up, trying to understand why Mrs. Browning would tell Carl I had bound the book. I'd never even seen it until that fateful day in Carl's shop. And even if I had, I didn't have that kind of power.

As I stood there a vision appeared in my mind of the lead-up to what I'd witnessed in the tunnels. I didn't want to see Carl wielding the baseball bat and slamming it down on the back of her head, tried not to hear the crack as her skull gave way just before she crumpled to the floor, but it tracked across my mind like a movie that had to play out. After she fell he dragged her to the open trapdoor and tossed her through. I heard Mrs. B call out to him and watched him hastily climb down to pick her body up, hurrying to the place where I'd seen him dump her. No wonder her leg was broken in two places.

I headed back toward Tarot and Tea, my mind reeling. Mrs. Browning had set me up for whatever Carl would do to get that book unbound. I was now a sitting duck.

20

By the time I got home that night I'd gone over the conversation between Carl and Mrs. B so many times I could have recited it in my sleep. And because of Jerry's relative, Jerry was also in Carl's crosshairs. I'd told Jerry about his doppelganger, but I was sure that in his present state of mind he would wave it off as one of my ridiculous dreams.

I waited until eleven o'clock before I locked the front door, giving up on the idea of Jerry coming home. His absence was like a heavy stone that rested against my heart. All of this over my reluctance to get a second pregnancy test? I paced around, my mood growing darker by the minute. Jerry wasn't here and I was clearly in danger now. Should I call him?

Outside the cottage the momentary calm weather had turned into a maelstrom, howling wind taking down tree limbs, trash whirling by from overturned cans. When the electricity went out I hurried to the doors, making sure they were all securely locked. I sat in the dark with my knees drawn up, a coiled snake of fear taking up residence in the pit of my stomach. When my cell phone rang I nearly jumped out of my skin. It was Jerry.

"The wind could shatter the windows—you need to close the shutters," he said.

"Jerry? Where are you? I'm in danger…I overheard Carl and Mrs.…." When there was a profound silence on the other end I realized he'd already hung up. I screamed and threw my phone across the room.

I thought of my conversation with Valerie after my experience in the tunnels, her look of horror when I relayed my vision and what I'd heard. "Why would Emilia say that?" she'd hissed. "She must have a reason—she loves you like a granddaughter."

"I don't know, but I'm nervous. At least I have Jerry to protect me," I'd told her.

But I didn't have Jerry to protect me and there was a storm raging—the perfect time for Carl to come and kill me. I pulled my coat on and went around the house to secure the shutters, but keeping my windows intact was the least of my worries.

By the time I went into the bedroom I'd calmed down, the storm calming with me. The electricity flickered back on just in time for me to turn the light off to go to sleep. But sleep eluded me, my wide-open eyes staring into the darkness as I went over and over the last two months. That's when I remembered what was mentioned in the article I'd read about Gjengangers.

I got up and searched through Jerry's things, finally coming upon the cross he'd had since he was a boy. It was solid wood and heavy, more difficult to nail to the door than I'd thought. But having it there made me feel better, especially after reading that a cross would keep me safe. Cutty curled up next to me on the bed, his warm body a comfort as the hours slowly marched by.

In the morning the clouds had massed again. So far they were holding their breath, but I had a feeling more nasty weather was on the way. By the time I left for Tarot and Tea my anxiety had reached alarming heights, and with the emotions came sleet and screeching wind that reminded me of a Banshee. In the back of my mind I had a strange thought—could I be causing this? Was I the Banshee? But despite what Marguerite had told me, I wasn't a witch. The wind was the wind and I had nothing to do with it.

Valerie was waiting at the door when I reached the shop, the shadows under her eyes indicating that she hadn't slept well either. Once we were inside she pulled me close and hugged me. "I was so worried," she murmured.

I remembered her warning about my death. But it had been Marguerite who died—was I next? "I nailed a cross on the front door last night."

"Good thinking."

"Have you seen Mrs. B? He said he'd release her."

"She wasn't at home this morning when I went by."

There was no police detail this morning and no sign that one was coming. "I think you should go," I told Valerie, worrying for her safety.

She shook her head. "I thought all night of possible reasons why Emilia would tell him that. One of them struck me as plausible—she wants to lure him out into the open. If she saw you there she knows you'll be surrounded with police. If he tries to hurt you they'll catch him in the act."

"Too bad Jerry isn't speaking to me and Sam hasn't bothered with my detail." I glanced into the back of the store. "Guess I should re-nail the trapdoor shut. Carl could get in that way."

"Yes," Valerie agreed.

By the time I'd secured the trapdoor there were several customers wandering around. Valerie was checking one out when I arrived at the desk. The woman was a petite blonde, her dark lashed eyes regarding me carefully. "I thought you'd be younger," she said, turning to go. I watched her leave, puzzled by her comment. Valerie and I exchanged a look.

When a man arrived with two bottles of essential oils I rang him up. As he was gathering the packages he glanced at me. "You aren't what I expected," he said, turning to leave.

"Wait! What do you mean—who said something about me?"

"Your father who runs the store a few blocks over? He told us all about you."

"My father's dead."

The man laughed. "He said you'd say that."

"What else did he tell you?"

"He told us you're a real witch with books on black magic, but I didn't see any. Where do you keep them?"

"I don't have any. He's the one who has them."

"He said there's one that's very dangerous. I think it's called *Black Magic and the Occult?* He told me that you know all the spells inside it—that you can bring the dead back to life or put a hex on the living."

What was Carl playing at? "I don't own that book. This man, Carl, is lying to you. And if you must know, that book is with the police right now."

"He said the police confiscated it from your store. He's having you arrested. Did you know that?" The young man gave me a sneering grin before he headed toward the door.

"What is going on?" Valerie asked.

"I have no idea, but I don't like it."

Several more customers came through, their furtive glances making me uncomfortable as they wandered the store. None of them bought anything.

At the end of the day I was exhausted and glad to close up. Fielding strange questions and having people stare at me like I had two heads had done nothing for my confidence. Valerie had stayed until the bitter end, her company keeping me from totally losing it.

I pulled on my coat and locked up, my thoughts going round and round in circles as I walked toward my car. When I noticed a police cruiser coming down the street I waved, assuming it was Sam. Instead it was an officer I'd never seen before, the look on his face less than friendly. When he stopped next to me I waited.

"Are you Summer McCloud?" he asked, stepping out of the patrol car.

"Yes."

He pulled cuffs off his belt and snapped them on my wrists. "I have orders to arrest you."

"What for?"

"Stealing and murder." He took my bag from me and shoved me into the back seat and closed the door.

"Who told you to arrest me? Do you know Sam Anderson? What about Jerry Brady? I'm his wife." He ignored my questions, the back of his head all I could see as we sped down the road. When I looked out the window a few minutes later I realized we weren't anywhere near the Ames precinct. "Where are you taking me?" No answer.

It was forty-five minutes of driving before we arrived at another police station in the town of Cummings. He pulled me out and marched me inside.

"I'm Jerry Brady's wife," I told the woman behind the desk. "Sam Anderson is a friend of mine."

"I don't care who your friends are. There's a warrant out for your arrest."

"But how could that be? I haven't done anything wrong."

"Says here you killed four people." She looked up. "Takes all kinds, I guess."

"I need to make a phone call."

"Sorry, that privilege has been dispensed with."

"What? Why?"

"That's what it says here," she said, pointing to the paper in front of her.

"But everyone gets at least one phone call."

"Apparently you already had yours." A moment after that a burly cop came to escort me to the cells.

"Please call my husband," I begged on the way. "You must know him—he's in Ames, used to be head detective? Surely you know Jerry Brady."

"Sorry lady. I'm new."

The cells were cold and damp, the odor of nervous sweat and piss greeting me as he pushed me in. He confiscated my bag, locked the barred door and pocketed the key. A moment later I was alone in the six-foot square cell with only a toilet, a sink and a steel cot for company. I thought of Cutty and the cats with no dinner. At least there was a dog door. Did they still have water?

What in hell was going on? I was sure Carl had arranged this, but how had he managed it? And how would me being in jail get him what he wanted? My stomach turned into a mass of knots just before I rushed to the toilet to be sick.

❧

My questions were answered the next morning when Carl arrived dressed in a suit and carrying a briefcase, an officious air about him. Despite my protests the cop opened my cell and let him in.

Once we were alone he sneered at me. "I'm your lawyer, Summer. If you want out of here you need to cooperate."

"I know what you want but I don't have it."

"You may not have it but you can get it for me—Emilia assured me that you can unbind that book."

"Did you let her go?"

He chuckled. "She's free as a bird."

"What did you do—is she all right?"

His eyes narrowed. "Let's talk about you, shall we? I want that book and the spells it contains. I will pay your bail and in return you will get me the book and open it. If you don't, I'll bite you. And you know how that goes."

I stared at him, trying to think. Nothing came to mind. "Okay," I finally said. We left the police station a half hour later after he signed some papers, retrieved my bag, and paid my bail. I had no idea how he'd managed to skirt around the law.

"You're in my custody," he said, shoving me into his car. "And if you don't do as I say there will be repercussions. Where to first?"

"Ames police station."

"Good girl."

"I'm not sure how to get the book."

"You can make something up. It won't be hard for a witch like you."

"I'm not a witch and I don't have that kind of power."

He gave me a look. "Are you being funny? It's shimmering all over you."

I thought of the room tilting, the trips into the past and being invisible. I had to admit strange things had been happening, but I had no intention of handing that book off to him. My stomach twisted as we navigated the slick roads and when I realized I was about to be sick I yelled for him to pull off.

He looked at me and did as I asked, stopping next to a weeded area. "Don't try anything funny."

But I was already out the door bent over and retching. Once the sickness passed I wiped my watery eyes and turned back to the car. "Do you have any water?"

He handed me a bottle, the look of distaste on his face plain to see. I took a swig and rinsed out my mouth before climbing back in. "Why do you want that book? Didn't you come back because of something left undone?"

He laughed. "Yeah, my life."

"How'd you die, anyway?"

"Murdered by one of my own men."

"Because?"

He shrugged. "Because I cheated him, I guess."

"But why don't you stay as you are now? Why do you want to be alive again?"

"What I am now is temporary. Once it wears off I'm gone."

"As in really dead?"

He nodded, his eyes turning dark with some unknown emotion.

"And when will that happen?"

"Soon."

The rest of the trip was made in silence as I tried to think. After two nights with no sleep and no food my brain was mush, no insights presenting themselves. Had Jerry noticed my absence? When I glanced at my cell phone the battery was completely dead.

When we reached the Ames police station Carl marched me inside, standing right behind me as I asked for the book. The first time I tried the female officer on the desk just stared at me. "You have no authority to take police property."

Carl gave me a little nudge. "You need to do better than that," he whispered in my ear.

The second time I asked I visualized the book in my hands. This time the officer's eyes seemed to glaze over. She rose and went to hunt for it, coming back with the shopping bag, which she handed over. I scanned the station hoping to spot someone I knew, but the place was filled with strangers.

Once we were outside I held the shopping bag out to Carl. He frowned and shook his head. "You need to open it."

"It won't open for me—I wasn't the one who put a spell on it."

"I don't care if it was you or not, I know you can open it. You told me you saw the copyright page. Didn't you see the author listed there?"

"No."

"McCloud. The author is Fenella McCloud."

"What? I didn't see that. How do you now that if you can't open it?"

"Emilia told me. It was written by a very powerful witch with your last name."

In the car I pulled the book out, surprised at how mild the tingling had become. I studied the worn leather cover covered in tooled crescent moon and stars, visualizing the pages lying open. When it flew open I gasped in surprise. Carl grabbed it out of my lap, but as soon as his fingers touched it, it snapped shut.

"Open it again," he hissed, pushing it back to me.

Again I visualized it open and again it unlocked. "Now what?" I asked him.

"Find the necromancy spell."

I thumbed through, searching for what he wanted. When I found a spell on bringing the dead back to life he leaned close, trying to read what was printed there, but as soon as he did, it closed.

He frowned. "You'll have to copy it out for me."

"Fine, but I want to see Mrs. B before I do."

He stared at me, his eyes narrowing. "I can bite you right now, you know."

"And then who will help you?"

He shook his head and started the car, his heavy booted

foot pressing down hard on the gas peddle as soon as it roared to life. We spun in the leftover slush and careened away.

He drove straight to his store and hauled me inside. "Sit there and copy it down," he said, pulling out a piece of paper and a pen and placing them on the desk.

This time when I asked it to open it went to the dedication page.

The spells on these pages are for the pure of heart; anyone who wishes to do harm or misuse the magic that lies within will be prevented from doing so.

I glanced up at Carl pacing in front of me with his fists clenched. "Not sure I'll be able to help you," I said gesturing for him to come read the dedication.

He leaned over me, his watery blue eyes narrowing. "I don't care about that—obviously you have permission since you're related to the author. Write that spell down and hurry up about it. I don't have all day."

"Where is Emilia? You promised."

He let out a huff of impatience. He picked up the phone on the desk, hit a key and held it out. "She's on speed dial," he said as way of explanation.

"Hello?" A wavery voice said.

"Mrs. Browning—is that you?"

"Oh my dear, Summer. Are you with Carl?"

"I am and I have the book."

"Oh good. I knew I did the right thing. Now just do as he asks and everything will be all right."

I was about to answer when Carl grabbed the phone out of my hand and ended the call. He placed it back in the holder on the desk, his pale eyes swirling. "Your precious *Mrs. Browning* is just fine. Now get on with it."

I shuffled through the pages, my mind on Mrs. B's lack of concern. *Do as he asks.* When I found the spell I began to copy it, not sure what I was looking at as the words began to swim, the letters rearranging themselves. I didn't stop to think, writing down what I saw despite what was happening in front of my eyes.

I handed the paper to Carl.

"What in hell is this?" he asked, staring down. "It's gibberish."

"That's what it says," I told him, pointing to the page.

"God damn it!" He grabbed me roughly and dragged me into the back of the store and flipped open the trapdoor. "Maybe an hour or two down there will clear your mind about things," he muttered, shoving me.

I stumbled forward, grabbing hold of the ladder in the nick of time before he closed the trapdoor above me. It was pitch black and I had no flashlight. I took off in the direction I remembered that led to Tarot and Tea, but when I came to the turning there were several other tunnels leading off in other directions. I heard the hum of angry voices, looking up to see probably fifty ghosts wafting toward me. But these ghosts didn't respond when I tried to talk to them, their faces contorted in anger as they surrounded me. They clawed at me, their mouths open as they closed in. Their nips drew blood, their nails leaving bloody scratches.

I let out a scream that echoed, falling onto my knees in my haste to get away. But there was no getting away from them, their hunger for the living taking away any chance I might have had. They were all over me, their eyes like black holes, their sharp teeth breaking through my skin. I couldn't breathe, my screams muffled as they squeezed close. They were greedy, biting and making smacking noises that chilled my blood. My eyesight dimmed, my heartbeat slowing. "Stop," I muttered weakly. But it was too late.

21

"Are you ready to cooperate now?"

I opened my eyes to see Carl staring down at me. I was tied to a chair, my hands bound together in my lap, the book of spells on the table in front of me. My arms ached, my entire body sore. I let out a moan.

"How'd you like it down there?" he sneered.

I glanced at my bare arms where the flesh had been punctured and scratched. They oozed and pulsed with pain. "What are those things?"

"Failed attempts."

"Ghosts you tried to bring back?"

He chuckled. "They were more like my guinea pigs. Unfortunately the experiments didn't work quite the way I expected."

I shuddered, imagining it. "Why haven't I seen them down there before?"

His face shifted and changed, the skull that lay beneath all I could see for a moment. "Because I keep them locked up."

"They were ghost-like and yet they bit me and drew blood."

"They would have killed you if I hadn't stopped them."

I thought of the moment when I blacked out, sure I was dying. "How would my death help them?"

"They were feeding off your life force—if I'd allowed them to continue a few would have come alive—at least for a while." He pointed to the book, his nostrils flaring. "Time to get to work."

"I can't do it, Carl. That spell is bound. Only someone pure of heart, remember? And I wouldn't count you in that category."

"But *you* are. Why can't you copy it?"

"Because the book knows the spell's not for me."

He turned when there was a thump on the locked front door. "Don't move," he hissed.

I watched him glide away, heard the click of the lock followed by Jerry's voice and Carl's matter-of-fact responses. A moment later the door closed and he returned. "That was your boyfriend."

"My husband," I corrected.

"He asked if I'd seen you. I told him no."

"And he believed you."

"As you noticed this morning I can be very persuasive."

"Casting spells? I thought you couldn't do that."

"It's this spell I want," he muttered, his bony finger pointing. His face went cadaver-like for a moment before it returned to its current shape. "If you don't do this for me you will die," he continued. "Maybe if you relay this to the book it will be more willing."

I wondered if he was right. "You have to untie me."

Once my hands were free I leafed through to the necromancy spell, sending messages to the book as I got pen and paper ready. A warning was printed at the bottom of the page. **This spell is a last resort and should only be used in case of the accidental death of a person filled with light.** This time the text didn't change as I copied, the words lying still. The directions made no sense, ingredients I'd never heard of as part of the complicated recipe. There were steps to be taken about being aligned with the sun and moon, and certain odd objects that were needed. I held the paper out.

He took it, frowning as he read it over. "Strange, but doable," he muttered.

"Can I please go now?"

He glared at me, his eyes narrowing. "I'll let you go, but if you do anything to stop me someone you love will die. And that includes talking about my plan. Agnes is a good friend of yours, isn't she?"

My heart went cold.

"Agnes thinks I'm the new doctor in town who has all the latest and best information about giving birth. She's convinced that without me she won't make it to term. Even her husband is unaware of my real identity." He let out a cackle.

"How do you do this?"

"I'm a Gjenganger, remember?" He laughed.

"I won't say anything to anyone."

He hauled me to my feet. "You better not. And if you breathe a word of this to your husband, I'll…"

"I won't," I said hurriedly, glancing back at the book. "Shall I take the book or leave it here?"

He frowned in confusion. "Why would I let you take it?" He pointed toward the door. "Go before I change my mind."

I didn't look back as I hurried to the door and flung it open. Wind nearly knocked me over as I stumbled down the steps and took off running. My bag had disappeared, my phone in Carl's pocket. I had no coat. It was nearly dark now, the streetlights winking on as I ran by, trying not to fall on the slippery sidewalk.

The cottage was dark when I got there, my front door securely locked. I went around back and squirmed through the doggie door, greeted by an ecstatic Cutty on the other side. When I turned on the lights and checked I discovered that Jerry's big bag was gone from the shelf, his clothes as well. All his personal items were missing from the bathroom. A note had been left on the counter next to the spot where his espresso machine had been.

If you have a change of heart, please call me. If I don't hear from you in the next few days I'll assume we're over and begin the process. I'm sorry it had to end this way over such a simple and easily remedied disagreement. I'm about as desolate as I can get. Agnes and Sam have been notified and agree with my decision. I fed Cutty and the cats since you weren't here. Where in hell are you?

I burst into tears and crumpled it up, a keening wail rising up from deep inside that scared Cutty almost as much as it scared me. It seemed that from everything that had happened Jerry might be a bit more worried about my disappearance. He'd obviously been here—didn't he realize how long I'd been gone? Carl was about to get away with something unspeakable, my husband was about to file for divorce and my best friend was on Jerry's side. And I couldn't talk about what had happened to me, or what Carl was about to do. I'd never felt so helpless.

197

I knew I should be hungry, but when I opened the refrigerator and looked at the food I had to run for the bathroom to throw up. Not surprising considering what I'd been through. A cup of peppermint tea soothed my stomach, but nothing could soothe my mood. Jerry had said he was desolate—there wasn't a word terrible enough to describe what I was feeling as I curled up on the couch.

⟪⁓⟫

I woke in the morning sick as a dog, my body wracked with chills. The run home in freezing temperatures had done its worst. I threw up several times before managing to make dry toast and heating water for tea. I lay on the couch, a splitting headache keeping me from moving. It was sometime before noon when I heard a rap on the door. I stumbled to unlock it, hoping to see Jerry standing there, but instead it was Agnes. I sneezed a few times, backing away to let her in. "I'm sick—you'd better stay away from me."

She closed the door and followed me back the couch. When her cool hand landed on my forehead her eyes went wide. "You have a fever."

"Not surprising," I mumbled.

"Summer...I..."

I held my hand up, my eyes closed. "Don't bother—Jerry left a note explaining how you and Sam agree with his decision to get a divorce."

"I never said that. I told him I agreed that you should see a doctor, that's all. He's flying off the handle right now, convinced that you could care less about anything he says."

"I told him I did the early pregnancy test—why can't that be enough?"

"They're notorious for false results. Have you had a period since you stopped the pill—wasn't that in August?"

"No, but I figure my system's screwed up." When I glanced at her she looked skeptical.

"Do you have any aspirin or ibuprofen? You need something to take down that fever."

"I can't swallow anything but tea and toast right now."

Agnes sat in the chair. "How'd you get sick? Jerry said you weren't here when he came by yesterday morning."

I pushed up to sitting, my hand on my aching head. "You wouldn't believe me if I told you."

"Try me."

"Carl had the Cummings police pick me up for stealing and murder. I spent the night in jail."

"What? How did he manage that?"

I thought of Carl's warning, trying not to put her life in danger. "He's supernatural. He got me out by pretending to be a lawyer—paid my bail."

Agnes leaned forward, her hands on her knees. "And what was all this for?"

I let out a long sigh. "Too tired to explain. Would you make me some tea?"

She rose and went to the kitchen. "Jerry didn't say anything about you being in danger," she called.

"I think Carl made him forget. Jerry did talk to him at Carl's store when he..."

Agnes turned from the stove. "When he what?"

"When Carl forced me to copy a spell out of that damn book." I'd done it now.

"Jerry doesn't believe any of this. He says you're making it all up because you want control of the case."

"I wish that were true. Everyone I'm close to is in danger now."

Agnes brought the mug back and handed it to me. "Even me?"

I stared at her. "Especially you."

"If you did what he asked, why?"

"Because I just told you about it."

An anxious expression moved across her features. "You didn't really tell me anything, Summer. Copying a spell doesn't reveal much."

"I'd stay away from that new doctor you're going to."

Her eyes widened. "What do you mean?"

"I mean he's dangerous."

Agnes stood, her hands going to the bump of her belly. "My baby."

"Your baby and you. That man posing as a doctor is Carl, and he isn't human."

Agnes shook her head. "That can't be. I met him at a new building off Main Street. He had a nurse with him. He was kindly and caring."

I leaned back, my headache pounding. "You'd better call Sam and tell him what I told you. Carl warned me not to say anything, that if I did you'd be in danger."

Agnes pulled her phone out of her bag, her pale face turning chalk white. "He isn't answering," she said a moment later.

"Call Jerry."

But Jerry didn't answer either. I'd now put Agnes in danger. Tears welled and spilled down my cheeks. "I promised him I'd keep this to myself."

Agnes sat at the end of the couch. "I'm glad you told

me—he could have hurt me or the baby. Why didn't I notice?"

"Because he's a master of disguise. The only way to get rid of him is keeping that spell from him. But he has it now—I gave it to him."

"Why did you do that?"

"Because he told me he'd kill me if I didn't?"

"Jerry needs to be here to protect you."

I shook my head. "It's too late now. Carl is aware of everything and he already knows I broke my word. Go to the station and find your husband and tell him what I told you."

"I can't leave you here alone."

"Ask Sam to send a detail to the house. I'll be okay."

Agnes gave me one last look before she hurried to the door. "Lock the door," she said. A moment later I heard her car start up, her tires moving off down the street. I locked the door and stumbled back to the couch and closed my eyes, waiting for the inevitable knock on the door.

When I woke later I could hear someone outside. Adrenaline shot through me—Carl was here. A second later I heard a key in the lock and Jerry came inside.

"Jerry!" I croaked, my voice nearly gone.

"What in hell did you do to yourself?" he asked. "Agnes was hysterical at the station, refused to leave until a detail was sent over."

I tried to smile. "Are you my detail?"

Jerry grimaced and felt my head. "You're fucking burning up." He hurried off, reappearing with two pills and a glass of water. "Take these."

I did what he asked, knowing that if I refused he'd force them down my throat. "If I throw these up it's your fault," I muttered.

"You're throwing up too? How long since you've eaten?"

"I don't know—two days?"

Jerry shook his head and headed for the kitchen. I heard him banging around, the refrigerator opening and closing, and the scrape of metal on the iron frying pan. "Why is there a cross on the door?" he called.

"To keep the Gjenganger from getting into the cottage."

He made a derisive sound in the back of his throat. "Agnes was babbling some crazy crap about her obstetrician not being human. And where the hell is your cell phone? I've called you like ten times."

"Carl has it."

"Carl? Why does he have it?"

"Because he kidnapped me and tied me to a chair. I was there when you came by yesterday morning."

"What?" Jerry stopped what he was doing to turn and stare at me "He was completely calm and reasonable—I had no reason to suspect him of anything."

"And he probably put a spell on you. Did Sam notice that the book is missing from the station?"

"The occult one? No. No one said anything about it."

"Carl made me ask for it and the woman on duty gave it to me without even questioning why or who I was. I seem to be able to do things I couldn't do before."

Jerry brought over a plate and set it down in front of me, but as soon as I saw the scrambled eggs I had to race for the bathroom.

Jerry came in while I was still leaning over the bowl, his fingers gathering up my hair to hold it back. "This is morning sickness."

"I have the flu," I muttered, gagging.

When I was finished heaving he helped me up and wiped my face with a warm washcloth. When he was finished I pulled off the heavy shirt I was wearing, suddenly boiling hot.

Jerry stared at my arms, his forehead creasing. "What in hell happened to your arms?"

"Carl threw me in the tunnels with a bunch of angry ghosts." I gagged as the memory of my ordeal came up, afraid I'd be sick again, but luckily the feeling passed. "They attacked me."

Jerry examined my arm. "The scratches look infected. You need to go to the hospital. How could a ghost do that?"

"I don't know how a ghost could do it, but these did. As to the hospital, absolutely not." I headed unsteadily back to the living room and collapsed on the couch.

Jerry followed me, his eyes narrowing. "And why did he throw you down there?"

"To impress upon me the importance of copying out the spell."

"What spell?"

"Jerry, we've talked about this already—the spell to bring him back to life."

Jerry gazed at me blankly.

"He must have wiped your mind," I muttered, closing my eyes. "I did copy the spell and by now he's probably used it to come alive again."

"He looked very alive to me yesterday."

"You don't remember anything about the Gjenganger?"

"The what?"

I let out a sigh of frustration. "He did something to your mind. We've talked about this several times. Do you at least remember the bruising on the murder victims? I wish you'd believe me."

"I'm trying, Summer, but this entire story sounds outlandish—especially the angry ghosts. As far as the bruising goes—yes, I remember that. So far there's been no plausible explanation for how the victims died."

I glanced up at him. "Now that I've told on him he'll either come after me or Agnes. And that guy I saw in the tunnels in the past—the one who looked like you? Apparently he was an undercover cop. So now you're on Carl's list too. He made me promise to keep quiet about all of it. And there's nothing you can do to stop him," I added, watching his hand go to the gun strapped under his shirt.

"I don't know what you're talking about, but I can tell how upset you are. Could this be because you have a fever?"

"No, Jerry. He wiped your mind. We're all in danger now and it's my fault."

When I began to cry he just watched me, finally saying, "I'll get Sam to send a man over. As far as Agnes goes, Sam's with her." When his cell phone rang he pulled it out. "There's Sam now," he muttered, answering. He listened, his brows pulling together. "What?" He glanced at me. "Jesus. Okay. I'll be right there."

He ended the call, wiping a hand across his two-day growth. Normally this scruffy look appealed to me, but today all my thoughts were on what I'd set in motion.

"Sammie's missing and the young gal who was watching him is in the hospital in a coma."

I swallowed down bile. "Carl has the baby."

Jerry stared at me, his eyes glazed. "I've got to get over there, Summer. Will you be all right until the detail arrives?"

"How long will that be?"

"Sam said he's on his way—so ten minutes tops."

I nodded.

He searched in a drawer and handed me a gun. "This is loaded. Lock up when I leave."

"Jerry, I..." But he was already out the door.

I stared at the gun in my hands before placing it down on the coffee table. I let out a sigh and closed my eyes. If something happened to Sammie I'd never forgive myself. A few minutes later I locked the door and headed into the bedroom with Cutty.

An hour later I was sick again, vomiting up bile before I made stomach ease tea and drank it down. Weak and shaky I crawled into bed and pulled the covers over my head.

22

I woke in the night, sure that I'd heard something. Cutty was on alert, his ears pricked, his gaze on the window behind the bed. The two cats had come in sometime while I was sleeping, but they didn't react, curled into one another like a beast with two heads. Stripes of cool moonlight filtered into the room, lending an eerie quality as I rose and crept into the living room to get the gun. I moved to peek out the living room window, struck by how clear the sky was. The shutters I was sure I'd left closed were now open, one of them swinging in the breeze. And that's when I saw him—a man skulking around the corner of the cottage. I opened the window, aiming. "Stop or I'll shoot!" I yelled. When I lost my balance the gun exploded, the bullet leaving a large hole in the shutter.

"Mrs. Brady," a voice called. "It's me, Bill Harris."

"I didn't hit you, did I?"

"No, ma'am. I'm fine. Just checking things."

Thank the goddess, I mumbled, closing the window.

In the morning when I looked out again I saw the patrol car parked across the street, Bill asleep behind the wheel.

For the first time in days I was hungry. I made French toast and bacon, gobbling it down like a starving person before I dressed in tights, a long wool skirt and a red sweater that reached below my hips. I had to get out of this house and do something productive. Also there was landline at the shop I could use to call Agnes and find out the latest on Sammie. My heart did a little somersault as I imagined him in Carl's clutches.

I pulled on my Mukluks, grabbed my down jacket and headed outside, the cold making my eyes water. When I knocked on the window Bill rolled it down.

"Sorry to be sleeping on the job," he said, embarrassed.

"You had a long night. I'm heading to Tarot and Tea. Go home and get some rest."

Tarot and Tea was like a tomb, the interior cold and lifeless. I turned up the heat and lit my sage smudge stick and let the smoke drift as I walked slowly around. Once that was done I sat at the counter and called Agnes.

"No, he hasn't been found," her exhausted voice answered. "Sam is beside himself—he's sent three patrols out to look for him. They put a bolo out for Carl after I called Mrs. B and got her to describe him." I heard her indrawn breath followed by a sob.

"They'll find him, Agnes."

"It's all your fault, Summer. He told you not to tell and you did. How could you do that?" The phone went dead in my ear.

I called Jerry's cell after that, my heart fluttering in my chest. "Any leads on Sammie?"

"Not yet. Where are you? I just saw Harris come in."

"I'm at Tarot and Tea."

"Do you think that's wise?"

"I had to get out of the house. And I'm much better today."

There was a long silence before Jerry said, "I'll send someone over. I don't want you to be alone."

"Thanks, Jer, but I don't think that's..." He'd already hung up.

I sat at my desk wondering what Carl's plan was. He wouldn't kill that baby unless he had a very good reason. The police must have checked out his store by now. Where would he be if not there? I locked up and left the shop, a vague plan forming in my mind—first Carl's bookstore, and then...

I knocked on his door, my pulse racing as I tried to see inside. Less than a minute later the door opened. "What do *you* want?"

"I want Sammie."

Carl laughed. "I told you what would happen, didn't I? You just can't keep your mouth shut. Heard you were sick—that over now?"

"How'd you...? Never mind. Where's Sammie?"

"The boy is safe. I'm working on collecting things for the ceremony. Perhaps you can help me."

"If I do will you give Sammie back?"

"I wouldn't go that far, but it might look good on your resume." He let out a sharp bark of laughter. "Come on in." He held the door wide and gestured me inside.

I scanned the room, listening closely for the sound of crying, but I didn't hear anything but the tick of the antique clock on the shelf next to his desk.

"He isn't here. Now let's take a look at my list and see how you can help. I hope to get this done by Friday."

"What day is today?"

He shook his head, sneering. "My, my, you are confused. You were in jail Friday night, Saturday you spent with me, and Sunday you were sick at home. Today is Monday."

"How do you know everything? And what kind of a spell did you put on Jerry?"

He chuckled. "Jerry is very susceptible due to his skepticism. It doesn't take much to make him forget. I do wish you hadn't told Agnes. I liked being a doctor. And she was such a pleasure to work with, if you know what I mean."

I gagged, choking for a second.

He looked me over. "Something going on, Summer— something you haven't told me?"

"I had the flu."

He raised his eyebrows. "Hmm. Come take a look and tell me what you can help with," he said, grabbing my upper arm. When I let out a yelp he smiled. "Sorry, forgot about your sojourn in the tunnels."

At his desk I glanced down at the page of directions, trying to make sense of what was written there.

"I need a silver chalice. Do you think you could procure one?"

"I have one at home—I inherited it."

"Perfect. What about this item?"

I read what he pointed to. "One full cup of blood from a doe? Hunting season for female deer is over."

"Too bad—we need it anyway. Can you shoot?"

"No, and even if I could I wouldn't."

"Really? Not even to get Agnes's precious baby back?"

I stared at him, my insides writhing in hatred. "I could try but I'd never be able to hit one."

"I've seen what you can do, Summer. Don't sell yourself short. Use whatever it was you used to get the book."

"So you want me to go hunting? Why don't you do it?"

"I thought we were negotiating for little Sammie's life."

I went cold all over. "Okay. I'll do it. But I don't have the kind of gun I need."

He smirked. "A high-powered hunting rifle? I have one you can use."

I glanced down at the book again, horrified to see the need of blood from a human baby.

"Don't worry. I have that already."

I was suddenly sick, racing for where I hoped the bathroom was. I made it just in time to heave up my breakfast.

"My, my—we are sensitive, aren't we?" he said, arriving behind me.

I flushed the toilet and rose to my feet to rinse my mouth out at the sink. "Flu," I mumbled.

"I didn't need much blood," he continued, ignoring me. "Only a few drops. He cried but he got over it."

My teeth were chattering when I followed him back to the desk. "I'll bring the chalice and go hunting, what more do you want from me?"

"There's one more item on this list you can help with." He pointed down the page where I'd written, *human bones.*

"What kind of bones? I have a cemetery behind me—I could dig up a grave, I guess, or…"

"You tell me. You're the one who copied it down."

I glanced at the page. There was no amount listed. But when I scanned further down I saw that they were to be pulverized and mixed in with the blood. "Looks like any amount will do."

"That's what I thought. You can go now as long as you're back here by Thursday with these three ingredients in hand. Think you can do that?"

"I hope so."

"Know that if you don't, a certain baby boy will be suffering the consequences."

"Are you saying you'll kill him if I can't produce this stuff by Thursday?"

"That's what I'm saying."

When I grabbed his arm it was as cold as ice. He flung me off, his eyes turning the color of coal. "You wouldn't—you couldn't..." I gasped, terrified.

He laughed. "You should know by now what I'm capable of, Summer. Please don't underestimate me."

After I copied the items down he handed me a rifle with a scope and a sack of bullets. "Make sure you drain the blood from the neck."

"Can I take a look at the book again? I want to make sure I got it right."

Carl used a pair of tongs to haul it out of the bookcase in back. He placed it in front of me. When I asked it to open to the necromancy spell the cover flipped back, pages fluttering by until it reached the right one.

"Cool trick," Carl said, watching over my shoulder.

I scanned down the list, noticing that some things had changed since the last time I looked. Instead of blood from a doe there was bark from a rowen tree, the human baby blood replaced with a special moss that grew at the base of beech trees. I quickly closed the book, glancing up at him. "I wrote it down correctly."

"Good. I'll see you Thursday."

"Before I go, can I have my cell phone back?"

He reached into his jacket pocket and handed it over. "Not sure why people in this time find these things so useful. Yours wouldn't turn on."

"The battery's dead. Do you happen to have my bag? I think it was in your car."

He made a face and went into the back to search. He reappeared with my leather satchel and handed it to me before walking me to the door. "Make sure you're back here early Thursday morning. I have a lot to do before the ceremony on Friday."

Once I was through the door it slammed shut, the lock clicking into place. And that's when I heard the baby. I gazed up at the second story window to see a young woman's pale face. The terrified look in her eyes made my blood run cold. Sammie was in her arms, his little face red from crying. I hurried to the car and deposited the rifle into the trunk before speeding back toward my store.

23

Rain was coming in again, the streets already flooded and my tires hydroplaning as I rounded a tight curve going fifty. When a siren sounded behind me I pulled over, hoping the officer didn't check the trunk. I had no license for a high-powered rifle.

"Where's the fire?" he asked when he reached my window.

Rain poured off the brim of his wide hat, his wet slicker bright in the gloom. "I'm sorry. I'm late for work."

"You were going fifty in a thirty, young lady."

I let out a heavy sigh. "I have no excuse for it, officer."

He glared at me for a few seconds before coming to a decision. "I'll let you go with a warning this time, but please slow down. You could get yourself killed or, god forbid, kill someone else."

"Thank you, officer. I will—I promise." After he drove off I glanced in the mirror, not surprised to see a pale haggard face surrounded with wild and tangled hair, my eyes sunken and bloodshot. The interior of my car was littered with wrappers and coffee cups, a couple of wires all that was left of my radio. The passenger seat of my vintage

Pinto was frayed and the stuffing was coming out of it. He must have decided that adding one more thing to my sorry life could possibly send me careening over the edge. And he was right. I put the car in gear and eased onto the street, driving five miles under the limit all the way to Tarot and Tea.

As soon as I got back I called Agnes from the landline, hoping she would answer. Her voice was less than cordial, but at least she was willing to talk.

"Sammie's at Carl's. I saw him in the arms of a young woman with long blonde hair."

"Is he okay?"

"He looked fine. I only saw him because I happened to glance up at the second story window."

"He's at Carl's bookstore?"

"Yes."

"Got to tell Sam," she said, hanging up.

When I called Jerry's cell he answered on the second ring, his clipped *Yes,* all business.

"Sammie's at Carl's bookstore—I already told Agnes and she's calling Sam. But Jerry, Carl will know before they get there."

"You don't have much faith in the police, do you?"

"Not when they're dealing with a supernatural being." I heard his scoff of dismissal.

"I'll go with Sam. Why are you wandering around when you're sick?"

"I'm better today and it's my fault Sammie got kidnapped."

"Not sure what you mean by that. Did you buy another cell phone?"

"No. Carl gave mine back."

"So you were with him, then. From what you've told me that doesn't seem wise."

"It isn't, but in exchange for Sammie's and my life I'm helping him gather what he needs to transform into the land of the living."

"Sounds like a very bad idea, Summer, but I'm not your keeper. Got to go."

Tears welled and I wiped them away as I replaced the phone in its cradle. It was obvious Jerry and I were through.

I was staring blankly out the window when Valerie walked in, her gaze going immediately to the rifle propped against my desk. "What is this about?"

After I explained the past few days her eyes widened in horror. "You're helping him?"

"I have to, Valerie. But how in the world can I kill a doe? Even the idea of shooting an animal makes me feel sick."

"A female goat is also called a doe. Perhaps that would work? I bet you could get the blood from the butcher at Ames Market. Mr. Riddle often has an entire animal in the back."

I stared at her. "Really?"

She nodded. "Now what else was on that list?"

"Human bones."

"Cemetery," she said. "Don't you have one right behind your cottage?"

"Digging won't be easy in this weather."

"Do you need my help?"

"As long as it doesn't freeze in the next couple of days, I should be fine."

"Pick an older grave in the poorer area—wooden

coffins tend to disintegrate."

I glanced toward the door when Mrs. Browning appeared. She looked stylish, a black beret set at a jaunty angle over her recently done hair.

She smiled. "How are you getting along with the book, my dear?"

I glared at her. "Don't you mean Carl?"

She pursed her red lips. "Did you know a long ago great great great grandmother of yours wrote *Black Magic and the Occult?*"

"The book seems to like me, but I figured…"

"You figured wrong. The book would not have opened for just anyone. Believe me, I tried."

"Carl wanted you to open it."

"Of course. And when I wasn't able to do it he threatened me."

"And that's when I saw you in the tunnels."

"Yes. It is because of you that I'm here today." Her smile widened.

"At least one person I haven't managed to harm," I muttered.

"Who have you harmed?" Valerie asked.

"Agnes, Jerry, baby Sammie, the young woman who's in a coma," I said, ticking them off.

Valerie frowned. "How could you keep all this to yourself? You couldn't have allowed Agnes to continue seeing a doctor who is basically a demon."

"Carl knew you had to tell her. He was expecting it and was ready to use it for leverage," Mrs. B added.

"I have to have his ingredients for the spell by Thursday—and it requires digging up a grave."

Mrs. Browning laughed. "I'm sure this is not the true spell. The book has changed it so that Carl won't get what he wants."

"I figured that too, but either way I have to provide human bones to be pulverized with the doe's blood and blood from Sammie. And he'll know if I fudge things."

"I doubt it will get that far," Valerie said, her eyes going opaque.

"What do you see?"

Valerie turned her gaze to mine. "I see chaos and fire and death."

"Can you be more specific?"

"I can't. I'm sorry."

"Do you have a timeline?"

She shook her head.

"It's of no consequence," Mrs. B said. "He will not get what he wants."

I was alone in the store when my plugged in cell phone rang. I answered, glad to see the charge at nearly eighty percent.

"Didn't find Carl or the baby. Are you sure you saw him?" Jerry asked.

"Yes, Jerry. I told you you wouldn't find him. He's taken the baby to a safer spot until he gets what he wants."

"And what does he want?"

"Is your memory going? He wants to come back to life. It's happening this Friday."

"He's coming back to life on Friday?" He let out a humorless laugh.

"He's having the ceremony on Friday—knowing him it

will probably be in the dead of night. But it won't work. I will probably be there since he has no other friends that I know of."

"So now you're friends with him."

"No," I said, exasperated. "I just think he'll want me there."

"You aren't making much sense, Summer."

"It's only because he wiped your brain, Jerry. If you remembered what's been going on you'd know why I have to be there."

"Are you still there?" I asked after several moments of silence.

There was a heavy sigh. "I'm not bailing you out of this one. You're on your own." The call ended.

Since when had he bailed me out of anything? And then I remembered the many times he'd saved my life, every case coming back to me in lurid detail. Okay—he *had* saved me, but I'd also saved him, I rationalized. I shoved the past into the back of my mind and concentrated on how to stop Carl from hurting anyone else. Where had he taken Sammie? There was no point in trying to find him. Carl was too adept at keeping one step ahead.

24

On Wednesday after work I went by the market, heading to the butcher counter in the back. Mr. Riddle smiled at me, his wiry gray eyebrows shooting up. "Haven't seen you in a coon's age."

"I've been pretty busy," I admitted.

He peered at me, a frown creasing his brow. "You seem a little peeked, Summer. How about a couple of steaks to invigorate your blood?"

I glanced at the meat in the case, acid rising into my throat. "I'm a vegetarian now," I lied.

"No wonder you're so thin." He let out a sigh. "So many young people these days starving themselves in the name of some silly fad."

"I do need some goat's blood—from a doe."

"You're in luck on that account, but I can't guarantee it's from a doe—most folks wanting blood get it for their pets. That what you want it for?"

"Exactly," I said, smiling widely. "I add it to his kibbles and he gobbles them down."

"How much did you need?"

"Exactly one cup...I mean, around a cup."

He glanced at me dubiously before he headed into the back. He returned a few minutes later, handing over a plastic container with a lid. I tried not to look at the dark liquid that sloshed. "Wish I could interest you in some steaks. They're on special—grass fed."

"Thanks, Mr. Riddle—maybe next time I'll feel more like meat." Right now all foods seemed to curdle my stomach, the mere thought of eating sending me running for the bathroom.

"Don't deprive yourself," he called as I walked away. "Eating meat will put the roses back in your cheeks and the sparkle in those beautiful eyes of yours."

I laughed, waving at him as I walked toward the checkout counter. He was right, though, I did feel weak and shaky, my stomach roiling. Must be the remnants of the flu and the days I'd spent without eating. I grimaced, thinking about the cell, the toilet that sat exposed for anyone walking by to see. The vision of the hungry ghosts came on the heels of that memory, my arms tingling in pain under my heavy wool sweater. The antiseptic salve I'd applied had worn off.

I left the market with the container filled with blood and some dog kibble, hurrying across the street to my car. *If only it was Friday*, I muttered to myself. *I want this to be over and done with. Please.*

I was halfway home when a bolt of lightning struck so close that it blinded me for a second. I slammed on the brakes and pulled over, watching a dead tree erupt in flames, a branch cracking and plunging to the ground not ten feet away. A heavy clap of thunder followed a moment later, an earsplitting hum in my ears as a strange light seemed to shimmer and then wink out.

By the time I eased onto the street again the flames were gone and sunlight filtered through the leafless branches as though nothing had happened. *The weirdest weather ever*, I thought as I focused on the road ahead of me.

At home I retrieved the heavily carved silver chalice from the breakfront, adding it to the box I planned to take to Carl. The rain had stopped, but I was sure the ground in the graveyard would be muddy and nearly impossible to dig. But I was expected at Carl's in the morning, and I had to be there with everything in hand in order to keep him from doing something terrible to someone else I loved—or to me.

I made yogurt with fruit for dinner, washing it down with a cup of tea. By the time I'd dressed in my warmest work clothes and mud boots, the temperature had dropped to the mid thirties. I clipped the leash on Cutty, went outside to grab the shovel and headed down the alley.

I was already shivering by the time I reached the cemetery. Shadows slithered out from under the trees, the night as dark as I'd ever seen. But on the other side of the graveyard the night sky was full of stars winking blue, a glow coming from the Milky Way.

The rusty gate squeaked when I pushed it open, unhooking Cutty's leash at the same time. He took off, his yips fading as he disappeared amongst the moss-covered stones chasing some unsuspecting nocturnal animal. Ghosts wafted about, peering at me curiously as I worked my way toward the oldest section of the cemetery.

Last time I'd been here was to talk to a ghost—Finlay

Ross McCloud, to be precise—my distant relative who'd been completely confused about the date of his death. It had taken a trip to Scotland for me to sort it out for him. My mind wafted backward to the ghost from *my* distant past I'd met on that trip, the hunk of a Scot who had taken me on the wildest ride of my life. It was lucky I'd come home at all. Poor Jerry had nearly lost his cool after that experience. But Jerry was a living breathing man, and Owen, although delectable, was a ghost, long since buried on a hillside. I'd seen his grave and wept for him, my heart nearly broken from losing him.

Now I wondered if I shouldn't have stayed in Scotland. Jerry was finished with me, and if I didn't get this right, I'd be finished too. My thoughts stopped midstream as a cold wind wafted around my legs. I heard it whispering in my ear but I couldn't pick up what it was saying. The trees weren't moving at all—the breeze must be coming from some other source—maybe a ghost was playing a prank. They did that once in a while.

I moved on into the dark, turning on my cell phone flashlight to find the oldest grave I could. Some here were from the seventeen hundreds. I stumbled over a grave and leaned down to take a look at the moss-covered stone, shining the light on the date etched there. 1789, I read. Liza Benton—age 15 year. It was a simple stone, hardly more than a marker. Whoever was buried here wasn't important and the coffin would have been simple. I cleared away the grass and weeds to find a place to put my shovel.

When I pushed the tip down into the mud, I was surprised when it came into contact with something solid. A ghost drifted upward, sad eyes meeting mine. Liza's brown hair was in pigtails with ribbons tied around the ends. She wore a loose dress covered with a white pinafore. "I'm sorry to disturb you," I said. She stared at me, her body shimmering for a second. "How did you die?" I asked softly. She pointed at her chest where a hole appeared near the heart. She'd been shot—murdered. "I'm so sorry," I murmured. Her gaze drifted away, her eyes going wide. "What is it?"

I was turning to see what she stared at when I was hit from behind, my knees landing in the soft mud. When I tried to get up a heavy boot came down on my back. The ghost took one more fearful look at me before she melted away.

"You ruined my life," Carl growled.

"I'm out here to do your bidding, Carl—looking for bones for the spell."

"You're a day late, Summer. The ceremony is tonight and I don't have what I need."

"Tonight? This is Wednesday."

"It's Friday, you stupid witch."

I thought about the last couple of days. "It can't be!"

"Shut up. I'm trying to decide what to do with you."

His angry voice brought Cutty running, the high-pitched barking music to my ears. A second later a gunshot split the silence, Cutty's whimper sending terror coursing through me.

"You better not have hurt my dog."

He laughed, a nasty rumble of uncaring. "Your dog? How about your life? Because you're next."

When his lips pressed against my neck I twisted to get away, but he was too fast. His bony hands gripped my arms, his cold breath in my ear as he bent to try again. This time I felt his teeth, blood trickling into my heavy coat as he bit deep into my neck. It really hurt, the pain radiating like lightning into the rest of my body. "Please…please," I moaned.

"Yeah, beg. It does my heart good to hear it, you bitch. But it's too late now. The deed is done. And by the way, little Sammie is dead."

I let out a sob, my fingers reaching for my neck. When I drew them back they were covered in blood. "Why? Why would you kill an innocent baby?"

"It was your doing, Summer. I told you not to underestimate me."

When I turned to face him he was gone. And that's when I noticed the flames and smoke coming from the direction of my house. As I tried to get up a sharp metallic taste entered my mouth. I felt woozy, disoriented. Blood trickled from the wound, dripping on the ground. *I must have at least a week,* I thought, my mind hazy. But then I remembered that this was not just a bruise—I'd felt his teeth sink into my flesh. A sudden rush of blood poured out, my senses loosening as my legs buckled. My life rushed by in a dizzying profusion of images just before the earth opened up to swallow me whole. I let go, plummeting downward through darkness.

I was in a space that had no perimeters, the edges misty and indistinct. When I looked around I saw my mother, her pale features looming out of the darkness.

"Summer! What are you doing here? It isn't your time yet."

"Mom…is it really you?" I threw my arms around her.

"You need to go back, child."

224

"How can I? Carl bit me. I'm dead."

"My dearest girl, I'd like to help but I can't. What has happened is beyond my abilities. But you...you are powerful now. Don't you feel it?"

"Not really."

"That book of spells belongs to you. It was always meant to come into your hands."

"That's all well and good, but I can't use it if I'm dead."

"You have to fight, Summer. You still have a link to life. See it there?" She pointed to a silver thread snaking off into the distance. "You have a life to live, a baby on the way, a man who loves you. Don't give up."

"A baby?"

"You didn't know?"

I stared at the rope of silver, wondering how I could catch hold of it. It was moving too fast, disappearing into the misty gray fog. I stretched and held out my arm, struggling to grasp it, but when I finally had it in my grip, it slipped through my fingers, vanishing into nothingness. I heard my mother's voice calling as I floated weightless, my life ebbing bit by bit until the blackness overtook me.

25

Searing pain behind my eyelids and inside my head. I felt like my body had been ripped apart and sewn back together with razor wire. Was this death? I let out a moan and opened my eyes. Blankness followed by blinding light and sickly green walls. I came fully to, my blurry gaze landing on a strange face belonging to a man with a stethoscope around his neck and wearing a lab coat. And the expression on his features was not hopeful. I heard a familiar voice behind me say my name.

When a hand touched mine I tried to turn my neck, but I couldn't move. I panicked, thrashing.

"It's okay. You're in the hospital." Jerry's face swam into view, his brown eyes filled with tears.

I put my hand up to the wad of bandages around my neck. "He bit me."

Jerry nodded. "The doctor did what he could. It was a very nasty bite."

"I was dead, Jerry. I saw my mom and I...how did you find me?"

Jerry sat on the bed and took hold of my hand, holding it between his warm palms. "Carl torched the cottage and the fire department came. If it hadn't been for Cutty…"

"Cutty! I thought he shot him."

Jerry shook his head. "That dog led them directly to you."

"Where's Carl?"

"He's dead."

When I tried to sit up Jerry pushed me gently back. "You've been unconscious for three days. You need to take it easy."

"I was trying to…Sammie! Is he…?"

"Sammie's fine. We found him upstairs in Carl's store along with the young gal he'd kidnapped to take care of him."

"I'm dying, right?"

Jerry's gaze turned sorrowful.

My eyes filled. "I wish I'd stayed in the underworld with Mom. I don't want to die here. Please take me home." When he glanced at the doctor I added, "You don't have to stay with me. I know you don't love me anymore."

Jerry shook his head, his lips tightening. "I never stopped loving you, Summer."

The doctor interrupted us to hand me a bunch of pills. "For the pain," he said, handing me a cup of water.

I thanked him and swallowed them down.

It took a while but eventually Jerry was able to get me released. He wheeled me down to the entrance, leaving me there as he rushed off to get the car. The sky was cerulean, fluffy clouds drifting by. It was a beautiful day. My eyes filled as I realized that I'd soon be gone from this wonderful world. My hand went to my belly, remembering my mother's words. I let out a sob, startling an orderly. "Are you okay, miss?"

"Yes, no. I'm just upset," I muttered, wiping at my eyes.

He smiled. "At least you're on your way home. That's a good thing, isn't it?"

I nodded, attempting a smile and failing miserably. I watched Jerry drive up in my car and park. A moment later he was beside me, helping me up and walking me out. I slid into the passenger seat, leaning my pounding head back. My body was on fire, aching everywhere.

"The weather's been horrible for weeks. Why does it have to be so beautiful today?" I asked once we were on the road.

Jerry didn't answer, his gaze on the road.

"What did they do to my neck? I remember it was bleeding."

"You lost a lot of blood. You nearly died when they were working on you. The doc said he couldn't do much." Jerry turned toward me. "The bite from that creature goes deep into your body—it's part of you now."

Not a simple bruise then. "You remember about the Gjenganger?"

Jerry nodded. "After the bastard died all my memories returned. I can't believe I let this happen to you. If I'd been there…"

"Don't blame yourself, Jerry. The guy was supernatural and very powerful."

Jerry let out a sound like a sob, his fingers wiping at his eyes before he turned to me. "I can't believe this is happening. I don't know what to do."

"I don't want to die."

Jerry wrapped his fingers around mine. "And I don't want you to die."

"There's no coming back from this."

Jerry focused on the road, tears tracking down his cheeks.

Once we reached the cottage I let out a shriek. One entire wall was missing, as well as a large section of the roof. A big sheet of plastic covered it to keep out the weather.

"It looks bad but it's already on the mend. The contractors were here earlier today."

"Can we live in it?"

Jerry nodded, the sadness in his eyes unbearable to witness. I knew what he was thinking—it would be livable until I wasn't here anymore.

Once we were inside I smelled the smoke, saw the blackened wall on each side of the fireplace. The guest bedroom was completely gone, tangled wires and pieces of scorched wood and ash in its place, the heavy plastic blowing in the wind.

"Your TV," I said, looking up at him.

Jerry pulled me into his arms. "Do you think I fucking care about that?"

Jerry was openly crying now, his face ravaged with pain. "You're pregnant, Summer. They discovered it when they were doing tests."

Our eyes met, both of us crying now. "I know. Mom told me."

"Your dead mother knew?"

I nodded. "She said I had to go back, that I had a life to live, a baby on the way and a man who loved me."

Jerry let out a sob, his face crumpling. He held onto me, his arms so tight I could barely breathe. "I can't lose you," he muttered.

I wanted to say something, anything to ease his pain but I was too overcome with grief myself. When his hand went to my belly I let out a sob, my knees buckling.

He carried me into the bedroom and helped me under the wool throw.

"I'm going to make hot mulled wine and feed the animals. Rest until I get back." Jerry smoothed my hair back and bent to kiss my lips before he exited the bedroom.

I wondered what resting would do for me, but I did as he asked, closing my eyes and breathing in the smell of him on the pillow. Jerry returned with two spicy mugs of wine. He handed me one and sat next to me, neither of us able to offer a word of comfort to the other.

Once the mugs were empty Jerry cradled me against him. I heard his sobs and the ragged inhales that indicated the depth of his grief. I was numb, my mind completely blown. When his cell phone rang he let go of me and fished it out of his pocket. He answered, rising from the bed, his brows furrowing as he walked into the living room. A few minutes later he was back.

"I have to meet with Sam. Can I leave you alone for like an hour?"

"Are you meeting about the murders?"

He nodded. "We're wrapping up the case now that Carl is dead. Funerals are being arranged."

"Do you know why he killed Daniel?"

"Looks like he was trying to keep us from identifying Louise. As far as Philippa goes, I think she was the woman you heard after Booker locked you in the tunnels. We found divorce papers in her purse—she must have been planning to get herself free. But why she stayed away all this time is anyone's guess."

"Where did you find Carl?"

"He was on the floor in his shop with that damn book and a bunch of weird shit around him. He'd drawn a pentagram on the floor in chalk. His body had aged—he was like a skeleton with only bits of flesh still hanging on the bones." Jerry grimaced. "It was really disgusting to tell you the truth."

"What day was that?"

"Saturday morning. Why?"

"Something he said before he bit me—something about the date. He seemed to think it was Friday, but I was sure it was Wednesday."

Jerry stared at me. "It was around midnight Friday night when the firemen found you, Summer. You were in the hospital for three days—today's Tuesday."

"That's very odd. How could I lose two days?"

Jerry shook his head. "In the grand scheme of things I don't think it matters much."

A few minutes later his motorcycle roared to life, the engine sounds growing fainter as he took off down the street. I thought of all the things I'd miss—the sound of that stupid motorcycle arriving at night, the smile on his face when he came through the door. His whistling, his snoring, his hands, his mouth…I doubled over in pain. I'd taken my life for granted, had argued with Jerry about stupid things and hadn't listened to what he wanted, neglecting his needs as I acted selfishly.

Being on the fence about a baby now seemed ludicrous. When my hands went to my belly it was already distended. How had I managed to ignore that? I was thirty years old—how long had I planned to wait? And now the baby would die with me, Jerry deprived of the child he so wanted. I let out a hollow keening sound, rocking back and forth as reality sunk in. It was my entire fault for not paying attention to the signs. If I had known there was a baby to consider, perhaps I would have been more careful.

It was sometime later that I thought about the missing days. Something told me that it *did* matter. I climbed out of bed and went to the kitchen, glad to see my little dog bounding toward me. I reached down to pat him. "You led them to me, little guy—you're a wonder dog." He licked my hand and gave a little yip. I gave him a doggie treat before heading back to the bedroom to dress.

I pulled on warm wool pants before unwrapping the bandage around my neck. The doctor had stitched it up but the telltale bruise said it all. I traced the stitches, running my fingers along the bluish coloring. The skin had turned gray under and around the wound, the bruise sending tiny fingers outward in all directions. I pulled on a heavy turtleneck sweater to hide my neck. I'd be lucky if I lived out the week.

I thought of the tiny being swimming in the waters of my womb, the future I would not have. I let the tears fall, sobbing as I pulled on my boots and found my winter coat. I grabbed my bag and my cell phone and headed outside, determined to make the most of the time I had.

26

Tarot and Tea was open and bustling with customers. When I came inside, Valerie was sitting behind the counter, half glasses on her nose. "When I saw how many people were waiting, I decided to open for you," she said. "Are you feeling better?"

She didn't know what had happened. "Flu is over, but..." I glanced around, noticing a young woman I hadn't ever seen before heading toward the counter. She handed a small goddess figure to Valerie. "Do you have books on this goddess?"

I glanced down at the figure of Airmid with her herbal pouches tied around her waist, long golden brown hair cascading down her back. The painting was meticulous and fine, her features perfect. "The shelf over there has books on the Celtic goddesses," I answered. She left the figure and hurried off.

Valerie stood to let me sit down. "The goddess of healing—the one who brings back the dead," she said, picking her up to examine her.

"What?" I frowned, trying to recall my Celtic mythology.

"Don't you remember? Bone to bone, vein to vein, balm to balm..."

"Oh—yes. Wonder if it would work," I muttered.

Valerie leaned toward me. "What are you talking about?" she asked, staring into my eyes. A second later she let out a horrified gasp. "What happened?"

I glanced at the customer approaching the desk. "I'll tell you later."

While I checked out the woman in her twenties I noticed other customers gathering things to buy. Of course now that I was dying my store had decided to rise from the dead. I checked out two more, watching Valerie wander through the store, her canny gaze on me every chance she could get. I knew if I told her the truth I would break down again—and so would she. I was still trying to decide how to break the news when Jerry entered the store, his eyes dark with pain.

He hurried over, his hand reaching for mine. "When I got home you weren't there. This was the only place I could think to look." He peered into my eyes. "Do you feel well enough to…?"

"I feel okay. I took some ibuprofen. I can't just sit around waiting, can I?"

He smiled a sad smile. "I'd planned to sit around with you."

I shook my head. "It's too much for me. I have to stay busy." I gestured to the customers. "Look what happened after Carl was removed from the picture."

Jerry scanned the store. "I'll run it for you after…"

I held up my hand. "Don't say it. I haven't given up."

He looked down, letting out a heavy sigh. "I got the book back from Carl's store. I took it home, but when you weren't there I decided to bring it here just in case." He held out a shopping bag.

"You still can't pick it up?"

"No, and neither can Sam or anyone else who's tried."

I reached inside and pulled it out, my fingers tracing the now familiar worn symbols on the cover. "It's beautiful, a work of art, really."

"It's dark magic and dangerous," Jerry muttered. "It doesn't hurt you to pick it up?"

"Not anymore. This book was written by one of my relatives—Fenella McCloud. It isn't dark magic; it's magic that illuminates and enlightens those who can understand."

He scoffed. "Obviously Carl wasn't one of them."

"Look at this," I said, opening the book to the dedication.

Jerry leaned in, reading aloud. 'The spells on these pages are for the pure of heart; anyone who wishes to do harm or misuse the magic that lies within will be prevented from doing so.' He glanced up at me. "That's why it didn't work for Carl. Then why were you out in the graveyard at midnight?"

"Because the recipe for bringing the dead back to life changed for Carl's benefit. The book never intended to bring him back."

"Then why were you digging up a grave?"

"I had to pretend that the words I copied from the book were the real spell. And how did you know I was digging up a grave?"

"The firemen told me they found you crumpled in the mud next to an open grave. There was a shovel there and bones had been removed from the coffin."

"Carl must have finished digging it up. I guess he made a last ditch effort after he dispensed with me. Did you notice a box in our kitchen containing a silver chalice and a container of blood?"

"What? No."

I stared into space. "He got what he needed but it didn't work. Wonder why he was so pissed—he hadn't even tried the spell yet."

"There was blood on the floor around him. We couldn't figure out where it came from." He looked down. "He had a mortar and pestle but the bones hadn't been pulverized."

"He must have known he'd be too late—that's why he was so angry with me."

Jerry twined his fingers through mine. "It doesn't matter now. The bastard's dead."

"We need to return those bones and say a little prayer for Liza Benton."

"Who is Liza Benton?"

"The young girl I was digging up. She was murdered back in 1789."

"How do you know that?"

"She showed me the hole in her chest."

Valerie approached, her gaze going to Jerry. "Summer hasn't shared the story, but I can see that things have healed between you and that something very bad is about to happen."

Jerry glanced at me and then at Valerie. "Carl bit Summer in the neck."

Valerie let out a little cry, her hand going to her mouth. Her eyes welled and she turned away.

"You should go, Jerry. I'm sure you have things to do today. I'll be home soon."

"If you start to feel odd or woozy, call me," he said, his dark eyes trained on mine.

I knew what he was referring to—he wanted to be with me when I died. "I will."

As soon as he was out the door Valerie wrapped me in her arms. She didn't say anything as she held me, and when she released me we just stared at one another. When her eyes filled she turned away. "I have to meet Becky," she said, pulling her coat on and hurrying out the door.

⁌∞⁊

I was up early the next day, rolling away from Jerry's warm body to dress for work. He'd held me against him all night, his even breathing stilling my anxiety and allowing me to doze as the night wore on.

"Where are you going?" he asked sleepily.

"I'm going to work."

He sat up. "Work? You don't need to waste your last days…"

"I can't just sit here, Jerry. I want to make the most of the time I have."

"What about me?"

"You have a job to do. And babysitting me isn't one of them."

He reached for my hand and pulled me down. "You're the most important thing in my life. I want to be with you as much as I can." He leaned in and kissed me, his mouth warm and reassuring in a world that teetered precariously.

After our kiss I pulled away. "It helps me to keep busy. If I sat here with you all day both of us would cry our eyes out. Come by Tarot and Tea around lunchtime—bring me a sandwich."

Jerry's eyes filled. "I can't stand this."

237

"Don't talk about it anymore. I still have a few days left."

"How's the pain?"

"Not great, but tolerable."

Jerry gazed bleakly into the distance, his fingers running through his hair and making it stick up. I leaned in and gently took his hands in mine. "I love you."

He turned, his eyes welling as they met mine. "I love you more than I can ever say," he managed before his voice broke. He buried his face against my chest. "Please don't leave me."

We held each other and cried.

⌒∞⌒

I cried all the way to Tarot and Tea, more upset about Jerry's pain than my looming death. I'd never seen him like this and worried about how he'd cope after I was gone. I knew that part of his grief was about the baby I carried, but I also realized that he'd changed dramatically over the past year. He was finally able to love deeply, feel grief and express it, abilities that hadn't been present when we first met. He'd grown and changed, and so had I. We would be having a baby together if I...a sob escaped, another one following it. I wiped my eyes and tried to see the road through my tears, swerving to miss a car coming the other way. *Now is not the time to kill yourself, Summer*, I muttered. I let out a shaky laugh at the irony.

During a lull from the steady stream of customers I called Agnes. I wanted to know the details of Sammie's rescue and check in with her...one last time. I punched in her numbers, hitting the speaker button before placing the phone on the counter.

"Summer…oh…I don't know what to say. I'm sorry I was mean to you…I had no idea what you were going through."

"It's okay, Ags. How is Sammie?"

"Sammie's fine and it isn't at all okay. You're a witch—can't you do something?"

"I'm not a real witch and I have no idea how to heal myself. Any ideas?"

There was a long silence punctuated by a ragged indrawn breath. "What about Valerie or Mrs. B?"

"Valerie mentioned Airmid's chant for bringing the dead back—but that's just myth."

"Are you sure?" her choked-up voice asked. "Shouldn't you at least try it?"

"I'll look into it."

"Now, Summer—right now. I'm hanging up."

I pocketed the phone and stared at Valerie who had just arrived. "Agnes thinks I should try Airmid's healing prayer." I let out a nervous laugh. "I told her it's only a myth."

I glanced down at the leather book on the counter, surprised when it abruptly opened. When I looked down, the entirety of the healing prayer blinked back at me, the letters moving into place. Valerie and I gazed at one another for a second before she came around to read it. When her fingers touched the book it remained open. "Did your mother tell you about this book?"

"What do you mean?"

"It was always supposed to be yours. I had no idea why

it was at Bookers or how it came to be in Philippa's possession."

"I don't remember Mom mentioning it. Mrs. B said something about that too."

"Lila kept it for you, but somehow over the years it was accidentally sold. But of course no one could open it. Maybe that's how Philippa found it."

"Could she open it?"

"I'm not certain if she could or couldn't." She glanced down, her long fingers tracing the now still letters. "Let's take a closer look at that healing spell, shall we?"

We pored over it together, noting the warning at the bottom that spoke again of using the prayer for evil. "Only for healing those who walk in the light, lest dark forces be brought forth."

Valerie smiled. "You definitely walk in the light, Summer."

"Not sure Jerry would agree with you."

Valerie's limpid gaze met mine. "That man loves you to distraction. He's completely heartbroken."

"I'm pregnant," I blurted.

Valerie's mouth opened, distress appearing in her eyes. "This is too cruel. We cannot let you die." She pressed her powdered cheek to mine, her arms going around my shoulders. "Lila always said this book would find you when the time was right. I'd say this is it."

She held me while I cried, handing me a tissue once I had control of myself. My body ached, the poison from Carl's bite showing up in my joints and in my spine. "How do we do this? We don't have a goddess here to read the words and perform some voodoo over me."

"It doesn't have to be a goddess, just someone who

cares. I can do it. I love you like a daughter, Summer."

When I looked at her I saw the clarity in her eyes and the glimmer of light all around her. "You...you're all glittery."

Valerie laughed. "You are too—didn't you know?"

"Carl said...he said my power shimmered."

Valerie studied me. "It's brighter now than it's ever been. Something has changed—something profound."

"Dying maybe?"

"Possibly. But didn't you say that Marguerite told you...?"

"She said Mom told her I'd be coming into my witch powers in my thirtieth year."

Valerie watched me, her head cocked to one side. "You may not even need this spell."

"Have you looked at my neck?" I pulled the collar of my sweater down and unwrapped the gauze to show her.

"Nasty. And the bruise reaches all around."

I rose to look in the mirror, alarmed to see how much it had spread, the skin beneath it gray and sunken. "It's getting worse."

"Well then," she said briskly. "Time to get to work to reverse it." She glanced at the book. "Read any and all instructions on spells—there should be a frontispiece about it. And in the meantime I'm going to call a special coven meeting to be held at the Victorian." She left the store and walked quickly in the direction of the bakery and Becky.

When I glanced down at the book it opened, the pages fluttering backward to where the words, *Instructions for healing* were printed in dark letters, each spell listed beneath. I scanned down, noting the need for candles and incense on some of them, pentagrams and a silver cup filled with aromatic herbal elixirs on others. All called for a sacred space and the complete cooperation of all those present. *IF DARKNESS IS PRESENT IN ANY FORM THERE WILL BE NO HEALING,* was printed in all caps at the bottom.

In the absence of a healing pool or well, the Airmid prayer called for a pentagram, within which the injured or deceased person would be placed in the center and surrounded by a clan of goddesses or white witches. They would chant the spell over and over until there were visible signs that the supplicant was healed. This could be seen in the color of the skin, movement of eyes or other parts of the body. *Be patient! Healing takes time.*

My hands moved to my belly, my silent prayer heard only by the small being that inhabited my body. *For your sake and Jerry's, please let this work.*

27

The day went by quickly, more than the usual number of customers arriving to browse and buy things taking my mind off the pain that kept getting worse. In late afternoon when Douglas arrived I smiled gratefully, glad to see a familiar face.

His normal light-hearted expression was troubled, and worry lines creased his forehead as he hurried to the desk. "Agnes told me," he said, reaching for me.

He enfolded me inside the comfort of his arms before I filled him in about our plan.

"I hope to all that's holy it works," he mumbled, watching me with a frown. "I've never encountered a Gjenganger—sounds like a nasty creature."

"It is, but ours is gone," I told him. "And everything is back to normal."

He shook his head. "With the exception of your life, Summer. Valerie has already contacted me. It's my job to alert all the witches and ghosts in residence at the Victorian. She wants it to happen on the night of the new moon."

"When is that?"

"Saturday night."

A flutter of fear went through me. If it didn't work, then…

"The new moon is all about manifesting your wishes and desires," he continued. "New beginnings and new intentions."

I let out a mirthless laugh. "Sounds about right. But if it doesn't…"

Douglas's hand landed on my shoulder. "Stay as positive as you can and allow the universe to come to your aid. It does, you know."

I smiled up at him. "I know it does. I'm just…"

"You're terrified and rightly so. And you're carrying a child, which wreaks havoc with your emotions."

"How did you know?"

"Jerry told Sam, Sam told Agnes and Agnes told me. You know how the gossip Internet works."

I nodded, unable to smile. "I'm more worried about Jerry than I am myself. He's…"

"He's come into his own this year—finally appreciating what he has and the people he loves. Lucia just mentioned it the other day." He glanced at me from under his heavy grey brows. "His love will help both of you through this, no matter how it goes." He patted me on the arm. "Is it all right if Lucia comes to the healing?"

I thought of my early dealings with Jerry's mother. "As long as she wants me to live, yes."

"She's very fond of you, Summer. She's told me several times how good she thinks you are for Jerry. Lucia attributes his recent maturity to his relationship with you."

I let out a sigh and stared down at my desk. "Glad to hear that—things were kind of rocky at the beginning. You've been good for her, Douglas."

He smiled, his eyes going bright. "I like to think so. She's what you call, 'high maintenance', but worth every minute." He turned to leave. "Have to get cracking on the preparations for Saturday." His eyes met mine. "Keep the faith."

"I'll try."

Fifteen minutes after Douglas left Jerry appeared, a brown bag in his hands. "Lunch," he said brightly, the pain in his eyes belying his tone.

"Come sit," I invited, pulling another chair up to the counter. "Did you go to the station?"

He nodded, pulling out a wrapped sandwich. "Tuna."

For once the idea of food didn't turn my stomach. "Yum," I said unfolding the paper.

Jerry eyed me. "Your appetite's back?"

"The Victorian is planning a healing," I told him, taking a bite of my sandwich.

His eyes widened. "A healing—as in keeping you from dying?"

I nodded. "It's from the earth goddess, Airmid. It's in the book."

He pulled out his sandwich and removed the wax paper. "But not the one Carl tried."

"No! That was a necromancy spell."

"What's the difference?"

"His was a summoning to bring life back to a supernatural being who shouldn't have been here in the first place." I leafed through the book, trying to locate the spell I'd copied down for Carl, but it wasn't there. "It's gone."

"The one he used isn't in the book anymore?"

"I can't find it."

"Is the one for you still there?" he asked worriedly, leaning forward to examine the book.

As soon as I thought of Airmid's prayer the pages began fluttering by. Jerry watched, his brows pulling together. "Are you doing that?"

"Apparently so." When the pages stopped moving I glanced down, turning the book so he could see. "This is Airmid's."

Jerry leaned close to read. "Wow," he said, glancing up a moment later. "I like it."

"But do you have faith that it will work?"

"Yes," he said without hesitation.

I smiled. "You've changed."

"I think it's better to believe than not, especially after what I've experienced recently." He took a bite of his sandwich, chewing and swallowing before he asked, "What's the plan?"

After I explained the timing and the place and the people who would be in attendance he took hold of my hand. "In the past few days I've prayed and bargained with a god I no longer believe in, and I've cried more than I have in my entire life."

"What kind of bargain, Jerry?"

He smiled sheepishly. "I agreed to never, and I mean never, dismiss your feelings or what you tell me, even if it goes against every rational thought I have."

Tears sprang to my eyes. Luckily at that moment a customer came in and I had to get myself together. The woman gave me a quick smile and went by, her gaze on the essential oils.

"Eat," Jerry said, pointing to my nearly untouched sandwich. "If there's any chance this prayer will work I don't want you starving to death before we do it."

I took a bite, savoring the flavors of onion, tuna, mayo and pickle relish. It tasted utterly delicious.

∽

That night Jerry tucked me in bed after making me take several painkillers, his worried gaze on mine. "That bruise is getting bigger."

"I know, Jer. Try not to think about it."

He climbed into bed and pulled me into the curve of his arms. "I'm praying this works."

I let out a snort. "Bargaining again?"

Jerry smirked. "In the past two days I've given up every one of my bad habits."

Attempting to maintain a light positive tone I said, "Don't give up too much—I like your bad boy ways—what would we do if we always agreed on everything? It would be totally boring."

When his mahogany eyes met mine the fear and pain he was feeling turned them dark. He moved a hand to my lower belly before he let out a sob and buried his face in my hair. Terror ran through me, my pulse racing as I relived the darkness of the underworld and watched the silver rope slipping away. I tried to find words of comfort but my mouth was as dry as a desert.

28

I took painkillers and ate a bunch of crackers with peanut butter the next morning before I slipped out of the house, leaving Jerry sound asleep. It was a little after midnight when I encouraged him to take a sleeping pill, noting his red-rimmed eyes and the cough he'd developed. "You need to be well enough to help me through the healing," I'd told him, rubbing his tense shoulders as he began to relax. I hadn't slept much, but I had drifted off for a few hours close to dawn, waking before it was fully light.

I left Jerry a note explaining where I'd gone before pulling on my boots and coat and heading outside to another gorgeous dawn sky filled with rosy light. He knew where to find me.

When I reached Tarot and Tea I noticed my door hanging wide open, my first thought going to Carl—but Carl was dead. Inside was a jumble of books scattered everywhere, as though someone had been searching for a specific one. I stopped to contemplate whom it might have been, my mind going over everything that had happened related to the book of spells—because that must have been what they were searching for.

I found an expensive man's leather glove on the floor and picked it up using a piece of tissue. I carried it to my desk and place it in a cubby. Maybe Jerry or Sam could get some fingerprints from it. For some reason I didn't have a terrible feeling about the break-in, as though what I was going through had rendered everything else unimportant.

A shadow took my attention, the black cat just disappearing behind a bookshelf. "If that's you Mischief, it's okay for you to show yourself," I said, but when I walked over to take a look there was nothing there but a lingering energy that seemed comforting somehow. Did I now have a familiar? I let out a laugh before a sharp pain in my neck brought tears. I stood very still until the pain passed, telling myself the healing would work and repeating it over and over.

I was picking up books and replacing them when Valerie walked in, her gray-green eyes widening in surprise. "What in the world now?"

"Someone broke in."

Valerie came over to help me. "Why?"

"Beats me. Maybe they want to bring back someone who died. Good thing I took the Grimoire home with me."

"Yes. You don't want to lose that spell before the healing," Valerie agreed, her smile slightly overdone.

"I'll call in an hour or so and tell Jerry about the break-in. He'll need to redo the locks and check for fingerprints."

Valerie frowned. "Why not now before customers arrive?"

"Because he took a pill and is probably still asleep."

"Shouldn't it be you who takes a pill and sleeps in,

Summer? For goodness sakes."

I met her clear gaze. "Jerry is terrified, exhausted and overwrought. He needed to sleep."

"And you aren't?"

"I am, but I seem to have more energy than he does—not sure why."

"Because you're a witch."

I shook my head. "I've never really thought of myself that way. I can talk to ghosts, but…"

Valerie scoffed. "What about the tilting room, going back in time and being able to cajole that policewoman out of the book?"

"Not to mention the two lost days," I muttered.

"What two days?"

"I was at the market on Wednesday to get the blood, and I just found out that when they found me in the graveyard that same night, it was Friday instead of Wednesday."

Valerie's almond shaped eyes narrowed. "Do you think you caused it?"

"I did ask the universe to speed the process along. And I added *please* while I visualized being done with it all."

Valerie nodded thoughtfully. "Anything else happen that day?"

"On my way home lightning struck a dead tree close to where I was driving and it burst into flames."

"I saw nothing about that on the news."

"So it didn't really happen?"

She gave a one-shoulder shrug, her head cocked the same way. "Could be a reaction to what you wished for. It seems your power comes from your emotions."

"So maybe if I wish to be healed I won't need the healing?"

"Your wound is from a supernatural being, which kind of trumps my theory."

I thought about things that had happened recently— going back in time—something I had wished in order to know the past, and even though it wasn't a conscious thought, the room tilting because I wanted to stop Carl. Not to mention the woman who'd handed over the book after I visualized it in my hands. The word *please* seemed to be involved, said silently and in desperation. But the please I'd whispered before Carl bit me didn't stop him.

When my cell phone rang I rose from the floor to answer it.

"You should have woken me," Jerry said.

"You needed the rest. Can you come by Tarot and Tea? There was a break-in."

"What? Why didn't you call me right away?"

When I didn't answer he let out a sigh. "I'll give Sam a call and we'll come by and dust for prints. Hope you didn't touch anything."

He hung up before I could tell him I'd already picked up all the books. I hoped the glove would help.

By the time Jerry arrived with Sam I'd cleaned up the mess and customers were all over the store removing whatever evidence was left. As soon as Jerry came through the door he shook his head, his mahogany eyes meeting mine. "Crime scene?" he hissed, coming close.

"Sorry. I did save a glove."

Jerry turned to stare at Sam, an unspoken communication

of frustration passing between them. "So where's this glove?"

I picked it up with the tissue and handed it over.

Jerry shook his head. "We might have gotten prints off the books that were handled, but off this glove? No."

"I didn't realize. Is it because of how thin it is?"

"Partly. Gloves hold grease and dust and so on, but this one looks like it's brand new. Not even sure it's been worn."

"How about tracing it back to where it was purchased?"

Jerry frowned, opening the inside to look at the tag. "Barneys in New York. Not traceable."

"Crap," I whispered. A second later I was doubled over in pain, my neck seizing up when I tried to turn.

"Summer? What's wrong?"

I tried to keep the tears from coming but I couldn't. "Neck hurts," I whispered.

Jerry's eyes went dark, his gaze going to Valerie. "Summer needs to leave," he said. "Can you check the rest of the customers out?"

Valerie's eyes went wide as she watched me, her hand coming onto my arm. "What's happening?"

"I don't know, but I can't move my neck."

"Go home and take a hot bath. As far as who broke in, it isn't that important."

Since I couldn't nod I gave her the thumbs up and let Jerry lead me outside. Once we were in my car I could see Sam inside talking with Valerie, both of them gesturing. "Who do you think broke in?" I asked, unable to move my gaze from the windshield in front of me.

But Jerry couldn't answer, a catch in his voice as he tried. I turned my entire body in the seat to face him, surprised by the tears running down his face. His apologetic gaze met mine as he wiped at the tears. "I'm sorry, Summer. I wanted to stay strong for you."

I tried to say something witty, something encouraging, something that kept me from feeling all the terror that rolled through me, but the stiffness was spreading and it scared me so much I was unable to speak at all.

Once we reached the cottage Jerry led me inside and drew a hot bath, helping me into the tub. After a good soak in Epson salts he assisted me with my pajamas and put me to bed, arranging several pillows behind me. "Can you drink some tea?"

"Yes, I'd like that," I told him, hoping against hope that this wasn't the end for me. *Healing is tomorrow* I chanted over and over. *I can hang on until then.* But I didn't know if that was true.

I didn't move from the bed for the rest of the afternoon and when night came I closed my eyes and slept, my dreams taking me to some horrible hell where I didn't want to be. Carl was there, an evil grin on his skeletal face as he watched me. "Told you you were a goner," he sneered. "Welcome to my world." I couldn't respond as paralysis spread from my neck downward. Terror took over, but when I tried to scream my mouth wouldn't open. And all the while Carl watched me, his grin growing wider and wider as the flesh fell off his bones.

29

The next morning I couldn't move my neck, my shoulders, or my upper body, the bruise taking up all the space between my chin and my collarbones. The skin under the bruise was sunken and gray, narrow blue lines snaking in all directions. I was so rigid that Jerry had to help me out of bed and into the bathroom. "Take these," he ordered, handing me a couple of muscle relaxants. His normally olive skin was ashen, his eyes red-rimmed.

"You didn't sleep?"

He shook his head. "I wanted to feel you against me."

"Oh Jerry." I wiped at my eyes, trying to let go of the rising dread.

He helped me back to bed and arranged the pillows to prop me up. "I'm making breakfast—stay here and rest until the meds kick in."

I wondered if meds would help with a supernatural wound, but I did as he said. By nine a.m. my entire body felt like it was paralyzed. When Jerry brought me breakfast I was barely able to open my mouth. His face went from ashen to bloodless, his eyes wide with fear. "I'm calling Douglas—you need that healing *now*."

I tried to nod but couldn't move my head at all. I was afraid to close my eyes for fear I wouldn't be able to open them again. I thought of my baby, hoping that my insides were still working.

Minutes later Jerry reappeared in the bedroom carrying a tray. "Douglas said he'd arrange it for as soon as he can. Can you eat?"

When I tried to reply my tongue had gone numb, my lips refusing to open. All I could do was widen my eyes.

"Holy fucking shit!" Jerry shouted, the tray with my eggs, toast and cappuccino clattering to the floor. He hastily reached for a towel hanging over a chair to sop up the liquid before he reached for me, one hand going to my forehead, his fingers on my pulse. "Jesus—you hardly have a heartbeat!" He stared at me, terror stricken. "What do I do?" he murmured.

But I couldn't help him, my throat like sandpaper, and the beats of my heart so far apart that I could barely register them. I couldn't move my hands, my legs or my arms. Jerry pulled off my pajamas and dressed me like an unwieldy doll, his hands trembling. He pulled a blanket around me and carried me to the car, placing me on the backseat where my rigid body could lie fairly flat. "I don't know what fucking time they expect us, but we have to go now," he muttered.

"Book," I managed to choke out just before he turned the key. He glanced into the back before he hopped out and ran for the house, returning with the shopping bag containing the Grimoire. He threw it on the passenger seat and a second later we were speeding down the road toward the Victorian.

We careened around corners, sending me from one side

of the seat to the other. I could hear Jerry muttering, his occasional oaths as a car appeared in front of us or some innocent pedestrian dared to be walking in our path. At one point he swerved sideways, propelling me off the seat onto the floor. When he glanced back and saw me he let out a shout and pulled off the road.

A minute later he had the door open, his arms lifting me back onto the seat. "I'm so sorry, Summer," he mumbled, his cheeks wet with tears. A minute later we were on our way again and I heard him on his cell phone, his hoarse whispers too faint for my ears. I closed my eyes, drifting in some nebulous place between life and death and entreating help from anyone who was listening.

When we reached the Victorian Jerry jumped out and began shouting. I heard running feet, worried voices. When Jerry lifted me out of the car I tried to open my eyes but they seemed glued shut. Jerry was openly crying now and I heard other familiar voices filled with emotion.

"Is the pentagram drawn?" Agnes asked. Someone answered her, saying yes. There was a frantic quality to all of it. Jerry had me in his arms, my body stiffened as though in rigor mortis. "Take her inside!" Agnes yelled.

I picked up the aroma of incense and candle wax before Jerry placed me gently on the floor. He arranged my hair, his fingers running through it to get the tangles out before his lips touched my forehead. "It's going to be okay," he whispered, as though trying to reassure himself. After that I entered a space that seemed neither here or there. I was floating, all pain gone. I knew it wouldn't be long now. I would die in the next few minutes.

My heart slowed even further, my breath growing

shallow and then finally stopping altogether. I heard Jerry sobbing as his hands went to my wrist. "Hurry," he muttered. "Pass the book around," someone called out. A moment later the chanting began.

I lifted out of my body and floated upward, watching the ceremony and listening to the words repeated, over and over, the voices growing louder with each iteration. My face was lifeless now, all color leached from it, my features slack.

Bone to bone
Vein to vein
Balm to balm
Sap to sap
Skin to skin
Tissue to tissue
Blood to blood
Flesh to flesh
Sinew to sinew
Marrow to marrow
Pith to pith
Fat to fat
Membrane to membrane
Fiber to fiber
Moisture to moisture

Black smoke hung all around my body like a poison that was unable to escape. I figured something should have happened by now—how long could I remain lifeless before there was no chance of coming back? I thought of the tiny being inside me—would she live or was she already dead?

My gaze moved around the room beneath me trying to

understand why nothing had changed. Something was wrong. *Please* I begged. A moment later a woman dressed in green velvet appeared next to my body on the floor. She frowned, leaning over me, several leather pouches tied around her small waist falling forward as she drew close. Her hair hung down her back in tangled gold brown waves, her hazel eyes leaving me to scan the room. When she pointed a slender finger toward a shadowy figure in the corner of the room, I turned to see who was there. But it was too dark to identify the man or woman who stood hidden amongst the flickering shadows cast from the many candles placed around the room's perimeter.

I wanted to shout for someone to notice Airmid and where she pointed, but no one saw her, their eyes closed as they continued to chant.

It was only when a beam of light stretched from Airmid's fingers to the figure that eyes began to open, gazes turning toward the corner of the room. "Who's there?" someone asked. By now the chanting had ceased and the entire group stared in that direction.

"Show yourself!" Sam called out, rising to his feet. Jerry was already up and running when the figure fled for the door and threw it open, slamming it shut in Jerry's face. Jerry opened it and gave chase, only to return a few moments later. He shook his head. "Got away," he muttered.

"Who was it?" someone asked.

"Don't know." Jerry sat down again, his face a mask of pain.

"The energy just changed," Valerie announced, placing a comforting hand on Jerry's forearm. "The dark force is gone now."

But Jerry was crying, his tear-filled eyes on the body that lay within the pentagram. He could tell my spirit had departed.

I tried to keep track of what was going on but I was drifting further and further away, as though I would soon become vapor and simply dissipate. I struggled to maintain what was left of me, staring down at Jerry who had his face in his hands, sobbing. If I couldn't be resurrected he would be lost. Not only was he losing me, he was also losing the baby I carried. I couldn't leave him…and yet…I had no control over any of it.

The chanting began again, this time with renewed force. Airmid's hands hovered over me, a flare of luminescence appearing from her palms to penetrate into my belly. But it was too late, any sense I had of this reality already turning into a hazy memory.

I felt the pull of the netherworld and the blessed sense of letting go as I turned into a million droplets of vapor. I was already walking into the dark when I felt the tug. Beguiled by the next life, where all pain and care were absent, I struggled against it. I saw my mother, my grandmother, their faces turned toward me…I was caught in between, one foot in the afterlife and one foot amongst the living. Memories rushed in. Jerry, the baby, my friends…

A second later I was inside my body with all the pain, uncertainty and fear. But there was also love, the enormity of it taking my breath away. As I relaxed into the shell that had held me for thirty years, I felt complete for the first time in my life. This body was my home, the place where I belonged. I felt the baby swimming in her warm sea, connected to me by the umbilical cord, our essences combined. I had a vision of what she would look like—dark hair and mahogany eyes, skin the color of milk and roses. I longed to hold her and yet it was as though she already rested in my arms.

When I opened my eyes Airmid gazed into them, her knowing smile sweet, and her hazel eyes filled with a special light. She had given me the glimpse of the child to come, allowed me to see the future. I watched her dissipate, her image growing fainter and fainter until she was no longer there.

A second later Jerry kneeled next me, his eyes filled with the same kind of light. His beautiful brown eyes met mine, the look on his face one of pure joy. He tried to say something and was unable to speak, his fingers moving to my neck to trace across the wound. "It's gone," he murmured. And then he pulled me up.

When I put my arms around him and felt his heart beating against mine, the truth of the world dawned. Life was a miracle.

30

Once I had fully awakened and was able to converse again, every single person who participated in the healing came to give me his or her blessing. Valerie and Mrs. Browning were among the first, holding me against them and murmuring soft words I could barely comprehend. It was tearful and emotional, my heart so full I thought it might burst from my chest. There was a giddy air of celebration at the Victorian, the sound of champagne corks popping and laughter.

Lucia came by, her warm smile like a balm to my soul. "I will be a grandmother," she murmured, kissing me on both cheeks European style. "I'm absolutely thrilled."

When she headed off with Douglas, Becky arrived with a sandy-haired man with an easy smile. "Shawn, I presume?" I asked, smiling.

His eyebrows rose before he glanced at Becky. "Another one?" he whispered.

"Yes," she laughed, a sparkle in her green eyes.

"If you mean witch, I'm not one," I whispered. "Valerie told me your name."

Becky shook her head, her mouth twisting in disbelief.

"Really, Summer? You can't admit it even after everything that's happened?"

I let out an embarrassed chuckle. "Hard to come to grips with."

"You've been one all along—you just didn't recognize it." She hugged me close. "I've hardly seen you these past months."

I glanced at the man waiting. "Looks like you've been busy."

Becky smiled up at him, her gaze full of love. "Shawn's helping with the bakery now."

"That's really good to hear—you were overworked."

As soon as Becky and Shawn left an overwhelming exhaustion came over me. "Can we go home?" I whispered to Jerry hovering beside me.

Jerry nodded, his arm going around my shoulders. "I was thinking the same thing." When he placed the blanket around my shoulders and led me toward the door many of those present called out to say goodbye, wishing us well.

I turned as someone shouted my name but Jerry tugged me forward. "You need to rest and recuperate, Summer. All these people can wait."

"Can you feel the baby?" he asked anxiously once we were in the car.

"It's too soon to feel her."

"But…can you tell if the baby's okay?"

I placed my hand on my belly. "If she wasn't I'd probably know it."

Jerry drove me home, his gaze drifting to me every few minutes. "I can't believe you're all right."

I turned from where I'd been admiring the bare trees, lost in the filtered sunlight drifting down to leave shadows along the soggy ground. The snow was gone now but small patches still remained near the base of the trees and in shadows along walls. The world sparkled as though illuminated by a magical hand. "I can't either," I replied. "I saw Mom again. She told me to go back—she was really worried this time. Half of me wanted to stay."

Jerry frowned. "You wanted to die?"

"It was seductive and there wasn't anything to worry about there."

"But what about me? Our baby?"

I smiled and twined my fingers through his, watching him steer with one hand. "It wasn't about making a decision—I was nearly there and I had no choice in the matter. It isn't something I can explain."

He pressed his lips together. "Guess I won't understand unless I have a near death experience."

I glanced out the window again. "The world looks lit up—full of magic. I feel excitement deep in my belly, like anything's possible."

He glanced at me. "Maybe that's our baby boy talking to you."

I laughed. "Yeah—maybe. But it's not a boy—it's a girl."

Jerry chuckled. "You know this, how?"

"I saw her, Jerry. Airmid let me see her and hold her."

Jerry made a face before catching himself. "Really? Tell me about it."

I giggled, remembering his bargain. "Airmid was there during the healing. She kept the baby safe when I died."

Jerry's head jerked around. "It wasn't just near death—you really died?"

I nodded. "I was up near the ceiling and I was drifting into nothingness when she pulled me back."

Jerry's eyes widened.

"Our baby girl has your hair and your eyes and my pale skin," I continued. "She's beautiful."

Jerry grinned. "I can't wait to see her. I feel…I feel like I've just been reborn."

"And yet it was me who got reborn," I answered, my fingers tightening on his. When I glanced at him he was crying, tears sliding down his cheeks. And then I was crying too, both of us completely overcome.

When we reached the cottage the plastic was billowing, bringing back all the horror. I began to tremble, my good mood fading.

Jerry hopped out and came around to my side of the car. "It's okay, Summer. We're fixing it. And I'm considering adding a room on for the baby. What do you think?"

"It…it isn't the damage, it's the memories. But another room sounds good—I was afraid we'd have to move."

"No moving. I've been discussing it with the contractor and I have some plans to show you."

"When did you do that?"

He shrugged. "After the house burned? I was pretty sure we'd need an extra room." He glanced at me. "If you lived." He pulled me against him, his face on my neck where the wound had been. The wetness of his tears was warm on my skin. He pulled me toward the front door, only letting me go to unlock it.

Cutty barked frantically when we entered. I reached down to pat him, tears welling before I noticed the many flowers. "Where did these come from?"

"Friends…me," Jerry answered with an embarrassed look. "I wanted the place to be cheery when we got back."

I glanced at the wall that still stood, the open door leading into our bedroom. "Seems like you were pretty sure I'd live."

Jerry's eyes went dark. "Not really. I just decided I had to have faith—that visualizing you here would serve me better than thinking about arranging a funeral."

"Oh "I love it," I whispered,, Jerry," I said, realizing the depth of what he'd been going through.

His eyes met mine. "I made a doctor's appointment for tomorrow morning."

"She's fine."

"Please, Summer. I only want to be sure. And we need the approximate birth date, don't we?"

"Okay, but I want a midwife when the time comes. No drugs and no hospitals."

"If everything's going well, I agree."

He led the way into the bedroom that he'd rearranged, anticipating my need for a change. The bed had been moved and was covered in a new spread in black and gray—Jerry's colors. He'd brought in a table and a chair and added a new rug that echoed the bedspread and had a stripe of red that ran around the perimeter.

"You like?"

"I do. It has a completely different feel. But when did you do this?"

"I had it all planned out before the healing. Bill Harris

moved the furniture and set it up after we left. And he arranged the flowers."

"I love it," I whispered, climbing into bed. I pulled the new red wool throw over my body. "Just a short one, okay?" I murmured as my eyes drifted closed.

Jerry tucked the throw around me and kissed me on the forehead before leaving the room and softly closing the door.

When I woke again it was light and I was naked and under the covers next to Jerry. I slipped out of bed and went to the window to stare out at the early dawn, my senses coming alive as I gazed at the drops of moisture sparkling on the bare branches. The sun wasn't yet up, a thin line of orange peeking over the eastern horizon. Streaks of gray and rose filled the space between that and the translucent sky. I let out a sigh and pulled my arms around my body, something akin to euphoria moving from my toes upward.

Jerry groaned. "You're killin' me."

I turned, surprised. "What are you talking about?"

He waved his hands. "I want you badly, and seeing you standing there naked isn't helping. I've been holding off until you see the doctor, so please have the decency to put some clothes on before I give in to my urges."

I laughed. "How did this happen, anyway?" I asked gesturing to my nakedness.

He chuckled. "I couldn't let you sleep in your clothes. You were so deep asleep you didn't even wake up when I undressed you."

I shivered as the chilliness of the room registered. A second later I hopped back into bed and snuggled against him.

He pulled away. "What are you trying to do to me?"

"Nothing. I just wanted to be close, that's all."

"Get dressed, Summer—your appointment's at nine." He pushed himself out of bed and went into the closet to dress.

"You honestly don't want to make love until I see a doctor?"

He poked his head out the door. "That's right."

"But why?"

"I don't want to make love to you and find out later that our baby's dead, that's why. Can you imagine how we'd feel? And if that's the case you'll need a procedure."

"I told you I saw our baby."

Jerry emerged from the closet wearing jeans with a long sleeved black polo in his hands. "Can you just indulge me without questioning everything? I've done a lot of thinking the past few days. It's easy enough to get an ultrasound." He tossed me my clothes and left the bedroom.

As I dressed I heard the sound of the espresso machine, the whir as he frothed the milk. I wondered about this new Jerry who worried and held himself back. I knew she was all right, but Jerry wanted proof. A hospital, and doctors to tell us what was going on was his way of feeling safe. I loved Jerry and I could deal with it, especially in my newly enlightened state.

When I arrived in the kitchen he'd set the table, my cappuccino next to a plate of scrambled eggs and toast. "Thought you might be hungry. You didn't have dinner last night."

"I am hungry," I said, pulling out the chair to sit.

He sat next to me, watching me eat. "Your breasts and belly are bigger, but otherwise you're way too thin."

I shook my head, staring at him. "You now keep track of my cycles *and* watch the changes to my body?"

"You're damn straight. This baby you're carrying is mine too. I want him to be healthy."

I forked eggs into my mouth, chewing and swallowing before I said, "I would never have guessed the carefree man I married could be so…I'm not even sure of the right word."

"Concerned? Caring? Loving?"

I laughed. "More like obsessed. I thought you were one of those men who'd ignore his wife when she ballooned out."

He shook his head, a grin appearing before his dark gaze met mine. "I can't wait to see you balloon out."

⸺

Our trip to the hospital was made in silence as both of us contemplated the possibilities. I'd been certain that the baby was fine, but after Jerry's insistence about the appointment and his warnings, I began to doubt. He parked the car and I followed him into the hospital and into the elevator to the ob-gyn department on the third floor. "How'd you find this doctor?"

"She was recommended by the doc who treated you after the bite."

"Even though you both thought I would die?" A few people in the elevator turned to stare at me.

Jerry shrugged and grinned. "Just in case."

Once we were in the office he led the way to the counter

and checked me in, handing over my insurance cards before we found seats in the waiting room. He'd thought of everything, had even filled out my health record over the phone.

It was twenty minutes before they called me in, Jerry trailing after me like a lost puppy. "Are you sure you want to come in with me?" I whispered, visualizing my legs spread and my feet in stirrups.

"What do *you* think?" he hissed back.

In the room I changed into a hospital gown and climbed onto the table while Jerry sat and thumbed through Parents magazine. I stared at him, still unable to wrap my mind around us being parents or how into it he was. I placed my hands on my belly, saying a little prayer that everything was all right.

The doctor arrived a few moments later, breezing into the room in six-inch heels and a blouse made of some gossamer material. The only thing doctor-like about her was the stethoscope hanging around her neck and the clipboard she carried.

"Hello, Mr. and Mrs. Brady," she said, holding out her hand to Jerry. "I'm Doctor Ralph." She glanced down at the clipboard. "I see you're here for an ultrasound. Are you interested in the sex of the baby?"

"Yes," we both said. "And we want to make sure the baby's all right," Jerry added.

She glanced at him as she wound the blood pressure cuff around my upper arm and pumped it. "What are your concerns?"

Jerry and I exchanged a look before he said, "Summer's been under a lot of stress lately and she hasn't been eating properly."

"Morning sickness?" Dr. Ralph asked, writing something down before removing the cuff.

I nodded. "I couldn't eat for a few days," I said, remembering my sojourn in jail and then my horrible day spent with Carl.

"Well," she said, pulling on her gloves and retrieving the ultra sound gel off a shelf. She lifted the gown and rubbed it on my belly before reaching for the machine. "How far along are you?" she asked, watching the monitor.

"I don't know—maybe two months?"

Jerry got up and came to look at the monitor. "Summer stopped taking the pill in August," he supplied.

Dr. Ralph frowned, moving the machine across my belly. "Baby's fine," she said. "A boy."

"A boy?"

"Yes. It's quite obvious, which means you might be farther along than you thought. I'd say closer to four months."

"I thought it took a while after being on the pill."

"It can. But in your case it seems you conceived in early September." She continued checking things, finally snapping off her gloves and handing me a towel.

I wiped off the gel. "So that means the baby's due in…"

"I'd say late May/early June is our best bet. I suggest prenatal vitamins and a diet filled with leafy greens, meat, if you're not vegan, and a lot of cooked vegetables. Don't scrimp on oil. You're very thin to be this far along."

Jerry gave me a sharp look.

"What about the morning sickness?" I asked.

"Are you still having it?"

I thought about the past few days since Carl's demise. "Not really."

She smiled. "Usually by this time in the pregnancy morning sickness eases. If you still have it make sure to have some salty crackers on hand. Also, your blood pressure's a little higher than I'd like it to be—high blood pressure during pregnancy can cause problems. I suggest a brisk daily walk and some calming exercise or meditation."

"Is it dangerously high?" I asked, worried.

She stopped on her way to the door. "No, not dangerously so. It could be a reaction to this stress you mentioned. Come back in a month and we can recheck."

Once she left the room Jerry gave me a significant look. "A girl, huh? I knew it was a boy."

I thought of the baby Airmid showed me. I'd only seen the face, the rest of him swaddled in a blanket. "I guess I just assumed," I muttered.

"You know what they say," Jerry said. "When you assume you…"

"Make an ass out of you and me."

Jerry laughed, his rich baritone filling the room with his joy. "I'm doing the cooking from now on. And you will eat well, milady."

We stopped to make another appointment and then left the building arm and arm.

31

In the car on the way home Jerry kept turning to me with an expression that I could only describe as abject lust. He fidgeted, readjusting in his seat, a pained look in his eyes.

"I was planning to head to Tarot and Tea," I murmured, teasing him.

"Not before I get my hands on you," he muttered. "Are you telling me you aren't interested?"

I laughed. "I'm very interested," I said, acutely aware of the sensation low in my belly.

"If it wasn't so fucking cold I'd pull off and ravish you in the car."

"And just as we got our clothes off a cop would appear and knock on the window."

Jerry laughed.

As soon as we were inside the house he tugged me toward the bedroom, closing the door just before Cutty rushed inside. "Not now, little guy," he told him firmly. He undressed me slowly, his fingers tracing across my breasts and my belly. "You'll soon look like a Madonna," he whispered.

"And that turns you on?"

"Hell, yes. The Madonna is a sex goddess."

I laughed. As soon as I stepped out of my loose linen pants Jerry lifted me and carried me to the bed. He lay next to me, his eyes meeting mine as he ran his fingers along my cheek and jaw. When he kissed me it was as though every cell in my body came alive at once. His gaze moved across my nakedness as though he'd never seen my body before, his dark eyes lingering to drink me in. And once he'd had his visual fill he began another slow exploration, every nerve ending turning molten under his delicate touch.

I felt some deep holding let go, the reality of being alive and pregnant and about to connect with the man I loved swallowing me up in emotions I'd never experienced. We became one being, lifting into a world without thought as we joined. My body shook with tremors, an earthquake of sensations moving through my trembling limbs as Jerry pulled me with him into an ethereal place where angels sang.

From then on it was only the sound of his breath and mine mingling as we pulsed together and apart, our hearts beating in rhythm. When I let out a little cry Jerry froze. "Are you all right?" he whispered.

I couldn't speak, could only nod as I pulled him close again, the feelings so intense I thought I might break into a million pieces and disappear. After that I lost all track of what was happening, my face wet with tears as we disappeared into a kaleidoscope universe that held us within its protective arms. We were separate and then we were one being, my awareness of him so strong that I felt like I was inside him, just as he was inside me. And when he moved deeper it was though I was moving deeper into him—there were no longer any boundaries between his body and mine.

When we crested the wave and I gazed into his eyes they were fathomless, dark pools leading to infinity that I fell into and lost myself. I heard him moan as the wave crashed over us, our arms tight around each other as the surf tumbled us over and over before depositing us on the shore.

Afterward we lay entwined, unwilling to move apart. What had happened between us was not like any sex we'd had before, the awareness of our profound connection penetrating deep into my psyche. "I can't believe this," I murmured. "It feels like a dream."

He gazed at me, his eyes filled with love. "I've never felt like this—not even when when we were first together. It's…it's like I just discovered what love really is."

I couldn't answer, my throat closing up as emotions swirled through me. I pressed even closer, running my fingers through his thick hair. "We got a second chance," I finally murmured.

His hands moved to rest on my belly, his dark eyes welling with emotion. He nodded, unable to speak.

We spent the rest of the day talking about the addition and planning how to manage it as we pored over the drawings the contractor had left. "Will we have to move out while they're working?" I asked.

"I don't think so. When they're here both of us will be gone. It could take several months, but should be done in time for the birth."

The birth. A frisson of abject terror moved through me as I contemplated the enormity of what was to come.

"It will all be fine," he said, as though reading my thoughts.

"I hope the baby inherits your mouth," I said, tracing his lips with my fingers. He grabbed my hand and kissed it. "You have a nice one too," he said, pressing his lips there to prove his point. It didn't take long before we were stretched out on the couch together, so enraptured with each other we couldn't keep our hands to ourselves.

"Will we ever get enough?" I asked afterward, basking in the feel of what we'd done.

"I hope not," he murmured into my tangled hair.

When evening came Jerry proceeded to cook as he'd promised, his meal of sweet potatoes, lamb chops and asparagus, delicious and satisfying. And when it was time for bed we took a bath together before he ravished me again, this time more thoroughly. That night I slept more deeply than I had in years.

☙

I woke in the morning to a cerulean sky, Jerry still asleep beside me. When I checked my neck in the bathroom mirror there was no sign that a bruise had ever been there. I slipped on my robe and went into the kitchen while Jerry slept, determined to make us celebratory cappuccinos. I was hard at work when Jerry padded in behind me.

He nuzzled my neck and pushed me gently away. "Let me do that."

"Happily." I watched his expert moves, a tingle of pure

bliss making it's way through me. This is how I'd felt when Jerry and I were new and so enamored with each other that we couldn't get enough.

When he turned toward me his mouth curled up in a smile. "I haven't seen that expression on your face for a long time." He handed me a cup and bent to the task of making the second one.

I moved to the table and sat down. "I feel...I don't know how to describe it. It's like I just woke up in another world," I said, gesturing to the window where a chickadee sat on a branch of our cherry tree. I watched him flitting about, wondering why I'd never noticed the sparkle of dew on the branches or the beauty of this common winter bird.

He finished making his espresso and joined me at the table, his clear gaze on mine. "I didn't know I could love someone so much."

"You've been holding yourself back. Maybe I have been too. Fear isn't good for anything. It's like we got married but didn't really understand what it meant."

He nodded. "I've been afraid for most of my life—worried that I wouldn't be good enough, or that I'd let you down, or that you'd decide you didn't want to be with me. I don't know if it's the baby or what, but all of it seems to be gone now."

"And I've been horrible to you, angry instead of loving when you had the worst scare of your life."

He reached across the table and took my hand. "That was not my worst scare, Summer. And I understand why you reacted that way. I was a prick to share it with Agnes and Sam and not tell you."

"I'm so incredibly happy."

He rose and came around the table to wrap me up in his arms

‿☙‿

When I arrived at Tarot and Tea Valerie had already opened the store and

she and Mrs. B were chatting. They turned when I walked in, both of them greeting me with warm hugs. "You look positively radiant," Mrs. B said. "The healing put the roses back in your cheeks."

"That and being pregnant," Valerie added, smiling.

My face went hot. I knew why I looked radiant and it had nothing to do with the healing or the baby. Several customers milled about, gathering things to buy. It was nearing Christmas, I suddenly remembered, glancing out the window at the sunny day. I was wearing a long sleeved cotton tunic and a pair of jean capris. Now the weather decided to turn warm? And then I remembered the conversation with Valerie about my witchy powers. Was it possible that my anxiety and stress brought on the early winter weather? I dismissed it as impossible and went to my desk to see how many sales I'd had.

"Did Jerry figure out who broke into the store?" Valerie asked, arriving at my desk.

I shook my head. "The glove is impossible to trace and I accidentally cleaned up the scene before he could find prints."

Valerie stared into the distance for a moment before turning back to me. "Why can't I see anything anymore?" she whined. "It's like my third eye has permanently shut down."

"You predicted my death and you predicted the fire and the chaos surrounding Carl's behavior. Since I've never had powers like that I wouldn't know, but it seems to me that you can't just call on it anytime you feel like it. Don't you need to have a really good reason?"

Valerie laughed. "Perhaps you're right. I'm not properly invested in the glove. So who could it be, Summer? Carl is gone and everyone else is either dead or has disappeared."

"The only person who jumps out is Henry because of his interest in getting rid of all things pagan. I have a feeling whoever it was, was searching for *Black Magic and the Occult.*"

Valerie nodded. "I haven't heard a word about Henry since his jail time. I wonder…maybe I can figure it out later when I'm in meditation."

"I got the ultrasound—we're having a boy."

Valerie clapped her hands. "When is he due?"

"Late May, the doctor said. Do you know a midwife?"

"You do know that witches have little problem birthing their babies."

I stared at her. "I…"

"Don't start with your denials again, Summer. It's patently obvious now to the most unskilled observer."

"What do you mean?"

"Take a look in the mirror, my dear, and you'll see what I mean."

When I moved to the mirror hanging by the entrance I saw a woman with bright eyes and rosy skin, a halo of chestnut hair around the heart-shaped face. I did look radiant. But the most surprising part was the pulsing aura of golden light that surrounded me. When I moved my hands tendrils of luminescence trailed from my fingers.

"Are you saying everyone can see this?" I asked nervously.

Valerie laughed. "Only those who also walk in the light."

"Is the baby causing it?"

Valerie laughed again, a tinkling sound that reminded me of my mother. "The glow is all you, Summer. You've come into your own."

∞

A few days later I decided to take Liza Benton's bones back to her grave. Jerry insisted on coming with me, afraid to let me out of his sight for even a moment. "The place holds dark memories," he said, helping me on with my coat. "I don't want your fears freaking out the baby."

I laughed, clipping the leash on Cutty. Outside Jerry retrieved the shovel and we walked together down the alley. We paused at the gate, the squeak of the hinges setting off a frisson of fear before Jerry's hand on my arm calmed me. Cutty ran off yipping as we worked our way toward the older section, shafts of light from the gibbous moon showing the way. "Here it is," I whispered, noticing Liza's ghost watching us. I smiled at her, eliciting a look from Jerry.

"Who's here?" he asked.

"It's Liza Benton."

"Does she know who killed her?" Jerry asked in cop fashion, bending to point his flashlight at the open casket where her pale bones lay in a jumble.

I pulled the clavicle and the upper arm bone out of my pocket and placed them as correctly as I could, attempting to straighten the rest of them.

Jerry was shoveling dirt when I noticed Liza pointing to

another grave close by. I grabbed the flashlight propped to shine on the grave and moved to check the headstone. Bailey Benton was the name on the stone, the date of his death several years after hers. "This must be who did it," I told Jerry. "She's pointing to this grave."

Jerry moved to see, his eyebrows furrowing. "I read about this in the historical archives, Summer. This was a famous murder. Bailey was her father and swore up and down he didn't do it. Some other poor sap took the rap—they hung him."

My hand went to my mouth. "That's terrible."

Liza's sad look was back, her eyes filling with tears. "And now she has to sleep next to her murderer for eternity," I muttered.

Jerry gazed at me before bending to shovel the rest of the dirt in. "Maybe we can move her," he finally said.

"With or without permission?"

He grinned. "What do *you* think?"

It was a week later that Jerry and I entered the graveyard in the dead of night and dug up Liza's bones. Luckily we'd had a thaw, the ground turning soft under the layer of snow that had melted. Once I collected the bones and placed them in the garbage bag I'd brought along, Jerry filled the grave in and patted it down. He pulled the worn gravestone out of the ground, heaving it into his arms. "Where to?" he asked, knowing I was in communication with the ghost.

I looked at Liza who was already wafting away. "Follow me," I said, hurrying after her.

Liza came to a stop in front of another very old grave,

this one even earlier than the others. I could barely make out the name or the year, having to kneel and point the flashlight close and clear the moss away to see the marking.

Elizabeth Swan
1696—1785

I turned to Jerry. "The woman was eighty-nine years old." I glanced up at the ghost drifting around us. "Is this your grandmother?"

Liza nodded, a small smile playing around her ghostly mouth.

"It must be her maternal grandmother," I told Jerry. Next to Elizabeth's grave was a patch of grass. He placed the stone down and began to dig.

32

It was nearing the end of February when Jerry told me that Wendy Werner had been found murdered. We were engaging in our usual before dinner pastime of sitting in front of the fire with wine or beer for him, and tea for me, when he turned his gaze to mine. "She was shot one time in the chest. Some kid discovered her out by the graveyard near the Catholic church."

"Who did it?"

"We think it was Henry. Isabel was buried there and her grave had been tampered with. Apparently someone must have caught him in the act because he dropped a book when he ran off and it had his fingerprints on it."

"But why would he kill Wendy?"

Jerry grimaced. "A page had been earmarked that contained a spell to bring back the dead and it called for a human sacrifice. Not sure how he settled on Wendy—maybe she just happened along."

"Yuck! How many of these creepy books with spells to bring back the dead are there?"

"This one wasn't at all like yours. There was no warning about dark forces or anything like that."

"What was it called?"

"*The Power of Black Magic.*"

"But that's the one Henry and Isabel had me hold for them…he must have stolen it from Tarot and Tea. I didn't notice it was missing."

Jerry shook his head, a grim look arriving on his face. "Some pretty nasty stuff in there. You should probably screen your books a little more carefully."

"Come to think of it, I don't remember buying that book. I wonder where it came from."

Jerry shrugged.

"Did you catch him?"

"No, and Isabel's body is missing."

"That's even more disgusting. You think Henry is still hoping to bring her back?"

"I don't know. We're searching for him." He turned away for a second, his fingers running through his thick hair. When he met my eyes again, his had gone dark with an emotion I couldn't identify. "Last time Sam and I were in the tunnels we discovered a padlocked door set into one of the walls. The padlock was rusted and easy to break." He glanced down before he continued. "We found at least fifty bodies inside that room—skeletons, I should say. The ME calculated their deaths to around the same time as the bootlegging. Not sure if they were locked in there on purpose or what, but they didn't die a good death."

My hand went to my mouth as I remembered the angry ghosts. No wonder they were angry. I stared into space, thinking about all the horrible things we'd discovered in the past few months.

Silence filled the room, the only sound the crackle of the

flames and the thump as the pine logs moved and settled. As the minutes ticked by I tried to let go of this latest terrible revelation, focusing instead on Henry and Isabel. "I guess we'll know if Henry was successful if we see Isabel wandering around town," I finally said.

"Very funny, Summer."

"How do I know if the spell works or not? This is different than Carl—Isabel is really dead. I'll have to ask Valerie if she's ever encountered a necromancy spell that actually worked."

"How did Mrs. Browning end up as a ghost that lives?"

"Honestly, I have no idea."

"Maybe you should ask her."

I shook off the chill that went down my spine, my hands going to the growing bump of my belly. "Right now I want to concentrate on the living."

Jerry smiled and moved closer to place his hand over mine. "Kicking again?" he asked.

I nodded. "I fear he's going to take after his father."

Jerry stared at me in mock surprise. "I don't kick."

I lifted my brows. "You may not kick but you certainly make sure your needs are known and met."

He laughed. "And I have a need right now to take you into the bedroom."

"But look at me," I said, standing to show him how big my belly had grown. I was now wearing loose pants with elastic waists and oversize sweaters.

"I *am* looking at you," he said, his eyes going soft. "A Madonna."

"And what about the wonderful dinner you promised?" I teased. In truth I loved Jerry's attentions, his words and the way he touched me making me feel beautiful. He surprised me every single day.

Jerry rose to his feet and took hold of my arm, steering me toward the open door. "We can eat after."

On the way by I glanced at the new addition, my gaze drawn to the baby's room I had yet to paint. We'd already bought the crib and a rocking chair and several other baby accouterments. There was still work to be done on the roof and the clapboards, but the walls were closed in, keeping out the chilly weather. A moment later Jerry tugged me into our bedroom and shut the door.

Fin

If you enjoyed this book *please* leave a review!

If you want more information on Nikki Broadwell
or her books please visit her website:

www.nikkibroadwellauthor.com

www.ingramcontent.com/pod-product-compliance
Lightning Source LLC
Chambersburg PA
CBHW052029240626
47153CB00006B/2014